Home renovation, like romance, can cause its share of headaches. And in Louisiana's Bayou country, the path of love can be strewn with murder...

Between maintaining a home renovation business and patching up their personal lives, twin sister divorcees Sunny Taylor and Eve Vaughn are too busy to meddle in their aging mom's romantic affairs. That is, until the strong-willed senior makes plans to marry her retirement community's newest resident. Her cadre of buddies at Sugar Ledge Manor are worried that Mom's beau is only after her money. But when the groom-to-be's nephew, Edward, is found dead in the house he'd hired the sisters to remodel, the situation gets even stickier.

Everyone knows Edward and the twins disagreed about the upcoming marriage. The crime hasn't just thrown a wrench in their professional reputations—now the killer seems to be taking aim at Mom. That discovery, along with a second sudden death, sends Sunny and Eve sifting through motives thicker than a Louisiana gumbo...and trying to nail a murderer before all dreams of happiness come crashing down along with their family . . .

Visit us at www.kensingtonbooks.com

Books by June Shaw

Twin Sisters Mysteries
A Fatal Romance
Dead on the Bayou
A Manor of Murder

Published by Kensington Publishing Corporation

A Manor of Murder

A Twin Sisters Mystery

June Shaw

LYRICAL PRESS
Kensington Publishing Corp.
www.kensingtonbooks.com

For Bob and all of my family—You are my reason for being.

Acknowledgments

My family and friends, I don't know what I would do without you. Thank you for all of your encouragement and love.

For years I saw through SOLA, my RWA writers group in New Orleans, that becoming an author of books people wanted to read was possible and increasingly probable. What a tremendous group of friends. Vicki McHenry, you are the best!

I learned so much about writing mysteries from countless people in Mystery Writers of America, Sisters in Crime, and the Guppies. It's amazing how much other writers want to share with you and want you to succeed. Thank you.

Thank you, God, for all of the blessings in my life, especially the people.

Thanks to all the folks from South Louisiana. Y'all rock like no others, bless your hearts.

Working with Lyrical Press has been truly amazing. Marci Clark does an excellent job editing my work. Managing Director Renee Rocco is wonderful and has people continue to work on books until they shine, so I guarantee you any errors that might still occur are all mine.

To you, my readers, my words on the page would sit alone without you. I can't thank you enough for allowing me to share my imagination with you. I really love to have you contact me and write reviews. Reviews truly help authors survive.

Chapter 1

Dread filled me as I raced into Sugar Ridge Manor ahead of my twin. I found our mother seated on a sofa in a grouping of her heavily perfumed cronies.

"Mom, you aren't really thinking of getting married?" I asked.

"Well, hello to you, too." She gave her head such a hard shake her hair resembled a thick cotton ball whipped by a storm. "No, Sunny, I am not thinking of getting married."

A *whish* of relief left my mouth.

"I'm not thinking. I'm *doing*."

My sister, Eve, ran up beside me. "But you hardly know him."

Mom's normally soft chin tightened. "Maybe you two don't know him well, but *I do*."

"Mom!" I threw my hands up and leaned toward her, smelling her bath powder. "We just want to protect you. You introduced us to him, but it wasn't that long ago. If everything is on the up-and-up between you two, why was our customer the one to tell us about this important plan of yours instead of you?"

Stillness sat around us like newly hardened concrete. Her normally chatty buddies grew solemn. Only their eyes moved, shifting from us to our mother.

Mom stared at the tan, vinyl floor. She lifted her head and faced the members of her Chat and Nap group on sofas and loveseats in their three-sided arrangement. "Ladies, I believe it's time for lunch."

It was nowhere near the hour for the early lunch the cafeteria served, yet none of her friends questioned her. None looked at us. Those who could, pushed themselves up and strolled off behind her while others worked their way to their feet and used their walkers and canes, following her like gray-headed little duckies.

Here I was, a tall, divorced, middle-aged woman who felt instantly transformed into a small child whose parent didn't want her anymore while I watched my mother turn away and go. It was the first time ever that I'd been around her and hadn't received a kiss or even a brief hug.

She went scooting off as though she had been overwhelmed by the smell of a stinkbug or, even rarer down here in south Louisiana, a skunk. I looked at my identical twin whose wavy red hair fell over one of her clear blue eyes that stared at me. Were we the stinkbugs or worse?

"We need to stop her," Eve said.

"Of course."

Both of us loved our mother more than anyone could love any other person. Mom was adorable. She was medium-sized, but soft and cushiony with her age touching eighty. She took medication for her heart and had one hand with fingers knotted by rheumatoid arthritis, which she never complained about. And a problem with constipation. She had always been sweet and loving to us and Dad while he was alive. But now she had become rude? Dismissive? To her own daughters, her only surviving children?

No sounds of pots clacking or dishes rattling came from the area of the cafeteria and no smells of cooking food drifted. It was one of those rare periods between mealtimes in the manor. Our mother was going to hide out from us, but she couldn't stay hidden. Her buddies seemed to want to avoid us, too. Did all of them agree with what she was doing? If they had all the facts, I couldn't imagine they would go along with our mother marrying. Just thinking about it made my stomach coil. I felt like there was a rattler squeezed inside me, preparing to strike.

Deciding we needed help, Eve and I strode to the office. This was normally a pretty area—the whole place was—but today nothing about it felt attractive. This section was right off the wide foyer that was decorated with lush plants and cushioned seating and framed outdoor scenes on the walls. We'd known this place was a striking retirement home, one we couldn't have chosen any better after Mom's arthritis made living alone too difficult for her. We'd each invited her to live with us, but always independent, she refused and chose to take residence here. The sprawling building was modern and bright, filled with activities and lots of people to have fun and converse with. Only now one person had moved in that we didn't believe our parent was ready to marry.

A long counter blocked the entrance to the main staff members' offices. The counter held a sign-in book with a flared-tip, white pen standing beside it in a holder. There were a couple of pamphlets describing the place, a clear vase holding colorful wildflowers with sprigs of bridal wreath, and a stack of papers with the meal plan for the week.

We didn't come to this area much, since we seldom signed in anymore, and visitors were supposed to do that each time they arrived. Now I penned my name and my twin's. Placards above shut doors on the far wall to the rear told that those offices belonged to the administrator, assistant administrator, and nurse. It was possible to reach their offices by lifting a flap of wood at the end of the counter, but they preferred that people didn't.

I looked at my sister and then called out, *"Hel-lo.* Can anybody help us?"

As I'd hoped, the administrator's door opened, and she came out.

"Oh, nobody's up here?" Terri Hebert, a petite woman a decade younger than we were, wore a long skirt as usual. "She must have just stepped out. May I help you?"

"Yes," Eve said, her voice strained. "Something's wrong with our mother."

I nodded. "That's right."

Slim creases between Terri's eyebrows erased as her eyes widened. "Do you want me to call the nurse?" She twisted toward that office door.

"No," I said. "It's with her mind. It's that new guy. She thinks she's crazy about him."

Eve spread her hands. "Can you believe she even believes she's going to marry him?"

Terri's upper body appeared to sway back a pinch. "I heard a rumor about that." Her reaction suggested she was in total agreement with us against that event taking place.

"What do we do?" I said.

"Have you tried to reason with her?"

Eve shifted closer. "Of course."

"What's wrong with that man?" I asked, my voice growing shriller until Eve motioned with her hand that I should speak softer. "Maybe they could flirt a little like it seems they had been doing. But marriage. Why would he want to marry our mother?" The whole concept made me shiver. "He seemed all right when we met him, but that was briefly, and darn—*marriage*? What's he really like? Tell us about his background."

She leaned forward, her face remaining tight with concern since we began bemoaning Mom's plight, but now she shook her head. "You two know that all of the information we receive about our residents is private."

That privacy clause had made us feel secure when we helped Mom move in. But now it became an impediment, a wall to keep us from protecting our mother.

Terri greeted a young woman in casual attire who walked up to the counter beside Eve. Normally we would greet people, too, even those we didn't know—a custom most of us shared in south Louisiana—but at this moment, other things gripped our minds. The woman lifted the long pen from its holder, signed her name and the date and time and who she was coming to visit, and then moved on.

Voice and footsteps came from a distance behind us. I leaned closer to Terri, keeping my voice low. "But something's happened to Mom. He's done something to her." She lifted her eyebrows, and I added, "You know our mother has always been an enjoyable person."

"But he's made her belligerent," Eve said.

The administrator stood straighter, her eyes appearing to look into the distance but see nothing. She was trying to sort all we said to her, I imagined. Behind us, sounds picked up, or maybe they had been there all along. Footsteps traveled across the vinyl floor. Light padding sounds came from rubber soles of the nurse and other staffers hurrying along to help residents who needed assistance. The *click* of a walking cane striking the floor told me the person using it was a man, a large one. I glanced to see if its user was the person my mother supposedly would marry, relief filling me when I saw it wasn't. If I saw the man my mother seemed so interested in, I had no idea what I would do, but giving him the inquisition seemed most likely. My twin would probably do the same. Perhaps it was good that we didn't find him. The enticing aroma of chicken and sausage gumbo touched the air and the back of my throat.

"I need to get to work," the administrator said. "I'm not promising anything, but I'll find out what I can."

We thanked her. With Mom nowhere in sight, we left the building.

Eve stopped right outside. "I think I'm going to be sick."

"I feel the same way. Has a man Mom hardly knows taken control of her mind? Who is he? Who has *she* become?"

"What can we do to stop him?"

We stood behind my truck, a sultry wind pushing against us, making our wavy hair twist like bright red flags. This retirement home normally brought peace to us and most others we'd heard from who came here. But now I felt like our mother had stepped into the largest anthill filled with thousands of stinging red ants, and we needed to rush her away.

"Let's go see the person who told us about the whole thing." I flung myself onto the driver's seat, and Eve slipped into the other side.

With our small town, it didn't take long to get anywhere. We crossed the algae-scented bayou that was green today, passed a couple of sugar cane fields with thin white egrets foraging along them and a decaying plantation home, and reached the two-story house we had been remodeling. The traditional style sported fluted columns in front and old-Chicago brick and was lovely. Edward Cancienne had hired us to make quite a few changes before he was going to move in. Many of the dramatic homes here in the bayou country of south Louisiana were large, plantation-style with sprawling lawns teeming with massive moss-laden oaks—a comfortable feel most of their homeowners wanted to keep.

Not so with Edward, a single attorney in his mid-thirties. He wanted his place more contemporary. Eve and I made suggestions but mainly used his ideas to update the place we had been working on for months. We seldom saw or heard from him. He left messages on our Twin Sisters Remodeling and Repair number or on occasion, a note stuck to the fridge.

We were in luck and found his luxury car in his driveway. But another nice car also sat out there.

"Let's hope the other person leaves soon," Eve said, and I agreed.

After I parked, we stepped to the front door and rang the bell instead of getting the key from under the second potted asparagus fern to the right of the doormat, where we and all the subs normally retrieved it.

The voices of two males lifted once the chimes inside rang. Eve and I gave each other questioning looks, since the men seemed to be shouting at each other. Stomping feet neared. A middle-aged man with a dark beard and hard stare faced us. "Yes?"

My instinct to step back was quelled by the homeowner coming into view. "Come in, Eve or Sunny, whoever you are." His voice was rough and rougher still when he spoke to the person with him. "Carl, get out of the way."

His rude company turned and stamped farther into the house. Similar in age and with a healthy build like Edward's, he was as well dressed. Possibly another lawyer friend—or enemy. We followed Edward into the kitchen, where we'd had difficulties with the existing brick floor. We had remedied the situation by filling in the brick and using a gray stain and glossy finish to disguise any problems. The new small black geometric print on one wall accentuated the seamless white kitchen.

I'd hoped Carl would leave when we entered so we could get to speak with Edward about our mother wanting to marry; he had been the person to tell us about it, and we had rushed out to Mom immediately afterward. But farther inside, I could see Carl pacing the great room. He stomped from the brick fireplace to the stairwell with the newly installed custom iron stair rail and back again.

Chest heaving, Edward glanced back at him and then at us. "What do you need?"

To know more about our mother's interest in marriage and the man she'd supposedly marry. You mentioned it to us in the first place, I wanted to blurt. But my gaze shifted from one man to the other. Things pertinent in Edward's mind right now had nothing to do with our parent. Carl didn't appear to be leaving soon.

"We'd like to check on the game room." Eve came up with an excuse faster than I could. "The new floors were supposed to be put down in there yesterday."

"It's good. The room's good, now go."

I felt he hadn't even looked into his game room and wasn't concerned with it now. We moved away from the front door he shut behind us. No curtains hung on any of the newly designed windows, and if we peeked back in, we probably would have seen the pair about to resume their argument.

"Not much learned there," I said as we got into my truck.

"Nothing that concerns us. And we can't go back to the retirement home today, or Mom might tell us off."

What a horrible thought. I let out a sigh. "Let's go back tomorrow."

"Agreed. So we need to figure out how we can keep her from making a horrible mistake. Take me home. I'll try to come up with ideas."

I brought Eve to her place where she would change clothes. She'd go and workout at her favorite gym to clear her mind and try to get answers and then go home and into her art room to paint. Her paintings weren't good enough to show anywhere, but while creating the colorful hearts and flowers, excellent ideas often came to her.

After I dropped her off, I fast-dialed Dave Price, the man my twin and I both had feelings for.

"Hi, Sunny." His cheerful voice instantly lifted my mood. "What're you doing?"

"Hoping you're at your camp, and I can teach you a thing or two about catching fish."

"Then you're in luck."

"You are at the camp?"

"Yes, come on over. I'll have a rod and reel ready for you."

I headed out of the neighborhood. Like with many other towns down here, I was soon riding beside a slow-moving ribbon of fresh water called a bayou. My aim this time was to Bayou Boogie Woogie, which didn't take long, especially since there wasn't much traffic. I hoped I could get rid of concerning thoughts about Mom that kept clouding my mind.

Dave's camp sat almost at the farthest end of the slim road with not even a gravel path on the opposite side of the waterway. In my sour mood, I needed respite. I opened my windows. The unique smell of the bayou water and dried seafood peelings washed in, immediately making my tight cheeks relax. Shrimp boats moored with their trawls lifted like giant butterfly wings paused in mid-flight. Their knotted ropes held dried bits of crabs and shrimp with a sprinkling of fish that left an enticing taste on the back of my tongue. A snowy egret dipped and road a long current of air above the water. Small houses and camps spread farther apart until I arrived at Dave's with my spirit already refreshed.

The sight of his midnight blue truck sitting in his dirt driveway brought a smile to my face. He wasn't from around here and owned a nice house in town but had wanted a camp. He hired Eve and me to help him fix up this old one a bit. One of the first things we did was add a wharf. When Eve wasn't around, I helped him buy the right fishing gear and promised I'd teach him to use it.

Eve had been through three amicable divorces with men who still treated her like a goddess. My sole marriage had been to a man who made me dread intimacy. I had married him because low self-esteem from being dyslexic made me believe I couldn't do better. I never thought I would be interested in a man again. But then came Dave. Eve had me pretend to be her to check him out when his company installed the alarm system in her house. She had decided he was the reason God made the universe. He was her soulmate, she had sworn to me, and not being shy around men, had come on strong toward him. Which turned him off, he'd let me know later once he admitted an attraction to me but not her.

She had been wanting so badly for me to find true love. But she would not be pleased for me to find it with him.

Dave and I had been on a few dinner dates out of town, and sometimes the three of us ate together, all acting like close friends. Dave and I had been getting closer. He'd urged me to let Eve know about our relationship so we could be more open about it. I promised I would soon. But our older sister was killed beside me when I was a child, which made it urgent that I protect this one. That horrible experience also caused me to blurt or hum Christmas carols when I felt terrified and helpless, a trait I had been struggling to get rid of for years.

Dave stepped out of his carport that was still filled with boxes, a wide smile across his handsome face. His eyes were like hot chocolate on a chilly day. In jeans and a T-shirt that said *Gone Fishing* across his wide chest, he held his arms apart, a fishing rod in each hand. "Take your pick."

"You know which one." I gave him a quick kiss on the lips and took the lighter rod.

"I have our chairs set up." He waved me toward the yard on the side of the rustic building. When I sped ahead of him toward the back and onto the wharf, he said, "You sounded like you needed some comforting."

"This is perfect." I took the folding chair a couple of feet to the right of his, since I cast right-handed and he casts left.

He grabbed a small round container from under his chair, lifted its white top, and revealed black dirt. "Have one."

I shoved my fingers into the loose muck and felt around. My fingers touched a fat piece of slime. "Got it." With that, I pulled up a large worm.

"You had the first choice, so if I catch the most fish, remember I gave you a chance." We shared a smile and he stuck his long fingers in the loose dirt and withdrew a skinny one.

Content to be beside him instead of where trouble had greeted me, I gave the white skirt on my hook a little shake and then added my wiggly worm. Dave struggled a little, needing more time to get his bait where it needed to be. I gave my line little jerks. Moments later, he did the same.

A gentle breeze touched my skin. I peered over the peaceful water and heard a seagull cry. Seeing Dave's line go out made me check my small resting cork. Like it, I relaxed. "How's your day been?" I asked.

"Pretty good. We finished a big job. The boat you helped me buy is getting its final touches. And now I'm here with you."

The intensity of his smile and our pleasant situation made me believe it was okay to consider my most troubling one. I watched the swirl beyond my cork. A slap on the water meant a fish—probably a mullet—jumped. Mullet was good to eat but they didn't usually bite on a hook. I glanced farther out, thinking I might see a gator. None were in sight, but that didn't mean none were near. What might mimic a floating log could be the snout and eyes of one. It was still exciting to pick one out.

"My mom wants to get married again." Just thinking about it made my shoulders drop lower.

"She does? That's great."

I whirled toward him. "No, it isn't great. She's an aging woman, and he's an elderly man who recently moved into Cypress Manor, and we hardly know a thing about him."

"Sunny, just think about it." The smile crossing his face made me want it wiped away. "They'll keep each other company."

"They can do that right now."

"Yes, but then they would share a room. Or a suite. Or possibly he owns a home somewhere that they could move into."

I was on my feet. "You're speaking about my mother. My innocent mother." His smile pulled into a little smirk. "Innocence can mean many things. And just like him, I'm not from here. You don't know everything about me."

"And I won't." I threw my rod down on my chair and stepped away from his wharf to the side yard.

"Something's pulling your line!"

"Let it have the whole thing." I whipped myself into my truck, hoped he lost the pole and reel, and sped away from him and his horrible ideas knowing I needed to find better ones that would help my mom.

Chapter 2

Back at home, I had to move around and do something positive at the same time. I scooted to the kitchen, powered on the oven, and whipped out utensils and ingredients. In no time, the enticing scent of the vanilla eased my tight shoulders, and I was watching two light-textured angel food cakes fluff up above the tops of their pans. In the meantime, I got everything ready to set two more of the same in my oven right after those came out. Maybe when Eve helped me bring those four cakes to the manor in the morning, Mom would be her more reasonable, softer self.

Thinking of her situation made me furious. As did considering Dave, the one man who had attracted me, but now did not. Yes, I cared about him, but I didn't want him siding with a man who wanted to take advantage of my mother.

While the cakes cooled upside down on the hot pepper bottles I'd hung them on, I fixed two more and set them to bake. Considering the work we had already done ourselves and what we'd used subcontractors for, I made note of the details left to complete at Edward's house and then worked on bids for another project. Because of my dyslexia, I always had Eve check over my numbers, which normally came out right, but not every time.

It was hard to focus, since concerns about Mom kept returning. Eve and I had been fortunate with excellent parents. Our father was a good man who always let his wife and daughters know how much he loved them. He'd worked hard to provide for us as a building contractor and had us girls often use tools with him. It had been great to occasionally work side by side with him. But he had been gone—what?—almost six years? Did I want Mom alone the rest of her life?

Maybe not, but she shouldn't marry someone we knew so little about. The man she was so interested in was too new in town. My sister and I needed to keep her from harm. We would take care of that in morning, I decided, leaving the paperwork and removing the cooled cakes from their pans. I wrapped the cakes, cleaned the kitchen, and eventually slept, waking to a dream of a slimy worm nearing Dave's face.

Dreariness hung like a gray drape over town when Eve and I rode to the manor in the morning with my offering and then carried them to the kitchen. The cakes would be distributed to residents with diabetes during lunch or supper, while sweeter cake with sugary icing would go to those whose health allowed it.

Some of our mother's Chat and Nap buddies were in their normal places in their sofa grouping not far past the foyer, but she wasn't with them. Maybe now the others would talk.

"Good morning, ladies," I said, and Eve repeated. Most of them greeted us. I stooped a little to get more at eye level with them, wanting to hurry before Mom might show up. I used a quieter tone. "What do y'all really think about Mom wanting to marry that man?"

Some of their eyes shifted as though looking to see if she were coming. Gazes swerved to each other like they might be asking if they should talk.

"You know what a lot of men do?" asked the rather plump Miss Ida who had bluish hair. "They take advantage of older women. Old guys go after the women to get their money or anything else they can get."

The lady who wore three strands of pearls and always shook her finger said, "Right. A lot of women are receiving pension checks that are better than those old men get. The men just want their husband's social security or insurance payments."

Eve and I both sat on the edge of seats where women had shifted over to give us room and waved us closer. We leaned forward, urging them on with these arguments we could use with our mother.

"We hope Mom hasn't told him about her financial situation," Eve said. "And he probably hasn't said anything about his."

Ms. Grace stopped looking at pictures on her phone and dropped the device into her bra. It fell so low it resembled a budding third boob. "Yep, they're all just about broke. Only want older women's money."

The wheelchair bound woman had dozed a minute but woke, shaking her head. "That's not true. Some of them just want to get in your drawers."

Eve grimaced, her face surely matching mine when I considered our aging mother and some older fellow.

Miss Ida shook her head. "Yeah, but what about that woman Clarice? She wants him, too."

We only knew of Ms. Clarice as a fairly attractive, thin person with kidney problems who was assigned to eat meals at a table with our mother and two other ladies. Eve and I considered ourselves fortunate in the gene pool, since the only medicine Mom required was one pill a day for her mild heart problem. But if Ms. Clarice also wanted the man in question, possibly there was more hope that a proposed marriage between him and our mother would not take place. Eve's eye shift toward me suggested she began hoping the same thing. Neither of us would want our mother to get in a catfight for a man.

Rubber soles suctioned the floor beside us. The nurse, Belinda Hadley, stepped near. "I couldn't help hearing some of this conversation, so I think now is the time I should mention this to all of you. Cases of HIV and venereal diseases in the aged have risen tremendously. None of you are protected from those things if you're sexually active unless you use some protection, so we have decided to give condoms to any of our residents who need them. Just ask any one of us at the office."

I felt my jaw drop. Eve's did the same. Most of the women with us frowned. One especially lively woman in the group made a worried face like she might be concerned about what she'd heard. The nurse walked off saying she would soon have a talk about sex with all the residents. My stomach roiled, ready to pitch my breakfast.

Mom walked up with our client, the younger attorney, Edward, beside her. Eve shot to her feet. "You can't marry him."

"No," I said and stood. "Mom, you need to take your time and think about this."

A frown creased her forehead. She pulled her lips tight. She wasn't ready to agree with us.

Edward faced Mom. "I'll tell you what, Miriam. With this kind of support from your daughters about you marrying my wonderful uncle, I think you two should do it right away."

"No!" Eve and I shouted.

Mom gave our client a sweet smile. "That sounds like a grand idea. I'll talk to Mac about it. You'll get things prepared?"

"I can do that in no time." With a smile so wide it showed a gold-capped rear tooth, he brought her hand to his lips and kissed the back of it. "Let me go find my uncle and discuss arrangements."

"He just went to his room to freshen up," Mom said.

I gripped her free hand. "Please don't think of getting married yet."

She slipped her hand from mine. "I'll make my own decisions. I'm old enough."

"You are," I said and turned on Edward. "You're the one who's been pushing this wedding—probably from the start. You probably put that horrible idea in their minds in the first place."

"Yes, stop it," Eve told him.

"You two are finished at my place!" He pointed at Eve and me. "You're done. Get your belongings out of my house and bill me for the work you've completed. I can't believe you're so hard on your mother."

"It's because we love her," I said, but Mom only frowned at us.

A number of people who worked there and nearby residents all stared at us. Eve and I turned around and left the building.

* * * *

"One positive that might come out of what we've just been through," Eve said, half an hour later while we sat in a rustic restaurant with our soft drinks. We had ridden around awhile, not saying a thing, trying to let our blood pressures go down before attempting anything else. "Of all those people who heard us, maybe somebody will come up with information we can use to stop her from doing it."

Not wanting to face what might soon lay ahead with our parent, we ordered the boiled seafood trio: shrimp, crayfish, and crabs. The spicy aroma of seasoning arrived before our large round plastic trays. The warm pink shrimp were plump and easy to peel with just enough spice. Crayfish took a pinch longer to get out of their harder red shells, and the crabs took longest, but were seasoned just right. Using the dip, I found all the food perfect.

By the time we finished with our meal, we were stuffed but in better moods. It would be difficult to tackle food like we had just enjoyed and not find yourself in a lifted state of mind. Things would work out with our mother, we'd agreed. She was much too reasonable to rush into something as serious as marriage.

We would return to speak with her during a quieter time, possibly after she took a long afternoon nap, we discussed while I drove up to Edward's house.

"Darn, I had hoped he wouldn't be here when we came," Eve said when we pulled up behind his car in the long concrete driveway edged with bricks that matched his house.

"Should we come back tomorrow instead?" I tapped the brakes and then reconsidered. "No, let's get it over with now."

"Maybe we can get him to change his mind about rushing to get those two together," Eve said. "At least we should be able to learn more about his uncle from him."

We strode to the front door and rang the doorbell.

Eve tapped her foot while I watched the windows to see if he would come through the great room. I hoped his face no longer wore the anger it bore the last time we saw him, two or more hours ago.

"Maybe he's making bridal arrangements in there," Eve said.

That thought added to my ire. She rang the bell, and we waited more long minutes.

"He might be in the backyard," she said once we'd knocked and waited some more.

"Or he could have left his car here and gone off with someone else." I knocked hard and was ready to go for the key under the plant when Eve tried the door. It opened.

"Hi, Edward, we're here," she called out. "It's Eve and Sunny. We're just here to get our equipment like you told us to do. We rang the doorbell and knocked."

I also called out his name and announced ours. Possibly he was upstairs. We didn't come across him when we entered and didn't see or hear him when we walked up the stairs and made our way to the large main bedroom, a beautiful space that would look even more fabulous once he furnished it. He had allowed us to store the few tools we often used there for measurements in one of the closets. We headed for the closet when I noticed water on the newly restored oak floor.

I pointed at it and followed the slim trail to the adjourning master bathroom. We had designed this masterpiece with large oval-topped windows that revealed beautiful landscaping outside and a lavatory topped with black marble. A delicate chandelier glittered above a freestanding tub.

The Christmas carol I sang let my twin know I had found what caused the water spill. Edward was fully clothed and might have floated out of his bathtub that overflowed onto the floor. He lay face up with unseeing eyes open, so even if he was spread eagle, he obviously wasn't enjoying a relaxing soak.

Chapter 3

My misery with blurting carols when faced with a fearful situation stemmed from when I was eight and alone outside our house with our sixteen-year-old sister, Crystal. She had been talking to her friend on the phone when a drive-by shooter took her life. Shaking and terrified, I had no idea what to do, but wouldn't leave my sister. Her friend on the phone told me she'd send help, and I sat beside Crystal, not letting myself cry. I knew if I did, I would never ever stop. Anguish filling my throat with sound needed to come out. My petrified mind let me voice a soothing sound, a carol. Ever since then, I had struggled to end that horrible trait.

Added to my being dyslexic, I needed to work harder than most people to achieve results and improve my self-esteem.

I tried to tone down my song while I moved away from Edward's body. Eve was calling 911 and giving information. Possibly the person who killed him was still here, I realized, reining in the sound leaving my throat.

When she hung up, I placed my finger across my lips to signal for her to keep quiet. She lifted her eyebrows, and I pointed at the closet door and then outside the windows. Tall, thick bushes stood around the lawn. It looked like branches moving from where two of them met.

Eve tugged on my arm. Our next movements again reminded me of childhood when she and I took dance lessons and practiced crossing the floor on our toes. This time, we made our moves quieter as we rushed through rooms to get out the front door.

The cool air felt good on my skin once we'd run out without getting attacked. Edward's car was still in his driveway with my truck behind it. My instinct was to jump in my pickup and rush us away. Then we would be safe.

Screaming sirens that neared made the hair on my arms raise but assured me we didn't need to leave.

In no time, the driveway and lawn were filled with vehicles of every sort. Police cars and an ambulance carried people who scrambled out of them while Eve and I waited, giving information to those who asked questions. The first young deputy had a full forehead of pimples. Afterward, an unmarked sedan pulled in on the lawn. Its stocky driver walked to us. I had never seen a man roll his eyes. This day, though, Detective Wilet speared us with his dark-eyed gaze and then flipped it toward the sky. Yes, us again.

"Be in my office this afternoon," he ordered, and we nodded. With nothing more, he stomped into the house through the open doorway.

We slipped into my truck. "He knows the deputies questioned us already," Eve said while I backed up and maneuvered us onto the highway.

"My God, what do you think happened?" I said, driving away. "Edward couldn't have just fallen in, could he?"

She stared at me. "No. I believe he was murdered."

My breath caught. She'd voiced my belief. "But who could have done that? And why?"

She gave my arm a reassuring squeeze. "We don't know much about his life other than hearing him argue with the man who'd been there."

"And Edward was an attorney and Mom's wedding planner." Renewed thought of her marrying made my stomach pull tight.

"And Mom's beau was his uncle," Eve reminded.

That made everything worse. I focused ahead and steered toward a place of safety for us, my home or my twin's. With what just happened, or what we'd just discovered, we couldn't chance going out in public yet. Our conversation would be about a dead man, which was not something we would not want anyone else to hear. Even if we tried, I was certain we couldn't just talk about everyday events. Finding a dead body was anything but ordinary.

I drove to my house. We remained silent until we were locked inside. "That's terrible," I said. "The man shouldn't be dead."

"Of course not. It's such a pity." Eve took a chair at my kitchen table.

"I really did like him, even if we just had problems with him."

"I liked him, too."

I fixed us mugs of dark-roast coffee with lots of cream and sugar since we could use comforting. Then I gathered legal pads and pens for each of us and sat. "We'd just as soon write everything we know about Edward before we go downtown to get ready for the detective's questions."

We drank coffee and wrote. Sometimes we stopped and discussed things like asking each other when we recalled first meeting our client, which was different for each of us. Occasionally one of us would stare into space, thinking. We got up and walked, deep in thought. Still quiet, we returned to the table and wrote. Twice I grabbed snacks for us. I kept a stash of chips and chocolate chip cookies for times like this. Not really like *this*, like expecting a person we knew to get murdered. It was more that sometimes I just wanted to stuff a bit of unhealthy food into my mouth. My twin did not, so she stayed trim, while I spread out more in the waist and hips. Today she didn't complain about junk food and shoved much of it into her mouth like I did.

My phone's ring made me jump. I wasn't expecting a call and feared if I spoke to anyone, I wouldn't be able to hide my concern about finding a dead person. I certainly couldn't think creatively now and didn't want to have to discuss ideas with a potential customer. Instead of answering, I considered letting it ring, and if someone wanted to, they could leave a message.

I glanced at the caller's name: *Mom*.

Dreading how I would sound to her, I showed Eve her name and then clicked to answer, putting my phone on speaker.

"Hi, Mom," I said as though everything were normal and that she had not told us she had wedding plans and her intended's nephew was planning it all. And then he and Eve and I had argued, and he'd insisted he would rush the ceremony. And then we found him dead.

"Sunny," Mom said. "I tried to call your sister's phone, but she must have it off."

Eve nodded. She probably turned off the ringer right after her 911 call.

"Did you need her for anything in particular?" I asked Mom. In one way, I was pleased to hear from her. In another, I feared giving away what happened.

She hesitated. "It's just that you're a little more delicate than she is."

"I am not." I bit my lower lip. Why would I want to argue with her now? Eve kept nodding, like she agreed with our mother.

"Something's happened," Mom told me. "Somebody killed Mac's nephew."

"Oh no." My gaze shot toward Eve, and I realized I was reacting to Mom's news as though I hadn't heard it or experienced it firsthand. Hearing her say the words made the entire event feel fresh, deadly fresh.

"Yes. Since my fiancé is his next of kin, the police showed up here to tell him."

"Oh, Mom, I am so sorry."

"I know. It's awful."

I gripped the phone tighter, feeling her pain, so sad for our mother's anguish. "Is there anything we can do?"

She grew silent, making me fearful that she might say we had already done enough with having such harsh talks with the deceased. I dreaded having her discover we had found him. She surely didn't know it yet. But she would.

"Just say a prayer for his soul and for Mac. I'm sure the police will find out what happened, and justice will be served." Forever rational, she would believe that. But nobody ever discovered who murdered my older sister. Mom loudly exhaled. "I can let you know when Edward's funeral will be taking place. I hope you and your sister can be there."

"Of course." I lifted my gaze toward Eve. Her face mirrored my sadness. "Let us know."

"I will. And, Sunny, I really do love you and your sister."

Her words pulled tears from my eyes. She hadn't expressed those sentiments last time. "I love you, too, Mom." I worked my throat to get more words to move out past the new lump. "And, Mom, everything will be all right."

"I know, honey. I need to go now."

Once we disconnected, I wordlessly stared at Eve and she at me. Surely she was processing the words and feelings expressed by our mother, who felt loving toward us again. What caused the change ran through my mind, but I didn't want to consider it.

"Maybe I should have told her we knew he died, and we found him," I said.

Eve's lips pulled back in a grimace. "Will she still say that she loves us when she finds out?"

"She will. We didn't do anything wrong."

Eve turned her paper over and began to draw. She drew circles, small and increasingly larger circles that connected and then some that did not. She moved her pen tip over and created hearts, these similar to what she often painted.

I turned my sheet over. I drew a couple of simple flowers and then created crude stick people. One of them held a large stick knife. Another lay inside a large oval—Edward's tub.

"We need to go see Detective Wilet." I lifted my pad, hiding that page. We grabbed our purses and pads and headed to the station, both aware that what was coming was not something we looked forward to.

The sheriff's office had been spruced up since the last time we'd been there. Thank goodness no murders had occurred that we'd been involved with in quite some time. Actually, we weren't involved in murders. We'd only been around them, making Detective Wilet believe we were more connected than we were.

His office, down the hall, had received a fresh coat of pale yellow paint, already scuffed with dark scratches. The notices and awards now clustered together as we had suggested instead of being strung along the wall like broken snap beans. The odor of fresh coffee came from the new pot on a small table in the hall, replacing the incessant stench of the burned bottom of the last one.

Eve and I passed open doors, where people speaking quietly in rooms paid no attention to us, and reached the detective's unmarked open door to the left. He sat behind his desk that was cluttered with papers. He worked on some of them until he finally looked up at us in his doorway. "Come in. Sit." He nodded to the pair of gray metal chairs across from him. "I see you brought your homework."

We lifted our pads we had written on.

"We knew you'd want information," Eve said.

"We wrote the things we could think of."

He leaned back in his thinly cushioned chair, wide hands clasped behind his head. His thick lips showed some potential of a smile. "I never had anyone do that before. Go ahead, let's hear what you have."

"You first," I told Eve, who, after all, was the oldest. By six minutes.

"All right." She held up her pad. I saw she had written her information in paragraph form. I glanced at my notes. I'd numbered mine and made a list. Eve's ability to always read words in sentences and numbers in order was a talent our parents hadn't passed on to me. She told him about some man named Carl we had seen there arguing with Edward and described him and his car. As she was reading her notes to Detective Wilet, his hands lowered, his potential smile wiped away.

He leaned forward in his chair. "You were really involved with the victim." His eyes took in me and my twin. Then he wrote notes, leaving his words in the air. What were we to interpret from them?

"All right, now you." He pointed his pen at me.

"Could he have just fallen in his tub and knocked his head?" I asked. "The water was running. Maybe he tripped and fell backward?"

He gripped his chin. Letting it go, he pointed at what I held. "Your list," he said.

Once I began, starting with how Edward contacted us, wanting to talk about ideas we might come up with on how to restore an older traditional house he had bought and make it more contemporary before he would move in, Wilet's eyes narrowed. "Let me see that," he said, and I held up my pad, ready to give it to him. He held up a hand to stop me. "I only wanted to see how you have that written."

Maybe he thought Eve's style of writing was better, but I had learned to accept what I could do and what I could not. Things I mentioned about the few times we had been in the same house as Edward ever since we took the job made the detective's eyes appear to gloss over, possibly since Eve already told him most of it. He sat straighter, alert detective mode, when I told of the dead man's connection to our mother.

"Your mother's getting married?" he asked, penning notes.

Eve wore a grim expression. "That's what she said."

I was ready to blurt that we didn't want her to, but second thoughts told me not to. Letting him know our feelings about that and the ensuring argument with the man who was now dead probably was not something we'd want to mention.

The detective wrote more while Eve and I sat quietly. I became aware of the pulse on the right side of my neck. He stared at me. "You two had completed your work at Mr. Cancienne's house and were retrieving your tools when you found him, is that right?"

Eve had told him that, so much better worded than I could have thought of. "Correct."

"And all of the remodeling he wanted done there was complete?"

No, we had planned to remodel the downstairs bathroom, too. "We finished everything he wanted us to do." A bead of sweat ran between my breasts.

"Is there anything else you want to tell me?"

I shook my head and saw Eve doing the same, both of us with tights lips pulled low at the outer edges and eyebrows lifted in our innocent expressions. "No, nothing," I said, although the words came out higher pitched than normal.

I hoped he wouldn't notice, but then considered his job was to detect. Detect problems, inconsistencies. He kept a hard stare aimed at my face, and I wanted to squirm like a guilty student seated in front of a principal. I managed to swallow twice under his watchful eye. My exhale sounded too loud when he turned those hard eyes away toward my sister. I became aware that she was experiencing the same emotions I just had and needed to remind myself we were guilty of nothing.

"You know this isn't the first time you two have been around murders." Detective Wilet leveled his gaze from one to the other of us.

"But we didn't do anything wrong," Eve reminded.

"We became victims." I jutted out my chin. My body had finally healed after I'd been shot.

"Yes. Thank you for coming in. I may be talking to you again."

Relief swept like a downpour through my body while we left his office. Why, I wasn't certain, although I had a feeling he would tie us both to our customer's murder, and I did not want to deal with that.

No, we didn't do it. But would we again need to prove that was true?

Chapter 4

I drove Eve home and tried, with little success, to keep from looking at houses near hers where things had occurred that caused much of our stress. What was happening now was most important, I told myself, parking behind her garage door that she opened with her remote. We walked through the garage she kept as immaculate as her Lexus and lovely home and into the kitchen while the garage door rolled down quietly behind us.

Eve punched quick numbers into the alarm beside her door and spun toward me, hands flying up at her sides. "Sunny, what's going to happen once he finds out we had an argument with Edward and then he fired us from the job?"

I tightened my jaw. "I know. That'll look suspicious on our parts."

Her torso swayed back. "We're sunk."

That sentiment struck me, too, but only for an instant. "Oh, come on, sis. We didn't really do anything."

She kept eye contact with me for long moments. "Right, but there's the sin of omission."

Again, we weren't guilty, I reminded myself. I didn't need to tell her, but determined the painful experiences we would need to go through. A ring from her front doorbell drew our attention. On edge, I went with her to the door, where she looked through the peephole. Her entire demeanor changed. A smile brightened Eve's face, bringing one to me, too. She unchained, unlocked, and opened the door.

"You're here," Eve said and stepped forward, arms up and then around the neck of her caller.

Dave Price looked at me over her shoulder while a jealous tinge ran through me. He shared the hug with her, but let her go before she moved her arms away from him. Then he moved forward and hugged me. I hugged back, enjoying the feel of his broad shoulders and the comfort of being close to him. We stepped apart.

"I heard what happed and wanted to see if I could help."

"Come in," I said, and we all moved from the foyer into the den. As usual, my emotions started battling each other when considering him. Although we hadn't told Eve that he and I were a couple, planning to be a more committed one, he learned of a murder we were involved in and showed up at my sister's house, not mine.

"Have a seat," Eve said, and he settled himself in a cushioned chair. She and I took the marshmallow-soft sofa, she taking the side nearest him. "I'm not sure what you could do, or even anything we can do about what happened. Sunny and I haven't discussed it much yet. But it sure is nice for you to come and offer." She did something I hadn't seen her do in a while—my sister batted her eyes at him. She was leaning toward him so far she could have fallen off the sofa, and I was sure she would want to land on his lap. And she'd want me to leave. I would not.

"I knew you two would be together right now," he said. "Sunny, I went by your house and when I didn't see either of your vehicles, I figured you'd both be here."

I allowed a small smile on my lips. He had gone to my place first.

Eve's phone rang from her purse she had left in the kitchen. "Excuse me," she said and went to get it.

Dave spoke to me, voice lowered. "I hope you've gotten over your silly anger about what I said about your mother's engagement."

I really hadn't thought of it. Possibly I thought of couples being engaged after a future bride announced their exciting news and showing off her ring. I stared at Dave, realizing my mother had announced her news to us—or Edward had, and maybe that was a reason we'd been so shocked. And hurt? Did she have a ring? New brides didn't always have one for engagements, but we didn't even let our mother have time to show it if she had one on her finger.

"Sunny?" Dave's stare made me realize I had been in my own world, thoughts back at the manor.

"I'm sorry. No, I'm not mad anymore."

"That was Mom." Eve's quick return into the room surprised me. "She said arrangements have been made. The funeral's tomorrow."

Giving us a moment to let this sink in, Dave glanced from one to the other of us. "Will you be there?"

Eve and I made eye contact. We held it in place, neither of us changing expression, neither saying a thing.

"Of course," I said, and she nodded.

"I didn't know him, and I have a major job to take care of, so I won't go. But if I can do anything to help you or your mother, please let me know." He spoke to both of us and then stood.

Eve gave him a hug, holding on an extra-long moment. "You are so sweet."

I rose from the sofa and gave him a brief squeeze around the neck. "Thank you so much. Right now I'm not sure of anything you can do, but we'll let Mom know you offered."

We saw him out the front door, and then Eve gave me the little information Mom had told her about services. Neither one of us looked forward to being there.

* * * *

The funeral parlor's musty smell smacked the air right outside the timeworn building's door when it opened. Another parlor had been built in town, and most people now chose to use that one. I'd had run-ins with the mortician there and was relieved that we didn't need to go to that funeral home this time.

Few cars were parked near. A bus bearing the name Sugar Ledge Retirement Home on its sides sat behind the hearse. Nobody was on the porch of the wooden building that short brick footings had bravely held up over the years. Bumpy coats of white paint had been added, assuring that nothing had been sanded down first. The black trim of the porch railing and shutters lent an air of distinction to the place, reminiscent of some of the plantation homes that remained nestled in this region.

I had phoned Mom and spoken to her briefly, asking if she wanted us to pick her up and bring her here. She'd responded with a hint of disbelief in her tone, letting me know that instead of riding with her daughters, she would be there with the man she intended to marry. Her comment and attitude made us decide not to challenge her on that situation right now. She had a friend to bury.

We didn't know how long or how much she had known the deceased, but figured if he had been planning some sort of ceremony for her, she had been closer to him than we had. Just thinking about that made me hesitate before going inside.

Eve looked back at me when I momentarily hung behind. She wore a navy knit dress that showed off her svelte figure just like most of her clothes. She would need to be wearing chunky clothing for anyone to not notice how trim and tall she was. As usual, she wore more makeup than I did, although it wasn't excessive. Her bolder lipstick and matching blush brought out her clear blue eyes and shoulder-length wavy red hair.

I'd chosen lower pumps, black slacks with a black jacket over a white shirt, and a touch of pale lipstick and mascara. I nodded for her to go ahead and stepped inside after her.

The odor of spent funeral flowers and old smoke clung to the air and wallpaper, and swallowed the antiquated carpet. Voices were loud. A quick scan of people inside explained why. Most of them came from the manor, and others I recognized as residing in the local nursing home that housed people who were in worse shape than those at the manor. Large gray and tan hearing aids filled people's ears, and many others here needed them. Those who worked at the nursing home and the manor were accustomed to speaking loud to make certain the person they spoke to could hear them. My own hearing, I'd noticed more lately, seemed not as precise as it once had been. Maybe I would soon be sporting similar devices.

People were curious and turned to see who was coming inside and stopping to sign the memorial book. Mom's boyfriend, or whatever he was to her, would probably be getting this book since he was Edward's closest relative.

The place wasn't crowded, but people's wheelchairs and walkers took up a lot of space. Almost everyone in there stared at us, most not giving away any feelings or judgments. The few who did eyed Eve a long time. A handful of women frowned, possibly thinking she was too made up or maybe attractive. A handful of men, even the elderly, ran their gazes up and down her figure, their lips curving into small smiles. As I walked behind her, I nodded at many mourners, although I didn't hear or notice anyone crying or even looking too sad.

Women whose sense of smell had lessened had poured favorite perfumes on their bodies. My sinuses clogged as we walked farther through the small rooms where people sat. Gazes ran over and away from me. I wasn't showy enough to garner much attention, which was fine with me. Strange, though, I did not notice people giving us double takes. Obviously, almost everyone here either knew us or had previously seen my identical twin and me together.

One person I wasn't thrilled to see stood against a far wall near the hall. His eyes pinned us. I hadn't expected to find Detective Wilet here. He hadn't mentioned that he'd known the deceased. Maybe he was trying to uncover a murderer in this place. Some mysteries I had read and some movies said killers often returned around their victims. Was that what he was doing here? Looking for one?

A surprising number of floral offerings hung on stands against one wall in the viewing room. Normally when a funeral took place this soon after a death without a notice in our local paper's obituary, few people attended services and much fewer sent flowers. That so many offerings were here spoke volumes about the dead man, and I was sorry things happened so fast that we hadn't thought to send some ourselves. A tasteful small arrangement of white lilies with other white sprigs topped the part of the casket hiding the lower half of his body.

Our mother sat beside the casket. My shoulders pulled tight when I saw her. She was holding the hand of an elderly man she had told my sister and me that whether we liked it or not, she was going to marry.

I watched Eve's back stiffen in front of me when she came face to face with our mother and her beau, their hands clasped together, but now wasn't the time for confrontation. Mom gave us a reprieve from immediately needing to watch how we spoke to her and her man by using her free hand to wave us toward the casket first. Her kind eyes and soft smile told us she was pleased to see us here.

We kneeled side by side at the casket. Eve squeezed my hand when we looked down at the man inside. Edward's face appeared a little more swollen than usual, or possibly I hadn't noticed that closely before, or maybe it was the way they had set his face, leaning his chin down lower than normal. He looked at peace, so much calmer than the last times we'd seen him. I mentally apologized to him for the ruckus we had caused in the retirement home.

My peripheral vision let me see someone coming behind us, so I made a sign of the cross and stood; Eve joined me to face the bereaved.

We leaned to kiss Mom, who pushed her lips forward. She greeted us as normal instead of having us kiss her cheek or only give her a brief hug. How nice to feel her love again.

"Thank you both for coming," she said.

"Of course." We spoke at the same time. And then turned to the man beside her.

Alexander McCormick, normally called Mac, kept his eyes level at us. His silver hair stood out with his navy suit. The walking cane he used stood beside his chair. We had met him a couple of times at the manor. Being this close, I noticed the wrinkles that had deepened in his face. Possibly grief at losing his nephew put them there.

"I am so sorry for your loss," I said and took the hand he offered, his grip much stronger than I had expected from someone his age. I let go, and Eve nudged beside me and repeated the sentiment. We turned to step away, but he didn't let go of Eve's hand.

"You two found him, didn't you?"

"We did," she said, and my breath caught. Would he blame us for the death?

"Thank you." He turned his head to speak to both of us.

Glad to do it, came to mind, but I kept my mouth shut, thankfully realizing that was a normal response when anyone thanked me. In this instance, it wouldn't be true. I was not glad we had discovered Edward dead.

"Did you find out anything else since you spoke with Detective Wilet?" he asked.

Did we? I wondered but could think of nothing to say. I shook my head and saw Eve doing the same.

Mom looked behind us, and I was pleased to find a man waiting there to speak to Edward's uncle.

"If you think of anything else, please let him or me know," our mother's beau said and then glanced toward the door. "Oh, my daughter's here, but I don't see her now. I was going to introduce you."

Eve and I mumbled words and moved away to allow the man behind us to speak to the deceased's next of kin. And this next of kin had a daughter we hadn't known about—one of the many things about him we lacked knowledge of. I led the way out of the viewing room toward the rear hall, hoping we might find an unfamiliar woman who could be his child there or in the kitchen or restroom. I only wanted to look her over, not talk to her.

Only a handful of men stood in the rear hallway. Most of them were local lawyers like Edward had been. One was the city judge. All of them wore nice suits and ties and told us hello or nodded. One woman was visible ahead, but she was the wife of the couple who owned this place. She headed into the kitchen carrying packets of artificial sweeteners and coffee stirrers. Beyond her stood a man I had seen before, but maybe only once, a dark beard, hard stare. And then I remembered where.

"Come on," I told Eve as she was turning to enter the kitchen. She followed my lead as I rushed back to the entry of the viewing room, where Detective Wilet stood with his back against the wall to watch everyone.

I tapped his arm to get his attention. When he looked, I motioned for him to follow. He went with us into the hall.

"The man who was in Edward's house arguing with him is back there. Carl. He's standing alone behind the judge." I spoke in a low tone and nodded toward where Judge Callahan stood.

"I hadn't realized that's who he was," Eve told me. "If I had heard his voice, I would have known right away."

The detective gave us a level expression, his gaze sliding toward one and then the other of us. As always, I couldn't make out whether he believed me or not, but then he stepped toward the rear section of the hall where I had suggested he go.

Some in the clump of attorneys back there looked at him coming and started talking to him. Surely he'd only speak with them briefly and then move on toward the man I told him about. Maybe the detective had already found out who the fellow Carl was and interrogated him, but it didn't seem likely. Now he certainly would. I didn't expect him to give Carl the third degree in this place, but he could gather other information from him and do further questioning at a more appropriate place—unless the man made incriminating statements or actions now.

"I'll ask those of you who would like to, to please come up and say your final good-byes to the deceased," a loud male voice announced from the viewing room.

Eve and I stepped to the doorway to see. The person who had spoken was surely the man now standing between our mother and the casket in his gray suit, his expression a blend of bland and concern practiced over years of selling coffins and then doing what he was doing right now. Waiting for people who might cry or those who were friends of someone in the family, like many of the people from the manor and the attorneys. Some were merely curious or had nothing else to do at this time, so funerals and wakes helped fill the void in their days. Others found funerals an excuse to miss a few hours of work.

Elders with walkers and wheelchairs pressed into the viewing room. Some came from small side rooms and others pushed against us from behind, pressing us farther into the room with the body. The room also held Mom and the mortician I'd once had a run-in with moving near her. I didn't know he also worked here. He might spew angry words at me or at least throw angry glares if I approached. Mom had reacted toward us like our loving mother again. This wasn't a time to add any stress to our relationship.

"Let's get out of here," I told Eve.

"Yes. We don't need to be up there again." She squeezed through the crush of people who had pressed in behind us, and I followed close behind.

Reaching the hall, I tried to make our way to the rear, but people jammed together, blocking the way. Some who must have been in sitting rooms across the hall and others who'd probably been talking outside created an almost solid wall. Maybe some had come because in our small town, it was rare to see a dead body exposed that would not have a funeral service to accompany it, normally one in a Catholic church. Instead, this person's casket would be closed soon after everyone paid their final respects and left. Then he would be brought to the crematorium, where his body would return to ashes and his casket would return to the funeral home. It was being rented, Mom had told me, something Eve and I and surely most people in town had never heard of.

What would they do with a used casket? Eve and I had asked each other, but I hadn't asked Mom. Her time speaking to me when she'd called to tell us about the service had been brief. Loving, but brief. When she'd mentioned this casket rental that her alleged fiancé had ordered for his nephew, we couldn't believe it. But she was talking to us again, and kindly once more, so neither Eve nor I was going to question her about anything that might interfere with our renewed happy relationship with her.

Probably like we'd expected, the man she told us she would marry had little money to pay for a proper funeral and casket for his nephew. A rental would certainly be cheaper.

"I won't look at another casket holding a body in the same way," I said to Eve, as I'd said before, but this time we had walked out the front door and stepped away from everyone.

"I know. I might start checking them to see if I spot any signs of previous use now that we've learned about that practice." She spoke while we stepped across the porch and down the steps. "I didn't see Detective Wilet in the hall again, did you?"

"No, it was too crowded. I didn't see that other guy Carl, either. Maybe Detective Wilet took him out the backdoor. Let's go back there and see."

"Good idea."

I smiled as we walked around the pathway that ran alongside the building and to the rear. So many of my early teachers and classmates had made me feel dumb because I was slower than most in my classes. Testing revealed my dyslexia, and then tests were modified for my condition. I had gotten over some of the pain from being behind then, but still, whenever Eve or anyone else made me feel like I was bright, it felt exceptional.

My smile, though, felt out of place when we reached the rear of the building where some people were exiting. One elderly woman being pushed in her wheelchair down the ramp by a man about her age gave me a prune face, making my smile wipe away. She'd possibly heard us arguing with the deceased at the manor. Another in a wheelchair came out the door and behind her came the administrator and other staff members from the manor. Either they all had known Edward or more probably, had come to support his uncle, who lived there. Possibly they also wanted to show concern to our mother because of her relationship with Edward's uncle.

Mainly elders and those who worked with them came out the back door. They hobbled and rolled and otherwise got into cars and the manor's van. Detective Wilet and the man who might have killed Edward were not around.

Not wanting to wait for every person to come out the funeral home, especially Mom and her male friend, I nudged my head toward the front where I had parked. Eve and I waited until I was driving away before we spoke.

"Did you see anyone who could have been that man's daughter?" Eve asked me.

"I have no idea."

"Maybe she'd be about our age."

"Or older. Younger? Who knows that or what she looks like?"

"I didn't notice any female who resembled him." She stopped talking while I considered the same thing. I had searched faces I wasn't familiar with from town.

"Sunny!" Her yelling my name made me hit the brakes. "She might become our sister."

Returning my foot to the accelerator, I glanced in the rearview mirror, grateful to find no car or truck right behind me when I'd stopped so suddenly. Eve's words filtered into my mind when I recalled with clarity the sister we had lost, the one we'd adored who had been killed beside me. A tear escaped my eye.

And then I considered another female, one we had not seen or met. "We'll need to make certain that doesn't happen. No one could replace Crystal."

Eve nodded, her gaze distant. "I'm really sorry Edward died. He could be a nice man, and even when he wasn't, he was a person with a right to live."

"I know. We didn't know him that well but saw his darker side when he yelled at us that he would get them to rush and get married faster than they had planned. Why would he want to do that?"

"His uncle must have been in agreement with him. Possibly he's a lot like Edward." She sucked in a breath. "Maybe all of this commotion with Edward's death will give Mom time to pause and reconsider."

I gave my head a hard nod. "We need to make certain that happens."

Chapter 5

On the way across town Eve contacted her daughter, Nicole, who lived with her husband and baby Noah in Houston. With the widest smile I had seen on her face lately, she kept her cell phone on speaker so I could hear everything on the other end. Soon Noah was babbling and so was my sister. Eve called his name and kept repeating *ga-ga-ga* and *da-da-da* and *ma-ma-ma* in a singsong rhythm until he was making similar sounds back to her.

Eve and I went to our own homes, both in better spirits. I dropped her off at her place, where she wanted to change clothes and then go to the gym to work out. "I might get to talk to someone there who knows more about Edward or possibly even his uncle," she said.

"I hope so. We can use all the help we can get."

At home, I exchanged my low heels for flats. In my kitchen, I worked to clear my head and open it for ideas on how to proceed with Mom.

Edward's body might have been removed from the casket by now and what? I asked myself, inspecting the pecans I measured. I'd bought these even though I had a bag of others in my freezer that I had picked this past winter in a local graveyard where two large pecan trees grew. I'd cracked their shells and peeled them, but many had broken into small pieces, which was fine for including in fudge or cookies or snacking. Pralines, I thought, came out best with pecan halves.

I gathered the other ingredients and swiped a wet washcloth across my table to keep in place the waxed paper I pressed against it. In a large pot, I mixed sugar, margarine, large marshmallows, evaporated milk, and a teaspoon of vanilla. I stirred the mixture over a medium fire until everything melted.

Why would anyone murder Edward? I asked myself, adding the pecans.

My doorbell's ring startled me, making my hand jerk and splash some of the hot mixture from the wooden spoon I was using on my opposite wrist. The burn on my arm almost made me forget to turn off the fire, but I did it, I hoped not for long, and plunged my wrist under cold running water in the sink. The burn started to ease a little until someone gave my doorbell an incessant ring and then a hard pounding came from the door. I turned off the water, patted my arm dry, and went none too happily to discover who the caller was.

A frown bit Detective Wilet's face.

My instinct was to shut the door. Instead I asked, "Detective, what are you doing here?" When he didn't respond, I said with no enthusiasm, "Do you want to come in?"

The moment he stepped into my entry, his face turned toward the kitchen. His tense face relaxed a pinch and his nose lifted a little when he sniffed.

"It's going to be pralines for the gumbo kitchen. I can save some for you if you'd like."

He shook his head. "No, thanks." His gaze at me hardened, his tough cop face back. "Ms. Taylor, I didn't discover the person you described and said was at the rear section of the hall of the funeral home. And I never located the car you said he drove, although you didn't give me much to go on."

I felt my shoulders drop. "I'm really sorry you missed him. He seemed to be having a big argument with Edward when Eve and I went to Edward's house."

He said nothing, eyes intense, severe gaze not leaving mine. "Or maybe there was no man."

Frustration shot through me. That and having my wrist burn as much as it did when the hot candy mixture struck it made me raise my voice. "Oh, come on, Detective. You already thought my sister and I were guilty of murder when we weren't. Why in the world wouldn't you believe me this time?"

"I spoke with other people while I was there and discovered you and your sister had a big argument with Edward Cancienne before he died."

"We—?"

Before my mind could return to whatever he was talking about, he said, "At the retirement home, Ms. Taylor. There were a number of residents and staff members around when you and your sister got into an extremely heated argument with the victim not long before you two say you found him dead."

"That's ridiculous. We weren't arguing with him about anything that we'd kill for." I realized how that sounded and amended my words while his hardened face did not relax. "Not that anything would make us kill another person. We just raised our voices at him because he wanted to try to get our mother to hurry and marry a man who recently moved in there. And we don't know anything about him."

I didn't realize how my hands were flailing around until his eyes turned to my hurt wrist. A red spot the size of a quarter had formed.

He stared at my face. "I don't know all the details about the older gent you're speaking about. Yet."

"We don't either. That's the thing."

"But I have learned that the deceased was his nephew, his next of kin."

"Yes. And?"

"And possibly that relationship to someone you two don't want around added to his pushing to rush a wedding with your mother could be—"

"What? A motive for murdering him?" I spread my arms in the air, causing his gaze to momentarily shift to the red spot on my wrist and then back at my face. "We didn't kill him."

"You had the means. The opportunity."

"So did everybody else in town. Eve and I and all our subcontractors used a key to get in the house that we all put under a pot of fern in front of Edward's house. Any of them could have gotten inside." And what? Waited to kill him? A shudder ran across my shoulders, and my mind shifted to the subs we used. Could they, would any one of them do something like that to Edward or anyone else? I didn't think so, but what about all the fellows who worked for them? Many of them weren't local. Some came from out of state for any job or two they could get and then left town.

"I'll want a list of all of the subs your company used."

"Eve has the most detailed information on her computer program, but she isn't home right now. We can get it to you later today."

Detective Wilet stared at me. "Instead of a worker there retrieving the house key, someone could have gone into the house at the same time as Mr. Cancienne."

"That's possible."

"And maybe it was someone working for him."

My breaths slowed. Again he was trying to turn the blame on Eve and me. "Detective, you must be certain it wasn't an accident. How was he killed?"

He glanced toward the kitchen. "We don't have all of that information yet. But it shouldn't be long." His hard eyes nailed me in place. "You might want to finish your pralines. Get them to the community center while you can."

He whipped around and was out the door before I could think of a comeback. The most ridiculous thought came to mind—I hadn't even offered him coffee or to sit down. Giving my head a shake as though I could get that idea out, I drew a deep calming inhale through my nostrils and stepped into my kitchen.

My instinct was to call my sister and let her know what just went on, but she was probably running on a treadmill or pulling and shoving on some other heavy gym equipment that I sometimes promised her I would join her on soon. My *soon* and hers had two different timeframes.

Should I tell Dave? He had offered to help if we needed anything. I did need something. It was peace from considering what the detective just came and said. But how could Dave help with that? He couldn't erase the experience or the police officer's words or insinuation. The only thing that would destroy any belief that we were guilty would have to be from them finding the person who was.

Suppose Edward really wanted to take a bath. He could have decided to try out the new tub we'd chosen. He would have had a tub or shower or both at the house he lived in while the other was being remodeled. But he loved the large windows with rounded tops we had put in that bathroom and most of all, he'd been thrilled when Eve and I suggested that chandelier right above a freestanding tub. He was lying face up when I found him floating in it fully dressed.

Could he have started running the water? He could have planned to undress but then maybe he slipped. I envisioned him standing beside the attractive tub with his back toward it, his fingers going to the top button of his shirt. And then maybe he fell back. Something startled him. Maybe his phone's ring. And he slipped backward, knocked his head. The water kept running. He remained in it.

We came in. *I* walked in first and found him dead. The water was still running.

Reliving that fearful experience, I found myself humming "Silent Night." Then instead of sticking my finger in the candy mixture to find whether it was still hot, I touched the side of the pot. Feeling the heat remaining there proved the detective's interrogation had not taken nearly as long as it felt.

I reheated what was in the pot. Then, even if the recipe didn't call for it, I beat the mixture. I beat the hell out of everything, imagining it was all the detective's blame that he shoveled on us.

The pralines came out stiffer and more sugary than the smooth creamy ones I normally made, but I felt a slight release of my anger. I dropped them by tablespoons on the waxed paper.

While they cooled, I entered my dining room and made notes about all the subs we'd used on Edward's house. My sister would have more detail about them, like if they had ever worked with us before.

We didn't get to make all the revisions we had planned since he fired us—and died, I thought, intense sorrow once more swelling inside.

I wrote everything I could think of about the people we had hired and the men and few women who'd come around Edward's house with them. A couple of guys seemed somewhat suspicious, or was I thinking that only because of their long ponytails or the way they wore their pants slung too low for my style? Those who carried in light fixtures or flooring or bathroom fixtures or other equipment could have watched the people they worked for getting the key for the front door from under the pot of asparagus fern. Any of them could have returned inside or even told others of the place it was supposedly hidden. Edward had wanted us all to put it there.

Mentally exhausted, I left my notes. In the kitchen, I lifted each cooled praline and placed it with others in a large plastic container I didn't mind parting with.

Carrying the pralines outside, I took a moment to suck in fresh air. I looked at the blue sky, saw a large white cloud, and remembered how as a child, I enjoyed watching clouds and deciding what they looked like with my older sister who had died. This one reminded me of a bathtub.

I threw myself and the gift into my truck and took off.

Soon I arrived at our community center that had turned into a soup kitchen we called a gumbo kitchen because that's what was served most to the needy. Lots of other southern dishes were prepared, and I'd never heard of anyone who ate there complaining about the food. A light crew worked every weekday and on holidays and fixed meals. Some of us locals often brought in an extra item or two.

"Oh, your yummy pralines," Amy Mathews said when I walked inside and told her what I was carrying. Her skin was the attractive color of a rich cappuccino, and she wore flamboyant reds and yellows and purples as always. My friend since high school gave me a squeeze and took the container. "Maybe nobody else will get any."

I laughed with her, knowing the most she would take of my candy might be a pinch that broke off. She cared too much about the less fortunate to take any food that was meant for them. It was probably also the reason she became my friend. Even if most of my classmates knew by the time we'd reached high school that I took longer than most of them to complete work because of my dyslexia, most of them still didn't understand the disorder. Add to that my compulsion to blurt out or hum carols when I was scared, some of them just stayed back. I was mentally slow, some decided. If their minds hadn't changed, so be it.

Amy was always my friend. She carried the sweets I'd brought to a long table. A few remains of cakes and other desserts stretched out past the table that had held large containers of redfish court bouillon. Mainly a little of the brownish red sauce and chopped bell pepper and celery remained, along with small chunks of fish. The large dish of rice held only a little left for anyone wanting seconds or any hungry latecomer who walked inside.

Voices rose and lowered from the dozen or so people who had finished eating and were playing cards. Most were probably enjoying Hand and Foot, a game some could play all day and didn't like to be disturbed from.

Hey, y'all," Amy called to them, "Sunny brought pralines."

The few women but mainly men scrambled from their benches and rushed to where we stood. "Yum. Thanks, Sunny," some said. Each grabbed a praline, a few going for another but holding back, waiting until every person had one. Then a couple of men lifted their eyebrows to Amy as though asking if they could have more.

"Go ahead. Help yourself," she said.

They took them and returned to their card games. In the end, Amy and I were left with sugary crumbs that flaked off large pieces.

"These are nice, but not as good as your usual ones." Amy spoke to me as only a true friend should.

"I know." Pulling my thoughts back to Detective Wilet's interruption of my candy-making process, I inwardly shuddered. "I needed to stop for a few minutes while I was cooking."

Her large eyes kept contact with mine. "You looked bothered from the minute you stepped through the door. What's wrong?" She leaned close and cocked her head with her chin lifted like she always did when she seemed like a psychiatrist about to probe my soul. "Problems with your boyfriend?"

"Oh no, not him." I took her hands. "Amy, somebody we worked for died, and Eve and I seem to be suspected of causing his death."

A brief laugh left her mouth. "Well, if that's the only problem…" She grinned, then looked serious. "Who died?"

"Edward Cancienne."

She quirked a brow. "I don't think I knew him."

"That S.O.B.!" The man seated behind me threw his cards on the table. His back was toward us, but he turned his slim body to face us. His forehead was wide, his lips thin and twisted in anger. "Edward Cancienne screwed my cousin out of so much money it put him out of business!"

I hadn't meant for others to hear us, but since this man had, I was truly interested in what he told us. "What happened?"

"He messed around with my cousin so much he lost his company and started drinking again. His wife and kids left him." Fury made large veins stand out on the man's forehead. His face became edged with red.

I didn't want to urge his anger on but wanted to know more. "Who is your cousin?"

"Emery Jackobson." He shook his head. His teeth pressed tight together, revealing an overbite.

"Come on. Let's get on with the game. What's your bet?" the fellow seated across from him said.

"Okay." Emery Jackobson's cousin slapped the table and glanced back at me. "If you killed Edward, then good for you."

Returning his attention to the card game, he didn't see me shaking my head and didn't seem to hear me saying, "No, I didn't do it."

Amy grabbed my arm and pulled me away from all the others. "He's going to believe what he wants to. For now, you're his hero." She grinned. "Or heroine."

"Who is he?" I needed names for the detective.

"All he says is *Nelson*. They have to sign in when they come here, but that guy hasn't been coming for long. A first name is all he writes."

"Or maybe it's his last name."

"I hadn't thought of that. Anyway, it's what I've heard a couple of them calling him."

So maybe it was a first name, I figured after I shared a hug with Amy, told her good-bye, and drove off. I got Eve on the phone. "Are you home?" I asked, and when she said yes, told her I was coming over.

At her place, I had lots to say. "I had a visit from Detective Wilet. He seems to think we might have murdered Edward."

Eve's hands shot up as though blocking a basketball slammed at them. "Can't he find somebody else to blame? Good grief, you'd think he could come up with someone else in town—or maybe somebody from away from here."

"I know. First, we need to bring him all the information we can gather about the subs that we used on the house. And I made notes about all of their helpers I could think of."

She was nodding. "Great. I'll do a printout of their contact info."

"I'm also going to let him know about somebody I just learned had a motive to kill our client."

"Tell me about it while I gather the other information."

The sun was shimmering toward the west when we rode to the station and carried our papers in to the detective. We told him tidbits about people we had worked with on the deceased man's house and then I gave him the bombshell. "We know all of those men and the few women went around his place sometimes. But what I just found out was a person who could have wanted to kill him."

This officer who had made me feel like a criminal earlier today now looked at me with interest. Giving him a person with a motive for murder made him sit straighter, and lift his thick eyebrows at the edges. He wrote and asked questions of me and wrote more. When he inquired about whether Eve had anything to add, she shrugged her trim shoulders. She looked a bit younger than normal with her hair pulled back in a ponytail. She still wore her attractive emerald green workout suit.

"I didn't see anybody I knew today, but I'll try to learn more soon," she said.

Detective Wilet gave me a nod. "Did this fellow Nelson say what kind of business his cousin had?"

"No, and I'm sorry I didn't ask."

"But he goes to the gumbo kitchen. I'll check it out." The detective set down his pen.

Relief washing through me, I stood beside Eve. "You know we're happy to get you any facts that might help solve a case." What good citizens we were, I told myself, mentally patting my back and my twin's.

The detective's lips formed a half grin. He knew the main thing we were doing was trying to find somebody else for him to blame instead of us for that murder.

We also cared about who killed our client. "Let's keep in touch," I told the stout officer rising from his desk and coming to walk us out of his office.

Away from his stifling building, we decided a nice trip to visit our mother seemed in order. She had been pleased with us for attending Edward's funeral. Now she would probably still be in a better mood with us.

"We'll be able to decipher whether his murder made her decide to delay wedding plans," Eve suggested, and I agreed.

We hurried to the manor, cheerful since we'd shared incriminating information with the detective.

Not far inside, Mom's friends sat gathered. Those in the Chat and Nap group who took daily naps must have already enjoyed them, although Mom wasn't with them yet. These all appeared lively, their chatter echoing through the foyer. We exchanged greetings with them.

A woman at the outer edge of one sofa wiggled her fingers at us. "Hello, I'm new here. Y'all are so pretty."

We both thanked her.

"I imagine in time I'll learn which one is which of you. I'm Thelma."

"It's nice to meet you," Eve and I said.

"And this is my husband, Bud." She held up a brown urn I'd thought was her purse.

I swallowed, not knowing whether I should tell Bud hello. I decided not to, while Eve obviously did the same. "Where's Mom?" I asked. "Still napping?"

"She needed to go to her doctor for a checkup," the pearl lady said. "Mac and his daughter took her."

I exchanged a grim look with Eve. Our good moods were dead.

Chapter 6

"Sit down," the woman who scooted over on a sofa told us.

I felt my face droop into a frown, exactly as what just happened to my spirits. Eve and I planted our bottoms on the places given to us. Squeezed in to fit, I felt the end of the stuffed sofa pressed against one of my hips and a large woman against my other one. Somehow that felt comforting.

Eve perched at the edge of a loveseat. "What do y'all think about Mac?" she asked, encouraging a whirlwind of replies from women on sofas and wheelchairs.

"He took your momma to the doctor. That was nice of him."

"We've offered to bring her," I said, "but she always wants to go in the manor's van."

"She says she doesn't want to give us any trouble," Eve said. "We've told her it wouldn't be, but she refuses."

"Mac isn't bad looking," one of the ladies said.

"And he always wears khaki pants. I like men to wear khaki pants." This woman nodded from her wheelchair.

"He never has food on the front of his clothes like some men do," another one said in their spitfire discussion.

"And how about when they scratch themselves? You know, down there."

"Does Mac do that?" I asked. The correct answer could be something we could use in our argument to keep Mom from thinking of living with him.

Aging women looked at each other. Some seemed to concentrate before giving an answer. A number of them shook their heads no. One said yes.

"Shoot," she said then. "The word accidentally slipped out of my mouth." She shook her head at us. "He doesn't."

"What kind of person is he?" I shifted to a topic of much more interest than the clothes he wore or his personal habits, although those could also be important.

"Ooh, he doesn't tip the Bingo caller," one woman waving her hand said.

"He doesn't?" Eve asked, her tone as enthusiastic as my mood from that woman's reply. At least it was something negative we might use.

"Oh no," said Ms. Grace, whose cell phone must have again slipped out of her bra and was now forming a third breast jammed above her belt. "He didn't tip any caller who came in the manor from another place when he first got here, but after he saw everybody else giving a dollar to the caller after they won a pot, he gave them a dollar, too."

"But that's only if somebody comes in to call the games. We don't tip the people who work here," one assured us. It was something we already knew.

"Is he sickly?" I asked, causing some to give each other quizzical looks with raised eyebrows.

"Not that I know of," one said.

"Neither me. But I don't hear those things about men."

The aroma of homemade bread swelled, gaining the interest of most in our group. Some heads turned toward the dining area.

"Yum, that smells good, doesn't it?" This comment would have been most appropriate at the moment, except it came from Thelma. She looked at her urn when she asked it. Was she expecting the ashes inside it to give her a response? Or maybe it would shake to indicate yes or no.

Others began getting up and moving toward the enticing smell that now also included a hint of garlic in tomato sauce.

"Y'all are having spaghetti tonight?" Eve asked.

"Yes," said the woman whose hip still pressed against mine. "And zucchini and a bun and salad and milk."

"Sounds good," I said. "We need to place an order ahead of time soon so we can come and eat a meal with y'all here."

"They're all good." Her hip drew away from mine.

"Y'all enjoy," Eve called to those still close. Some replied, some waved back, and some of them didn't hear well and probably hadn't heard her.

Residents and staff members were moving toward the food. Who could blame them? The aroma swelled around us. My sympathy went out to those who never left their suites or rooms. Unlike the nursing home in town, this retirement community catered mainly to those capable of taking care of themselves. They needed to be mobile and not require medicine delivered to their rooms or baths by staff members. The few who were here and needed more help hired their own; these were mainly parents of local doctors. Thinking of that made me recall Nelson from the gumbo kitchen who said Edward ruined his cousin's life. Gaining a little optimism, I hoped Detective Wilet was finding information that would get his attention off us as killers.

Eve and I watched people entering this large space that was filled with white tables, each having four chairs. Residents had been assigned to their seats. Women sat together; so did men. Female and a few male staff members wearing navy tops and pants held up with drawstrings got trays of food and drinks from the wide serving window of the cafeteria and carried them to people's places. The trays had matching numbers with each seat so they knew what meal went where. Some residents who got heartburn from red sauce received baked chicken breasts instead. Others who were on special diets would receive a tray holding the type of food or drink they could have.

Even the nurse, administrator, and the assistant-administrator took part at mealtime, so everything moved swiftly and meals arrived hot. The assistant moved toward the kitchen. The administrator passed near us carrying a tray. "Hi, are you two eating with us tonight? Did you order meals?"

"No," I said. "We're just standing here getting hungry from this great smell." I sniffed the air and looked at the enticing plate of spaghetti.

"Really, we're waiting for Mom," Eve said. "We know Mr. McCormick took her for a checkup, but they should be back soon. Doctors' offices are closed by now."

"Mom is probably in her room freshening up. We'll just wait a couple of minutes to get to see her," I said.

She shook her head, rushing off with her tray. "Miriam said she wasn't coming back for supper. After the doctor's visit, Mac was taking her and his daughter to a restaurant."

I stared at Eve. How could we feel any pleasure toward the man and his daughter? Both were shoving us out of our mother's life.

"Do you want to eat out?" Eve asked after we had sullenly ambled to my truck in the fading light of day and then shut ourselves inside it.

There were only a couple of restaurants in town where a man would have probably taken a woman he cared about for a date. "Humph, a date." I snorted, and Eve gave me a look, like that's not what I asked. "Not today. I wouldn't want to run into our mother and her new man and his child."

Eve's shoulders slumped. "I know."

"I've got leftovers if you want. You can come over." She seldom cooked but liked almost everything I prepared.

"No thanks. I think I'm just going to throw a few slices of baked chicken on a salad." That type of food was her normal diet, the reason she stayed so trim.

I, on the other hand, preferred food that added fluff over my bones. She and I rode in silence toward our homes. I considered turning on music but shoved off that thought. Remaining sour was more my mood.

Right before I dropped Eve off, she looked at me. "I'll bet she's pretty."

I knew who she spoke of—our intended new *sister* whose father was judged by at least one of the residents as good looking. "Probably so."

We gave each other slight good-bye waves once she reached her front door. It was as though that was all either of us could muster at the time. *But when would that time be over?* I wondered, driving the short distance to my house on the street parallel to hers. Suppose Mom married him and moved into a little house with his pretty daughter and him? I considered, getting out of my truck in my carport and slamming the door. Would we get to visit her often? Would they want us there? Would they still live around this town?

"No, we need to stop any of that from happening," I told myself, unlocking the door to my house and going inside.

The moment I shut the door, the doorbell rang, making me jump. I stuck my eye against the peephole.

Dave stood outside.

"What do you need to stop?" he asked when I yanked the door open.

An overwhelming need washed through me. "Not this." I threw my arms around his neck and planted a kiss on his lips. Feeling relief but somewhat shaken, I let him go.

He pulled me back into an embrace. "Good. Don't stop this." The man who was becoming most important to me drew me closer and gave me a warm kiss that lingered against my lips.

"Oh no, I won't," I said, responding to his statement about putting an end to us doing that. Instead of standing in the open doorway, I drew him inside. He was lifting his arms to me again, growing passion in the darker tint of his eyes, his neck shifting with his swallow. He closed in.

"No." I placed my palm against his firm chest.

His shoulders pressed back. His happy composure collapsed. "No? Sunny, what's wrong?"

Reality set in. "It's been a rough day."

He took my hands, his face tight with concern. "Tell me about it."

"Sit down. I'll get us some coffee." Second thoughts came. "Or wine instead?"

"That sounds good."

I poured cabernet into two stemmed glasses and sat next to him. With a grim smile, I tapped my glass against his and took a sip. The rich flavor felt good going down.

"It's good," he said after a swallow. "Okay, now tell me what's going on."

I thought a moment. How much of all that happened should I tell him? Did I really want to replay any misery? "Somebody asked me about you today."

He cocked his head. "Really? And who was that?"

"Amy Mathews, my friend who runs the gumbo kitchen."

He gave me a tiny uncertain smile. "Somebody knows about me? You told somebody about you and me?"

"Amy's been my good friend since high school. We don't hide anything from each other."

He lifted an eyebrow, seeming impressed. "Then I guess you told her you and I care about each other." The corner of his lips lowered a pinch. "You do still care about me, don't you?"

I touched his hand. "Of course I do."

Dave drew in a breath that made his chest rise and then he relaxed. He took another swallow of drink. "Then you might tell me what's bothering you besides your friend inquiring about me."

"Today I almost walked in on my mother and someone else who might be replacing us as her daughters."

He cocked his head, forehead creasing. "Where was this?"

"At a restaurant in town. I'm not sure which one." He narrowed his eyes as though he were trying to figure out what I was saying. I knew my brief comment must have been confusing, so I spilled out all of what happened at the manor—how Eve and I had gone and spoken with some of Mom's friends and then waited for her in the dining room. Then we'd learned that instead of eating at her usual place there, she hadn't come back but remained gone with those others.

Dave watched my face with no change in his, absorbing all the things I was telling him. Once I finished, he gave me a moment to calm my emotions. Then he reached over and brushed back the wave I realized had fallen to my face. "You're afraid of losing her."

"Yes, I am."

"Your own mother." He kept looking at me. "You think she'll stop loving you?"

"No. Absolutely not."

"But you're jealous."

"Of who?" I pressed my upper body forward, ready for a major argument with him. Jealousy wasn't a trait I was fond of, not one I thought I possessed.

"A man that your mother cares about. Ever since I've known you, you and Eve and your mother seemed to have a close, loving relationship."

"We always did."

Dave leaned closer, the manly scent of his skin attracting me. "Do you believe your mother could ever stop loving both of you just because she might want to let a man enter her life? Don't you think she has room in her heart for all of you?"

"Yes." I pressed back in my chair. "No. Or I don't know. But what I do know is that he seems pushy if he's trying to marry her so fast. Or marry her at all."

"Ah, I know." He took a swallow of his wine. I did the same. "You want to keep them from being intimate."

"Intimate?" I shoved up to my feet and slapped the table with my palm. "That's not it. But hey, you're talking about my mother here."

A grimace tightened on his lips. "I know it. Everybody's mother is sacred." He stood and took a step back from me while anger broiled around in my chest. Dave picked up his wineglass. "Thanks for the drink."

"You don't have to do that," was all I thought of saying when he carried the glass to the sink.

He headed for the front door, and I followed. "May I kiss you good-bye?" he asked.

I needed to check in with my anger. I wanted a kiss from this man much more than I wanted to argue with him.

"Yes."

Neither of us revealed any passion with the brief kiss. It was the same kind I normally exchanged with my mother.

Busying myself, I washed and dried and put away our glasses, then remembered I hadn't eaten supper. The experiences I'd had made me feel that I didn't want a meal, especially when I considered my mom had gone out. I grabbed a handful of chocolate chip cookies and gobbled them down with a glass of cold milk. Then I swept the floor and went for a shower.

I stood under steamy hot water with strawberry shampoo making my eyes burn before I allowed myself to consider Dave's visit and words. Was I jealous about Mom's situation? If I admitted the truth to myself, it was yes. Whether male or female, I was jealous of anyone who stole my mother's love from me.

And I had hurt Dave, the man I believed I may have fallen in love with. Pain held in his tone when he'd spoken of mothers being sacred. Now, while

I could see my arms turning red from the steam, I considered how those words and our discussion must have hurt him. His mother and father had died when he'd been a young man. The woman Dave had married died from an illness some years back, too. They never had a child, and since his only sibling was a wonderful sister who adored him and was now wheelchair-bound, he would not understand my twin and I being uneasy about the possibility of gaining another one. Our other sister died. Nobody else could replace her.

The skin on my back stung by the time I stepped out of the shower. I would have to work with myself and my sister so I could come to grips with what was happening in our lives, or else we would need to change it. After a good night's sleep to clear my concerns, I hoped I would face a better morning but feared I would not.

Chapter 7

Eve's phone call came soon after I woke up. "Hey, girl, we need to go finish the job at the diner. You want to do it this morning?"

I didn't have enthusiasm for anything. "We'd just as soon."

"I'll be there in an hour."

She wasn't giving me enough time to push through all the haze of confusion that came yesterday and stayed with me this morning. I couldn't fall asleep for hours last night. I tossed around the bed. Images about what Dave and I spoke about kept grabbing my mind like a robber and holding it ransom. Finally freed of those thoughts, I'd slept maybe one hour, possibly two. I shuffled my dragging body to go and put some clothes on so we could finish our work at the diner. We had previously sanded and refinished the chairs around all her tables with high-gloss varnish that made them look almost new.

The face that glanced at me from my bathroom mirror made me look away. That person had deep folds in the skin from being pressed against a pillow or sheet. Her eyes were bloodshot, and her hair was pushed up on one side and lying limp on the other. She didn't move as fast as most of the residents of the retirement home.

Since our main mission today was completing work for our Twin Sisters Remodeling and Repair business, I made an easy pick of clothes to wear. I pulled on jeans, and tennis shoes, and a purple T-shirt with our logo on back. That done, I sat on the edge of my bed waiting for Eve to come. Getting dressed hadn't taken long even though my movements were sluggish. I waited and waited for Eve.

"Sunny, it's late. What's the matter?" She stood next to my bed, arms waving around like she was trying to grab sacks of air. "Are you sick?"

She leaned in and did like Mom, pressing her lips to my forehead to check for fever.

I waved her away. "No, I'm fine." I took long minutes more to enjoy the luxury of lying in my bed pushing up. I managed to support myself on one elbow, but it wanted to drop me back again. "I just didn't sleep well."

She backed away while I got to a seated position, rested there a minute, and then stood.

"I'd better get out of this bedroom before I flop on that bed again."

She had walked over here since she lived around the block and only gave me time to grab a small glass of milk and a banana for the road. I needed coffee but since we were going to the diner, I could get a cup or two there. We went in my truck because it held the tool chest, but she insisted on driving while I had my small meal and tried to wake up.

Josie's Diner sat like a small red dot at the end of Sixth Street. Around it, most buildings appeared drab. They were barbershops, and a uniform store, and dry cleaners, and others that had been there for years. Most of those businesses bore small signs with the names of their places as the only way to tell them apart on their unpainted old cypress storefronts.

Josie's place grabbed a person's eye. When she'd wanted to update her diner and make it stand out a little from the others, Eve and I had suggested the bright chartreuse posts that stood on both sides of the welcoming door that we painted sunlight yellow. We designed a fairly large sign with its color matching that of the posts and JOSIE'S DINER across its center.

The inside was normally bright as well, with all the colors and lighting we had suggested, although this morning one corner of the fairly filled diner was faintly lit. I noticed right after opening the door two extra-long fluorescent bulbs above that section had burned out. There was lots of talking, and enticing scents of bacon, and powdered sugar on the beignets I saw a few customers in the crowded room eating. Mixed with the aroma of breakfast sausage and smothered onions, Josie's food called to my attention almost as much as the two people I saw seated together under the diminished section of light.

"That's him," I said, elbowing Eve.

"Ow." She rubbed her side that I'd hit. "Who?"

"I'll tell you about it later. Come on." I stepped ahead of her to the table at the far end of the room, right up to the man who had watched us ever since we stepped inside.

He squinted, giving me a cautious look. His small lips pushed forward in the middle and twisted toward the left. He pressed back against his chair as we neared.

"Hello, Mr. Nelson." I offered my hand, which he looked at as though it were some creature coming to attack him. Mr. Nelson stared at it, but did not offer his. "I'm Sunny Taylor," I said, although it was obvious my name meant nothing to him. I wanted to bring up where we had met, but I didn't in case the man with him did not know of Nelson's frequenting the gumbo kitchen. "You might have heard of me. I make pralines."

Like an old-time cash register, his eyes rolled down and then just as quickly rolled up. His mouth opened without making a sound, but I could imagine it saying, "Ah." Yes, he remembered I had brought some of them that he'd eaten at the center.

"This is my sister, Eve Vaughn. Of course you could tell we're sisters, since we're identical."

Eve stood back a bit. I grabbed her hand and tugged her forward so these men would have to also respond to her.

Eve eyed Nelson's hand, which remained on his fork instead of up accepting mine. She nodded but did not put out hers.

In case Detective Wilet hadn't gotten any information about Nelson or his cousin that Edward had supposedly put out of business, I wanted to know more. Probably this wasn't the time to ask Nelson about it, but I needed to learn all I could, and he was here now. Maybe I could get Nelson's last name if that was his first. Whatever, I wanted his full name.

I reached my hand out to the man seated across from him. This person was small, pale, looking almost as frail as a china teacup. His dark brown eyes stood out. So did his hand with a surprisingly tight grip. His smile was quick.

"Hello, I'm Emery Jackobson, Nelson's *friend*." The grin he gave Nelson and the light in his eye when he looked at his eating partner suggested Nelson might not be only a casual friend. He was not this man's cousin, either. And if I was right, Nelson and now the deceased Edward Cancienne, was the reason for this fellow losing a wife he probably shouldn't have married in the first place.

"It's good to meet you, Emery." I chose not to mention what Nelson had told me about him.

"Same here." He could give lessons in southern manners to the man seated with him.

I returned my attention to the man I had previously met. Or I hadn't met him but had spoken to him. "And Nelson—?" I left the name hanging, anticipating another name to go with that one.

He pressed his lips tighter together until only the thin outer rim was visible.

"There are my lady friends." Josie's words boomed over the raised volume of other voices and noises from scraping chairs and skillets slapping on stovetops. She was standing two tables away, using a spray bottle to squirt liquid on the red tabletop and wiping it off with a dry towel. Josie was a whirlwind tall enough to clean the top of a refrigerator without needing anything to stand on. Eve and I were relatively tall, too, for being females, but we needed to look up to Josie. Her hair was blue today, clashing with her deep wrinkles that said she was a little old to dye her hair different colors, but she was her own person. On her, the cotton candy hair looked charming.

"Did you want us to fix that stool today?" Moving toward her, Eve pointed at the empty stool with the tilted seat at the counter. Whenever Josie asked us to do some fixing up in here, she didn't care whether customers were around. That made working much better for us than if we would have to come after closing hours, but I didn't know how people eating felt about her policy. So far, I had never noticed that anyone seemed to care.

The men I stood beside had resumed their eating. Emery poured thick, golden cane syrup on his bacon slices and the stack of French toast that was already coated with powdery sugar. The tempting dish made my taste buds dance and my mind question how he could eat like that and remain so thin.

Nelson stuck his fork into eggs that had been scrambled with bits of mushroom, onions, and bell pepper sticking out. He kept his face and shoulder turned away so I knew he was not wanting to converse with me any longer.

"I saw you looking at that food mighty hard," Josie said when I walked up to her. "I think you need to put something in your little belly before I can put you gals to work."

"No, that's okay. I ate at home," Eve said.

"I'd like a couple of bites of something. And coffee." I sat in a chair at the table she had just cleaned.

Eve sat with me. "I'll have a coffee."

"Be right back." Josie swirled away and snapped her fingers at the teen walking around with a half-filled carafe. When the girl looked at her, Josie showed two fingers and pointed at us. The girl nodded. She grabbed two thick white mugs and carried one atop the other one to us, still gripping the carafe in the other.

"Thanks. I could never do that without dumping coffee or dropping a cup," I said.

She set our cups down and filled them almost to the top. "You're welcome. I've gotten used to it."

On the other side of the eatery, I noticed some people's eyes aimed at us. When I met their gazes, two of them smiled and nodded in greeting, which I did in return. Others, though, rushed their stares away. Maybe they had heard Eve and I found Edward dead. Some, like Nelson, might believe we killed him. If that was the case, I didn't blame them for turning away from us.

I shook powdered creamer and a spoon of sugar into my coffee. Then I stirred, not so tempted by its scent or hungry for food anymore. Eve started drinking her coffee black. "This is good." She lifted an eyebrow at me. "Weren't you in a hurry to have a cup?"

After a little shrug, I took a sip of mine. Then while she took her time having small sips of hers, I took one big swallow after another. The liquid was warm, soothing, only not giving the relief I now sought. "I can't until till they find out what happened to Edward," I said.

"Here you go." Josie had moved up beside me. She set a plate in front of me. "Since you didn't say anything, I got you your usual." The plate held a fried egg that was soft in the middle but crispy, almost burned at the edges. Buttered toast sat at the edge of the plate next to three slices of bacon and two beautiful plump strawberries.

"You're wonderful," I told her. The colors and aromas drew me to lifting my fork, wanting to fill my stomach.

"I know. So tell some good-looking guy so he can sweep me up and marry me and pay all my bills." Josie was gay and did not really want a guy. She flipped up a plaid towel over her shoulder. Its violet and orange colors clashed with her hair. "They're still working on finding out who killed Edward, huh?" she asked, obviously having walked up when I'd spoken to Eve.

Eve nodded. "You wouldn't happen to know anything about who killed him, would you?"

Josie kept her lips tight. "You know me," she said and shook her head. "I don't know anything about anybody." That's what she always told people. Not taking part in gossip sessions in your establishment was a good way to stay in business.

She startled me by leaning down, her blue hair tickling my ear. "I think one of his lovers could have gotten jealous of the others."

Before I could pull my head back to question her, she was striding away. "Who?" Eve called to her.

Still facing forward as she moved on, Josie jerked her thumb toward the table where Nelson and Emery Jackobson sat.

Josie must have given the pair their check right before she served me. Nelson picked it up. Wearing a smile wide enough to create a big bracket of shiny, white teeth that made him look even paler, Emery reached over and snatched the ticket from him. Nelson shook his head and tugged at it as though he wanted to pay it himself, although I couldn't imagine why since Nelson frequented the gumbo kitchen where he received some of his meals free. Then I recalled Emery also supposedly lost his business, so his income must have greatly diminished. If any of that story was true.

To my surprise, Emery placed his hand on top of Nelson's. He tilted his head and made sweet eyes like a baby learning to accomplish that feat. The last time we got to see Eve's little grandchild, he carried out that incredible action that tore into our hearts and made Eve plant kisses all over his face and make those goo-goo eyes back at him.

The two men stood, and we both tucked our chins, keeping our gazes away from them. I chewed a slice of tasty bacon that was cooked crisp like I enjoyed best. Out of the corner of my eye, I saw when the men were coming this way and then heading for the door.

The minute they were out, I got up. "Have some breakfast," I said, pushing my plate toward Eve. "I'm going to get our tools." I rushed outside, wanting to see if both men came in one vehicle or if each had their own and arrived separately. I wasn't certain why that was important, but felt it was something I needed to learn.

They walked a few steps ahead of me. Probably hearing my footsteps or the door shutting, Nelson looked back. He eyed me with a frown.

I grabbed the small toolbox out of my truck's cab and held it up. "We need to fix some things," I said, not knowing why I felt a need to explain.

He didn't respond and gave no evidence that he even heard. Nelson and Emery reached the corner and walked around it, disappearing beyond the palm reader's little building. The sign out front that showed an open hand had lost a letter so that it read *Pam Reader.*

Even though I was tempted to step to the corner to see where the men went, I realized Nelson might be watching for me. And then what? He might suspect me of something? He already believed Eve and I killed Edward and at the gumbo kitchen praised me for doing it, although I'd protested we had not. Maybe he believed we were murderers, and I was stalking him. I backed off, returning inside the diner.

Eve was chewing when I reached our table with a toolbox. "Great bacon," she said after swallowing. "But your fried egg isn't so good, since it's gotten cooler." She shoved my plate back to me.

My appetite was mostly gone, but I eyed my egg with its yolk runny now that Eve had cut into it. I ate the final slice of bacon with a few bites of toast. "I didn't see what they came in," I told her.

"Maybe they walked."

I hadn't considered that, but there were a couple of older houses and apartment buildings in the area. "That's possible." I left what I knew my meal and Eve's coffee cost plus a tip on our table. "Let's go fix that stool." She touched the side of her face. "I forgot to tell you. Someone I work out with at the gym told me Edward was gay. Not that that means anything."

I looked back at the place where two men I believed were also gay just sat. Was that a coincidence? Just gossip or an assumption of something more?

Three people from the right of the barstool with the tilted seat had left, giving us more space to work. We apologized to others sitting around, but they said they weren't bothered.

"I like to see a gal work with tools," the postman with the big belly said. He rode in a truck to deliver our mail.

"Well, there you can see two for your money," Josie said, slapping his ticket down in front of him. "And hire them sometime. You could get to watch them use all kinds of tools." She gave us a wink. Josie knew we could use more orders to help our business thrive.

We only needed to use electric screwdrivers to remove the bent metal plate under the seat. We had known what we needed here, so had purchased another plate. We took little time to screw it in and make certain the seat was balanced.

"All done," Eve told Josie. "Anything else you need?"

"No, I don't. Girls, y'all are so quick. Send me your bill."

I waved that thought away. "Just give us some nice, warm goodies to eat next time we come back," I said, and she grinned. "And get us a couple of fluorescent bulbs right now. We'll go change those burned ones."

With our heights, we didn't need a ladder but could stand on the chairs Nelson and Emery had used. The table had already been cleared and spray cleaned. I checked the floor beneath the table and chairs before getting up, thinking I might find some bit of paper that might shed some light on the two who'd been here. Only a small piece of biscuit lay against the wall.

Standing on one the chairs, Eve loosened the edge of the light's plastic cover and let it hang from the opposite side from me. I twisted out one long burned bulb and then the other. She gave me the new ones. In no time, we had those bulbs enclosed with the yellowing plastic cover that had been used here for years. Getting more thanks from Josie, we wiped off the chairs and left.

I drove straight to Detective Wilet's office. Soon we sat across the desk from him, the stench of burned coffee again in the hall we'd passed through. Papers lay strewn across his desktop. "Okay, so what is your new information regarding Edward Cancienne's case?" He had his pen out and was ready to write.

"He was gay," Eve said.

"So?" He didn't jot her words.

I spread my hands. "We don't care about that, but we believe he had two or possibly more lovers around here. One of them was probably Emery Jackobson."

The detective quirked a thick brow. "Wait, hadn't y'all told me that Edward caused Jackobson to go out of business?"

Eve leaned forward, hands clasped. "If those men were involved together, that certainly would have also been a reason for Jackobson's wife to leave him."

Dark eyes swerved from one to the other of us. He watched us while voices and quick footsteps sounded from another room. With a sudden motion, he bent over and wrote. His notes were quick before he faced us again. "And if word leaked out, and Emery Jackobson lost his family, then what? It would have been a reason for him to kill Edward?"

I wiggled my index finger like a pen. "It also made him lose his business. Don't forget that." I watched but did not see the officer making another note. "I don't even know what kind of business he had."

"He owned a machine parts shop. The oil slump with prices dropping so much is what caused it to close, just like so many other companies down here."

"Oh." I lowered my hand.

He set down his pen. "If I would decide to pursue these things you suggested, is there anywhere in particular you believe I might look?"

Eve got to her feet first. "Go eat at Josie's."

"And we," I said to my twin once we walked outside, "are going to go check on our mother. Maybe we can take her out for an early lunch. We need to find out what's going on now with her and her fellow."

"And his daughter," Eve said, lips compressed and down at the corners.

Yesterday Mom went to eat with them. Now if she wouldn't come with us, I couldn't imagine the deep disappointment.

Chapter 8

I pulled in at the manor, turned right on the lot, and took my time driving along it, slowing behind a few of the parked cars. "Do you recognize anyone from Edward's funeral?" I asked Eve.

"So that's why you're going so slowly."

"Yes, let's see if we can tell if that fellow Carl that we saw arguing with Edward at his house and then in the hall at the funeral parlor is here."

"It would help if we could remember what he drove." But neither of us could. She stared out the window on her side where people had parked. We passed beyond a dirt mount holding a blooming crepe myrtle covered with profuse pale pink flowers. Eve pointed beyond it at the parked truck and older model car with a dented rear fender. "Maybe Mom's beau drives that car." She looked at me and shook her head. "I have no idea what he drives."

"I know."

Two women I recognized as residents moved away from a car one of them must have just parked. These ladies walked with springs in their steps and seemed just as spry as our mother. They were probably her age or maybe a little younger. Possibly they moved in here because of an ailment like our mother's. Some people only chose to live in this pleasing environment because they were past their prime and decided on a place where their rooms were cleaned, their meals purchased and prepared, and their dishes and pots scrubbed. They didn't need to worry about having the grass cut or attractive flowers planted outside. Everything worked, or if it did not, it was soon fixed. They had socialization with games and bus trips for anyone who wanted them and hairdressers who came in and religious services and lots of people to become friends with. All of this was provided in this charming building we walked into. The aroma of sweet jasmine growing right outside the door followed us in.

"I think I want to move in here," I said to Eve.

She gave me a strange look, surely thinking here we were, angry with a man in this place, with residents much older than we were, and I wanted to live here?

A few of Mom's buddies sat around their space not far past the foyer. Mom was not one of them. A shiver of dread ran through me. I didn't want to ask where she was.

Eve obviously didn't feel the same way. "Good morning, ladies," she said and received many similar replies. "I don't see our mother. Does anybody know where she is?"

A couple of them shrugged and shook their heads, but the eyes of two of them darted to our right. Down there was a hall that Mom had emerged from the day we first saw the man she now thought she might marry. She had not told us where she was coming from but had hurried to the bank of elevators, insisting she needed to hurry because a good movie was about to come on. That would be a showing on a much larger television than most of them had in their rooms or suites. The viewing room was a nice size with several chairs. It was often used as a gym, though its two treadmills and all the weights stayed along the outer walls.

At that time, right after our mother got into the elevator and its doors closed, a senior male we had not seen before came from the same hall where she'd come from. *Dapper* might be a word to describe him. Although that depiction wasn't used much these days, it was my first thought. He looked lively and well dressed in nice clothes and holding a walking cane. He followed right behind where our mother went and looked happy waiting for the elevator.

Mom had said the movie they were showing was about an older couple falling in love.

A mild profanity left my lips.

"What?" Eve said, leaning close to me.

I rolled my thumb toward that hallway on the right. "You know Mac's room is down there." Our mother's room was to the left and on the second floor. "She went out with him last night. What if—?"

She shoved a hand across my lips to keep me from asking the rest.

No, neither of us wanted to consider that our mother was sleeping with a man. The idea of that occurring sent shivers along my back and goose flesh sprouting on my arms.

"You're afraid?" Eve whispered, making me realize I had begun humming a Christmas tune.

I quieted my throat. "I'm afraid for Mom. Having someone take advantage of her could ruin her life. She's too old to start over again."

"I know."

Eve was the one who loved men and had surely done some things I would prefer not to think about. It was only that now we were talking about our mother. Our mother! And suppose this stranger drained her bank account and took all her savings? She had always been so trustworthy. We could take care of her if that happened, but she might be destroyed if that occurred. The medicine she took for her heart could only do so much.

"Sunny. Eve." It was Terri Hebert, the manor's administrator who had stepped near. The hem of her long skirt still swayed when she stopped. "If you two aren't busy right this minute, could I ask you to check out something?"

"Of course," we answered together. Anything that would draw our minds away from where they were going down that hall would be a pleasure.

We followed her to the office area, where she raised the square section at the end of the countertop that ran across the room to keep every person with a question or complaint from rushing right up to the office doors to the rear. The square she lifted seemed a little wobbly. That square was only locked with a small sliding bolt, so actually anyone with agile fingers could open it and go back there. Most residents didn't seem to know this, or maybe seeing the offices blocked, they got the message not to try.

As usual, a secretary sat back there near the sign-in sheet. She would give answers to guests and direct visitors to residents they wanted to find.

What seemed different this time was the open doors to all three of the offices—the nurse, administrator, and her assistant. Normally they kept those rooms closed off. One shut door wore a sign saying *Supplies*. The other shut door was unmarked.

The nurse didn't appear to be in her office that I could see, although I didn't poke my head in the room to determine whether she was stooping at the bottom of a filing cabinet. If she left her door unlocked when she left her office, she mustn't leave medicine out in the open. While I was considering this worrisome thought, she stepped out of the room with no sign on the door, and I could hear the sound of the final flushing of a toilet. I imagined she needed to go in a hurry and hadn't taken time to lock her office or even shut its door. Or wash her hands?

She walked into her office and shut the door. What attracted my attention before that was the trio of framed pictures of azalea bushes that hung on her rear white wall. The flowers were profuse, one bush filled with white blossoms, one with pale pink, and one with fuchsia, the most common color down here along the bayous. Seeing them made my stomach hurt, and I needed to turn away. I might have been the only person in south Louisiana, or possibly anywhere, who not only disliked azaleas but experienced anguish whenever I saw them.

"Sunny?" The administrator had stopped walking and now stared at me. Eve looked at me, too, lifting an eyebrow.

"Are you like some people who enjoy Christmas books or movies anytime of the year?" Terri asked with a small smile.

"Or tunes," Eve said, a flash of concern in her eye toward me. "Yes, my sister can sing those carols all the time."

Having them call attention to my problem of humming or singing a holiday tune when something brought up my fear got me to stop the sounds from coming out my throat. Seeing all those azaleas, I realized, had brought me back to the terrible long moments when I was little and stooped beside my dying sister on our driveway to wait for help to come for her. Momma's azalea bushes next to the drive were bright pink and too pretty and shaking in a breeze—and I hated them. Nothing attractive should have been living.

I needed to go back to counseling to deal with that problem.

"Let's see what you've got that concerns you," I said. As we walked close to the room with a plaque above it saying *Assistant Administrator*, I glanced inside that office. Rita Picou was not in her office that I could see. My view automatically ran over the rear wall of the room painted pale blue to find photos of beach scenes. "Nice pictures in there," I said without a song, and pointed. "She must love to go to beaches."

Terri nodded. "As soon as she can retire, she plans to spend most of her time there."

Reaching Terri's office, I inevitably scanned her back wall first. Besides noting that it and the whole room were covered with dark paneling, I noted the floral prints were less clear, possibly with water lilies and some other flowers on land, although I would have needed to put my glasses on to tell. They were obviously Monet prints.

Not surprising, she kept everything in place. No papers lay scattered on her desk, no file cabinets were left open, no family pictures stood out, and nothing hung on the wooden coat hanger standing in a corner. We weren't experiencing winter, but many women with offices had a tendency to keep a light jacket hanging in theirs in case they got chilly.

"I'd like a change in here." She swept her arm around the room.

I didn't see anything wrong with the space. It was functional with a nice large oak desk, a brown cushioned desk chair for her, and two side chairs for guests. A tall file cabinet stood beside the coat rack, but otherwise the room was bare.

"Okay," Eve said. "What kind of change were you thinking of?"

"I don't know. It's too plain." That was a statement I wasn't going to argue with. "It looks sterile, almost like it belongs in a hospital, and I don't want people who come in here to inquire about possibly living in the manor thinking of it like that."

"You want it friendlier," I offered. "Maybe painted in a welcoming color." She opened her eyes wider. "You can paint over paneling?"

Eve nodded. "And it would help to add a few live plants in here. Greenery oxygenates a room, and the green reminds people so much of nature that it helps them relax."

She was nodding, looking from one to the other of us. "I didn't know you knew so much about human nature."

"We continuously study about color and other things used in remodeling or making repairs," Eve said.

I pointed to her laminated floor. "That looks nice, but a pale short-napped carpet would capture sound and give warmth to your space."

She gave me a broad smile. "That's a nice idea. Even if carpet isn't used so much anymore, I love the feel of it under my feet."

"So would potential clients," I said. And then while she was smiling and so agreeable, I needed to ask, "Ms. Hebert, what can you tell us about our mother?"

She jerked her head toward the door. Eve and I did, too. Was Mom standing at the doorway, listening? She was not. Neither was anyone else. A few people moved past—some fast-walking staff members and some residents traveling at slower paces.

Terri returned her attention to me. "It would be terrible if I would spy on our people who live here and tell about everything they do—unless we discover someone really has a problem and requires help. You know your mother's a grown woman who can make her own decisions and choices. She also has her full senses, so you cannot claim she's a person who doesn't have her full faculties." While I was frowning and shrugging, she added, "You're aware that I should not be telling anything about her business, which I know is what you're asking about. Whatever she does is her choice."

"But," I said, pointing a finger at the woman running this place, "suppose it was your momma we were talking about. Would you feel the same way?"

Her eyes rolled shut. Seconds later they opened. "I can't tell you that. She died of cancer when I was three."

"I'm so sorry," I uttered.

"I am, too," Eve said in a soft tone. "That must have been tough."

"It was. But now I'm a grown woman, and I need to get on with my life." Her sharp words and pointed stares at each of us made it clear that any discussion about mothers had ended. "Now. Do you want to do some work here in my office?"

My twin and I took only a moment to glance at each other. We needed no words to each other for approval. We had shoved back any other job offers, since we had expected to take much longer to finish work on Edward's house. "Yes, we'll do it," I said.

"When did you need it done?" Eve asked.

Terri looked at something on her computer. "We have a number of things coming up soon, and I'll be giving an address to the state Chamber of Commerce in a couple of weeks. I want minimal distractions so I can focus on my speech. I'll let you know after that."

"Okay, we might have to work you in-between jobs by then, but that shouldn't be a problem. This won't take a lot of time." Eve gave her a nod and walked out the door.

I waited until I had left the office before speaking. "At least coming here to remodel her office will give us a good excuse for being around Mom and seeing what she's up to." My gaze darted from the seating area she normally sat in to the hall on the side. She wasn't apparent. "We could go up to her room."

"But then what if she's not there?" Eve spoke the rest of the words I was thinking. "Possibly we'd better just leave today. Maybe she'll contact one of us later."

"Yeah, maybe." My tone didn't sound any more assured than hers had, but each of us was attempting to make ourselves and each other believe them.

I drove my sister to her house and dropped her off, declining her offer to come inside. I wasn't in the mood for chitchat and didn't believe she was either. On the way to my house, I called to make an appointment I did not want to tell my sister about.

To my satisfaction, Dr. Lesley could see me that afternoon.

Chapter 9

"Sunny, do you want to remain seated," Dr. Lesley asked, "or would you prefer to lie down?"

I tightened my lips. Yes, I would have liked to lie on her green velvet sofa with its soft texture, but I believed I would want to squirm more and feel like a bug under a microscope, especially with her staring at me with those slim rimless glasses perched at the tip of her nose. A light lavender fragrance from potpourri in scattered small dishes must help patients relax. I glanced around her room, which appeared cozier than last time. The lighting was different. This time instead of having bright lights overhead, there was more area lighting with a small unique lamp here and there on her desk and end tables. Another lamp, almost four feet tall with a slim tubular shade, stood on the floor not far from this sofa I sat on. She sat beside me on a cushioned matching chair.

"I'll stay here."

"That's fine." She peered down at the pad in her hands and made a small smile come to my lips. The part down the center of her jet-black hair made me imagine someone had poured a slim row of powder there. It looked funny with her bangs and ponytail and pencil skirt. She was a kind person. I liked for her to look good.

Her eyes, which seldom missed anything, shifted up at me. "Why are you smiling?"

"The top of your hair. You need a touch up."

Her hand went up to her roots. "Thanks for telling me. I appreciate it."

"I know." I wouldn't have said it if I didn't know she would want to be made aware of that fact.

She lowered her hand. Her gaze grew steady. "It's been awhile since you came to see me."

The urge to squirm wriggled inside me. "I've been busy."

She gave me that familiar tight-lipped knowing smile. "Haven't we all?"

I spread my hands. "Okay, I know. I should have been coming to talk with you more often, but I put it off. I thought I could get rid of the problem on my own."

"Has it gotten any better? Worse?"

I flipped my hands around as though I could grab answers. "Oh, I don't know. Sometimes I think I've got the whole singing thing under control and I've stopped doing it, and I'm normal. But then it flares up and happens again."

She nodded, jotted a brief note, and peered at me. "It's still always Christmas carols?"

I lowered my face. "Yes."

She was the first person who'd ever heard me blast out one of those tunes. When I was eight, Lesley Babineaux had been sixteen like my sister, Crystal. They were best friends. Lesley was the girl Crystal was talking with on the phone when someone shot Crystal. Lesley soothed me then, saying she would send help. Years later, I hadn't been surprised to learn Lesley went into this line of work.

She was a popular psychiatrist. I had seen others before her over the years. At first, they didn't try to discourage the singing, since it was an outlet for me after being with my sister when she was murdered. Combined with my struggles with dyslexia, they didn't attempt to pressure me to change.

"Sunny." She waited until I looked her in the eye. "What's been frightening you?"

"Oh, Lesley, there's been a death. A murder, really. You probably read about it or heard about it."

"You tell me about it."

I released a small cough. "Eve and I were remodeling the old Danos house on the edge of town that Edward Cancienne had bought and planned to move into once we got everything completed."

"But?"

I went on a roll and told her everything that happened with Edward and how we had found him in his tub, but then we had become suspects in his murder. That had mainly been because so many people at the retirement home heard us arguing with him once we found he was pushing to marry our mother to his uncle even faster than they had considered before.

Lesley knew our mother and looked pleased when I said she wanted to marry again. "But you and Eve don't want her to."

When I told her about the man we barely knew also having a daughter, Lesley's lips pulled down a little at the edges. Her lips made the slightest quiver, and she nodded.

I ran out of words.

She gave me a minute or two to relax. "How are you handing the dyslexia?"

"I pretty much have that situation under control. I've worked at forgiving those teachers and classmates who didn't understand that condition and made me feel I wasn't good enough. Now I know I am, and I get Eve to check anything for our business that I'm not sure of."

"Good. It seems like you've handled it pretty well." Her wide smile made me feel a mental pat on the back. "You can do it with the songs, too. Keep working at it. Try to pay attention to any Christmas carols that come to you and avoid singing them. I know it's hard. But so is anything that's worthwhile."

Protests came to mind. I didn't voice them. "I'll try."

"That's all anyone could ask for."

We both stood, and I gave her a hug. "Thank you. I'll see you again when I see you."

"That sounds good enough."

I was out the door feeling relieved of pressure, much more aware that I could do it. I only hoped that positive attitude and the achievement of that goal worked out.

On my way home, I stopped at our town's nursery. Since it was the only one, its owner gave it the clever name of The Nursery. Quite a few flats of multi-colored flowers were out and lovely, but I didn't want to dig in my small flowerbed today. Instead, I went straight to the section of taller plants, the bushes that mainly stood in plastic buckets and weren't so showy. The few offerings of trees stood just beyond.

"You getting azaleas, Sunny?" The nursery's owner, burly Big Bub Richards with a small gray ponytail and slim beard, knew without asking that I was Sunny, although he also knew Eve. He was well aware that I was the twin who purchased and planted flowers. With no other business now, he stepped up behind me while I stood near the bushes.

My back went tense with the thought that I was about to do what he asked. "Yes."

He shook his head. "I heard about all that stuff with Edward Cancienne. Can't believe they were wanting to pin it on you and your twin."

I tightened my lips. "They had reasons, but not good ones."

"Yeah, I heard all about that. I got a neighbor who's got an old aunt at the manor. Tells him all about stuff that happens."

"Uh-huh," I said and pulled two bushes forward, one with a few white flowers and one with pale pink. I didn't want to hear about my mother and her man friend and all our commotion with Edward at the manor. "I'll take these." I pointed. "That one, too." A few fuchsia flowers bloomed on it.

"I could pick out some nicer ones for you." Big Bub had come on to me a little in the past, getting too close, making suggestive remarks. Now he stood so close I felt his warm breath on my arm.

I didn't want to encourage anything other than having him check out my purchases. "No, thanks. These are fine."

"You want a coral one, too?"

I gritted my teeth. "These are good. Now if you'll just ring them up, I'll be on my way." I reached for one of the little wagons to set them on. Before I could grab a plant, he had juggled them around until he tucked them all in his arms and thick hands.

"I got 'em." No use to warn him that his clothes would get dirty. His worn shirt and jeans already had their share of new stains. Inside the small building, he set the plants on the counter and used his cash register that printed a small receipt. "You know they do best with dappled light. I'll put 'em in your truck."

I handed him my credit card. "That's very nice of you."

"And that Edward guy, I can't believe the cops really thought y'all killed him." He tsk-tsked, gathered all my plants into his arms, and walked out front with me. I was eager to get in my truck and drive away, and not listen to any more mention of that horrible event Eve and I had experienced. Poor Edward was gone. His death was awful.

Big Bub set the plants in my truck's bed, close behind the wide tool chest that would give them more protection. I glanced at them again, trying to force down the anger azaleas always brought up when I recalled seeing Mom's so pretty, moments after Crystal died. "And he knew about those pimps and all."

"What?"

"That guy Edward who died. The guy's aunt told him when Edward moved to New Orleans for a while, he knew a couple of pimps and girls they had working for them."

My head did a little bobble while I tried to imagine this.

He kept nodding. "Yeah, and he almost got his butt ripped off. One girl's daddy out here found out about it and then learned Edward knew. He was ready to kill that dude right then."

I stared at Big Bub's moving lips, barely able to grasp the words coming from them. "And what happened?"

He rolled his thick shoulders forward. "The only thing that kept him from doing it was his daughter begging her daddy to keep it away from the cops so it wouldn't get all over town with her friends and the rest of her family around here. She promised she'd be good and go on to college like she was supposed to be doing over there."

"What a horrible thing to happen to your child."

"Yep, some little ol' folks from right here. You know what I believe? I believe everybody's got a lotta secrets." His eyes appeared hooded while he shook his head, and I could imagine him considering some of the things he had done and kept well hidden.

"People got a lotta secrets," he repeated like he was springing to life. "Even if this isn't a big city, everybody hides things." He nodded, his ponytail bobbing. "Bet you know that girl's daddy, Tommy Jeansonne. He runs the Best Prices Gas Station up on the other side of the bayou."

I started to nod, since I had been to that station a couple of times, but then recalled I had pumped my own gas and couldn't remember ever seeing the store's manager. I felt sorry for the family while also starting to consider what else this might mean. I stayed so busy deep in my thoughts that I hadn't noticed at first that he had stepped closer to me. Checking his face, I saw a lewd smile.

I yanked on my doorknob and pulled the door so wide open between us it bumped against him. "Thank you." I slid into my truck and backed away. Then I considered whether I was thanking him for carrying the bushes or the information. I determined it was both. Being polite was our Southern way.

On the road, I called Eve. "Come on, come on, answer," I said to her ringing phone. What I had to tell her was too important to put off. Frustrated and about to blurt that she should call me right away, I heard her voice.

"Hey, sis. I've been talking to Nicole and my adorable little grandson who was babbling away. I put them on hold."

"Oh, tell them hi for me. I'll need to tell you about something I just found out about our dead customer."

"Then I'll tell Nicole I need to go."

"No. Let Noah babble to you a little longer. I'm going to hurry and call Detective Wilet and tell him what I know."

She protested again, but I insisted and almost hung up on her. We disconnected, and I got the investigator. He answered much quicker than she had. "Detective Wilet, this is Sunny Taylor." The minute I said it, I imagined he'd already known. He must have caller I.D.

"Yes." He waited.

"I just found out about somebody who might have had a motive for killing Edward Cancienne."

Maybe I'd hoped he would get excited, eager to discover what I'd learned. Instead, he only said in his bland tone, "I'm listening." But he didn't sound interested. Was he doing paperwork while we spoke? Looking at notes about another case? Filing a jagged fingernail and feeling the tips of his other fingers in case they needing smoothing while he had the file out? Possibly he had somebody sitting in his office, maybe in one of the chairs Eve and I had sat in. Would he take calls while he had someone there?

"Do you know Tommy Jeansonne, the man who runs the Best Prices Gas Station?"

He wasn't saying a thing, so I couldn't imagine whether he might be shaking his head no or nodding, although I imagined he knew almost everyone in town and the towns around here. I rattled on with my story, pleased to have his interest when he asked a question.

"And who gave you this information?"

Then I knew he'd be writing. While I resumed my statement that should make him look at someone else besides Eve and me as possible suspects, the detective said, "You said this person *might* have had a motive. Your uncertainty here is because?"

While he waited, I needed to search the thoughts I didn't want to visit. "I think the person who passed on a lot of this information resides in the manor."

His exhale was loud. Abrupt. His tone when he spoke again was different. "You don't know whether this information you're passing on is reliable or not. Do you know the resident's name?"

"No." Then quickly I added, "But I can probably find out."

"If you discover anything of value, keep in touch. And stay around town."

"Wait. Do you still think Eve and I could have killed him?"

Right before he hung up, he said, "Just don't schedule a long trip."

Chapter 10

After speaking with the detective, I took a moment to tremble with rage or fear, or probably both. I shook off most of those emotions and got Eve on the line.

"What did he say? What did you tell him? I want to know everything." She sounded much less calm than before.

I ran through everything Big Bub Richards told me.

"That's awful."

It was strange to see the gray clouds that sat low in my vision while I drove. Curlicues of white looked like scalloped potatoes on their edges.

When I said nothing, Eve went on. "What did Detective Wilet say when you told him?"

"He sounded pretty interested—until I said the woman who had passed on at least part of that story lives at the manor."

"Oh. And so many people still think of it as a nursing home. Maybe he needs to visit the place and realize most of the residents are fully capable of using their bodies and minds. Like Mom."

Thoughts of our mother's youthfulness flashed into my thoughts. No, I didn't want to think of her as being so young at heart as to want to start a new family. One that didn't include us.

"I can't believe you bought azaleas. Good for you."

I pulled into my driveway. "Tell you about it later. I'm home. Gotta go." With my sunken spirits, I didn't feel like speaking about my session with Lesley or even thinking about it. I was afraid—a little. Of remaining suspects in a murder. Of having others taking my mother away.

But I also didn't feel like singing or even letting out a soft hum. Instead, I went to my truck bed and started unloading the bushes I would try to learn to like. A few of the white flowers had flown off during the ride.

I hauled the bushes to my backyard and set them at the right edge of my flowerbed that held snapdragons and tulips in bloom. I retrieved my shovel from my carport's closet. I remembered what Big Bub told me about a person who might have a motive to kill Edward but forgot what he'd said about dappled light being good for the bushes until after I already had two of the bushes planted in bright sunlight. That's where they would stay.

"Hello? Are you back here?" Dave's voice carried while he walked from the side of my house into the backyard. "Ah, there you are." Since it was late afternoon, he had changed from the dress clothes he normally wore for work into jeans and a Saints T-shirt. As good as he looked all dressed up, he looked even better in his casual clothes.

I stabbed my shovel into the ground. "Where were you looking for me?" I offered my lips for a kiss, and he obliged.

"I've been ringing the doorbell. Since I saw your truck was here, I figured you were, too, although you could have walked over to Eve's house."

"It's good to see you. I'm glad you thought to look back here."

His slow-spreading smile told me he was glad to also see me. "I won't ask what you've been up to, since I can see that." He picked up the shovel from the ground. "I'll get this last bush in for you."

"You don't need to. I'm already dirty."

"A little dirt won't hurt me, either. Where do you want that one?" He nodded toward the final plant. "About a foot away from the other one?"

"That would be fine. Thank you."

"Should I remove this broken branch?" Two leaves that had turned orange on a small broken branch clashed with the fuchsia flowers of the bush. When I nodded, he snapped off that section.

While he dug, I unwound the garden hose I kept connected to the faucet behind the house and gently sprayed my flowerbed, starting at the opposite end, making sure not to create mud that would splash on him. In no time, he dug the hole. He set the bush into it and filled in the dirt, patting it down once he finished. Then he stepped away so I could water that bush and spray more on the two other azaleas plants.

"Nice," he said, admiring my garden.

"Now you're dirty, too. Come on, we can wash our hands with this." I changed the setting on the hose to get a gentle cool sprinkle to do the trick. "Thanks for your work, now come on inside."

"Not with my shoes like this." A little dirt coated the edge of his tennis shoes.

More dirt than that coated the bottom of mine. "Let's just leave them out here," I suggested. We sat outside my backdoor, tugged our shoes off, and walked into my kitchen in our socks.

Dave stepped close to me. "I wanted to ask you out for supper." He glanced down at his clothes and gave me a smile. "I thought we might just go to the diner. Josie makes the best crayfish poppers. Or if you'd like someplace nicer, I could go home and change." He clasped my hands. "I'd just like to be with you awhile, Sunny."

I gave him a tight hug. Right that minute, I didn't want to think about Nelson or Emery Jackobson, the two men I had seen together at the diner. After a sigh, I drew back. "Tell you what. I have the best shrimp jambalaya in my freezer. I could warm some for us. And I've got French bread and a little bread pudding that I made."

He placed his hands together over his heart. "You are a woman I could grow to love." His face became solemn, his eyes intense. "Maybe even more than I already do."

My heart stopped. As tempted as I was, I wasn't ready to say I loved him. With one sister dead and Eve still caring for him so much, I was striving to keep myself from feeling quite so intensely yet.

He insisted on helping. While I took a package of jambalaya out of the freezer and defrosted it in my microwave, he gathered our utensils and plates and glasses that I directed him to. Once our entrée was almost ready, I grabbed a long loaf of French bread and sliced some, getting butter from the fridge. "Beer, wine, soft drink, or milk?" I asked, holding its door open.

"A beer would be fine."

"Me, too." I set them on the table next to the place settings he'd set out nicely in front of two chairs beside each other. I smiled at our paper napkins he had folded into triangles. "Good job."

He moaned and praised my food as though it were the best he had ever eaten. When I served the bread pudding, his eyes opened wider with his smile of appreciation. He took a bite, set his fork down, and looked at me.

"I do love you." He gave me a kiss on the lips that was quick. Then, keeping his gaze away from me, Dave resumed eating.

That kiss and his sentiment might have been done playfully, but I was still tied up from the feelings of both. We didn't speak for the rest of the meal, but once we were done, he insisted on helping with dishes.

What a sweet man, I thought, watching him set each glass and plate gently into the warm soapy water. He gave me a smile that was also warm and handed each item he washed and rinsed to me so I could dry them and put them away.

As soon as we were done, he said, "You must be really relieved you're not a person of interest in a murder."

"How do you know that?" I was excited about this wonderful news.

"I've told you to let me know if you had any more problems connected to finding Edward dead. I wanted to help." He gave me a tight grin. "Since you haven't mentioned anything about it again, I figured the police are homing in on who killed him. They'd know it wasn't you or Eve."

My relief was short lived. If he was a detective or anyone connected to police work, I might have told him all that happened, and that my sister and I were still suspects. His concern and offer to assist us were comforting. But he owned a company that installed security systems in homes and businesses, and apparently did it all very well. Also I did not want to think about murder or the troubling situation with my mother.

"How about a movie?" I asked, changing the subject. "I have a few recorded ones that I haven't seen yet. Maybe you'd find one that you'd like."

"That sounds fine."

He settled himself on the sofa, and I found the remote. I sat a little away from him and channel surfed through my recorded shows. It didn't take long before we agreed on one. The movie was a mystery with some romance. Dave scooted closer and wrapped his arm around my shoulder with his hand resting on my arm. He made me feel relaxed, comforted.

I snuggled my head against his chest, and he drew me closer. The music on TV intensified, drowning out the sound of the heartbeat I felt against my ear. And then a phone rang. It must have been in the film. But the scene changed to a prison escapee charging through a forest. The man was alone and without a phone.

"Sorry," I said and reached beside me for my cell phone. I had brought it into the den out of habit, especially since there was always the chance Mom might need me. "Hello." I hadn't checked to see who the caller was.

"Hey, sis, what are you doing?"

I pulled farther away from Dave. "Just watching a movie."

"Is it good?" She was crunching on something, probably a diet rice cake.

"Pretty good." I eyed Dave, who was watching me.

"Okay, then I won't keep you. I was just checking in. Anything new happen?"

I looked deeper into the warm brown eyes of the man next to me and swallowed. "Nothing I can't tell you about tomorrow."

She did a little cough. "Just choked a pinch, but I'm okay."

I made her insist that she was fine before I let her go. We agreed to catch up with each other in the morning. Once we hung up, I set the phone down.

"That was your sister, wasn't it?"

"Yes, that was Eve." I lifted the remote. "Ready to watch this again?" He gazed at me, at my tensed shoulders, my tensed jaw. "I'm really not as interested in this film as I thought I'd be." He shoved up to his feet. "Maybe we can do this another time. If you'd like to?"

"Absolutely. We'll plan something. Maybe we'll rent a movie of your choice."

He surely knew our mood was gone, the romantic emotions destroyed by my twin. As I walked him out, I feared that if I did not commit to a more open relationship with this wonderful man soon, I would lose him.

Chapter 11

I slept later than usual. When I awoke, I stayed in bed, replaying events from last night. Dave had come over and helped me plant. Then he'd helped with dishes before we began to watch a film that probably wasn't his favorite. Since he'd dirtied his shoes like I'd dirtied mine while we'd planted my azaleas, we'd needed to get his from out back before he left.

The little dirt on them had dried, and even though I had offered to wash them, he deferred, thanking me and saying they were fine. He had sat right outside the door and slipped them on, tied them, and gave me a quick kiss before walking to the side of my house to get to his truck parked out front.

Positive feelings and negative ones played through me while I got up, showered, and dressed, still replaying some things from the day before. Dave had been loving and helpful. He'd dug a hole and planted an azalea. Noticed and removed a broken branch with two dried leaves that had turned orange.

"It was orange!" The words blasted from my mouth as the scene came to me. The object I had seen but forgotten was that color. I was sure of it.

Breathless from my discovery, I grabbed my phone. Lesley's secretary told me she had just stepped in, but a client was waiting to see her. The pleasant young woman said she could take a memo for Dr. Babineaux. Maybe she would be able to call me between appointments or if not, she would probably return my call after office hours.

"No!" I insisted. "Get her now! Tell her who I am, and that I need to talk to her right now." When no response came, I thought of how many patients might say that to the person who needed to act as a buffer between them and their psychiatrist.

I lowered my tone. "Please, it'll only take a minute. Just tell her what I said." She still offered nothing, so I added, "She and my sister who died were best friends."

A long second passed. "I'll pass on your message. Hold please."

Soon Lesley picked up. "Hi, Sunny, what's the matter?"

"It was orange. Lesley, I remembered that when you were speaking on the phone with Crystal and somebody drove by on the highway and shot her, I hadn't thought I'd seen anything or anybody around. But it came to me this morning—I had glanced at the road when something from there made a *Pop!* It was a truck. The truck was orange."

She didn't say a word.

My heart continued to race. "Lesley, is it possible that I really saw one? Or is my mind just trying to figure it out?"

"You were a child then. But yes, even years after a traumatic event takes place, people can recall something their minds blanked out at the time."

I tightened my grip on the phone even more, attempting to push my thoughts back there. To find another image. To envision the person who killed her.

"Sunny." Her tone was soft. "Good for you that you've recalled another memory from that day. Maybe you will even think of more." She allowed me a moment and then asked, "Did you sing when you remembered it?"

My thoughts shot back. I envisioned the orange, just like the orange leaves on the azalea bush. "No. I didn't even hum."

"Good for you." She was letting me also congratulate myself for that achievement. "Now I need to get with a client."

I understood, thanked her, and sat in silence. Time moved on while I tried to squeeze any picture or sound or even a scent from then. All I thought of was sitting beside my sister, watching blood spread on the back of her favorite turquoise shirt, and later hearing the sirens.

Eve walked into my house before I heard her. "Hey, what's up, sis? You didn't hear me ringing the doorbell?" She wore a royal blue jogging suit that brought out the red of her hair and held up a house key. "It's a good thing the key to your place is with the keys to mine so I could get in here. I was about to call the police and tell them something happened to you."

I raised a hand toward her and waved it like a windshield wiper. "Oh no, don't call the police." Seated at my kitchen table, I pulled out the chair beside me. "Sit. Let's talk about some things."

Looking even more concerned, she sat and placed her fingers over mine while I relayed everything. I told what I recalled about the truck and how that memory came because of a dying azalea leaf. This wasn't the time to tell about Dave, so I left out the part about him being here to plant it and then staying awhile. "I wasn't sure if an old memory like that could be true, but I called Lesley and she said they could and often do."

"Sometimes that happens with people who've been abused as children," Eve said. "I've heard a number of women and men on talk shows telling about how that happened to them. Repressed memory, the professionals call it."

We looked at each other. Silent moments later, we both lowered our gazes toward my oak table. Our thoughts stayed inside ourselves. She, surely like me, went back to that most awful day when we lost Crystal. Her killer drove past. This we knew before. Now I could picture him moving beyond our house that sat along a bayou with empty lots on either side. I couldn't see the man's face but imagined a gun he pointed at her. He could have just as easily shot me.

But he kept rolling along in that orange truck. Yes, I was certain it was a truck.

"Do you want to go tell Mom?"

"That might give her a little peace. But I don't know."

"It was something we're both satisfied to discover. It's something, Sunny. And that was her child, her daughter."

"Okay, we'll go."

"Oh, first I want to see those bushes you planted. I can't believe you put azaleas in your yard."

We went out back. The dirt was still dark and moist from my watering last night. I stared at the last bush on the right, the one Dave set in the ground. Maybe this would be a good time to let Eve know that happened—to make her aware that he and I cared about each other.

She wrapped her arms around me, held me in a tight hug, and pointed to those bushes. "Do you know what this means? Besides getting more memory back from that day, you're overcoming another situation that event caused. You've gotten over hating azaleas that everybody else loves."

I stared at mine. "I didn't say I like them."

She gave me a one-arm squeeze. "I am so proud of you."

My small smile was the only response I could give. No, now wasn't the time to tell her about Dave and me.

Eve decided she'd jog home and change clothes. She would pick me up in her car.

It wasn't until a few minutes after she was gone when I realized I could have jogged with her. Waiting, I stared out my backdoor's window at my flowerbed. A lot more people could see those azaleas if they were on the side of my house or out front. But back there I could watch them grow. So could my sister when she came over. And Dave. And anyone who visited and Mom, the next time I convinced her to come to my house.

When Eve arrived, she was dressed much better than I was, but that was nothing new. I wore casual slacks and shirt with flats while she had put on a swingy dress and little heels.

Mom was sitting with her friends in their normal grouping when we walked in. The enticing aroma of cinnamon rolls from breakfast or the upcoming lunch pulled me forward, along with the pleasant laughter coming from their gathering.

"Ladies, what's going on?" Eve asked. "Sounds like fun."

The Chat and Nappers nodded with big smiles—at least most of them did, although one or two couldn't hear well and today might not be wearing their hearing aids.

"You look nice today, Eve." This was spoken by the woman whose thin white hair was curled tight, revealing her ears with no aids in them.

"Thank you. You can tell us apart now?"

"Of course." She swerved her finger up and down at Eve. "You dress better than her."

Even though I normally didn't care about things like clothing, I felt a blush tinting my cheeks.

"That isn't a nice thing to say." Our mother leaned forward and frowned at her. Having her come to my defense gave me great pleasure. "My daughters are unique. They might look alike, but they are individuals."

"Thanks, Mom," I whispered at her ear when I leaned down and kissed her.

"It's true," she said. "I wouldn't have it any other way."

Those words brought even more comfort to my heart. My mother loved the person I was. I gave her a big, warm hug. Her eyes were gentle when she looked at me. Eve bent down and kissed her, but I was the one who right now felt extra special.

"Where is your male friend?" Eve abruptly asked her.

"He's out. He got a virus or something and went to the doctor," the newer woman with her husband's urn on her lap announced without waiting for our mother to answer.

"I would have taken him if I still owned a car." This came from Miss Clarice who had been walking next to the group. She wore a nice pantsuit and looked younger than many others here. "But I would take him anywhere he wanted to go."

Two of Mom's buddies snorted at her. "You know he's Miriam's boyfriend, don't you?" the one seated beside Mom said, placing her hand on Mom's as if to help her show ownership.

"They haven't taken any wedding vows. Until they do, he's still available." Clarice shoved her pointed nose up in the air and walked on.

The women in Mom's group all started talking about how he was Mom's, and nobody else had the right to go after him. As Eve and I remained in the midst of this gathering, I also experienced the urge to complain about what that other woman said and stand up for my mother. But then I recalled our main mission was to stop any wedding from happening. Who was the man really? What did he want? Would he hurt her?

People around the place started walking or rolling in wheelchairs. As if on cue, the cadre of ladies here stood and started moving toward the dining area. Our mother easily got to her feet. "I hate to run off so soon, but you know the meal is much better when it's first out. You two could come and sit with me in there awhile. A couple of the ladies from our table had late hair appointments upstairs this morning and said they'd be a few minutes late to eat."

We walked beside her. I leaned in close. "There's something I need to tell you."

Normally she might have urged me to say things in front of her close friends. This time she came to a halt, concern filling her eyes. "Sunny, what is it?"

"It's about Crystal." The second I said my dead sister's name, our mother appeared to wilt like a dried flower. I hated to go on and was sorry I'd brought it up, but she had to know. She was Crystal's mother and should learn everything we knew about her.

A couple of male residents almost ran into us. They had to take a sharp turn while we three stood still.

"Tell me." Mom's gaze gripped mine.

I swallowed, all moisture gone from my mouth. "I remembered something from that day. I had thought I'd only heard a shot, but then an image came back to me. I had looked at the road once I heard that sound. A truck was passing by. An orange truck."

Motion from her thin neck came from her throat's swallow. The news, this information I was giving, was having a profound effect on her.

"It's all I remember." I gripped her hand. "But maybe I shouldn't have brought it up."

Eve was leaning close in front of our mom as if to give her support. Mom lost a sixteen-year-old child that day. Her cold hand with the gnarled knuckles tightened on my fingers. "No, I'm glad you did." She gave me a tight-lipped smile with a nod. "It's something."

Both my twin and I wrapped our arms around our mother. Amid workers and residents, we stood there long moments, holding her, gripping each other. We were there. We were family. We all had each other.

Automatically, Eve and I went along with our mother to her table in the center of all the others. Chairs scraped the floor as people sat in them. The tempting aroma of fried shrimp filled the air. Staff members wearing navy shirts and the navy pants with a ribbon tying the waist served trays to the tables.

The woman who wanted Mom's man or whatever he was to her sat right next to our mother, no apology for her earlier comment on her face or from her lips. Mom gave her a brief nod. "I told my daughters they could sit with us a little while until the others get here."

We sat, and Mom lifted her glass that held ice and sweet tea. "Oh, I forgot to bring my medicine."

The other lady leaned closer as though she were inspecting Mom's shoulder and then every inch of the table to find something our mother couldn't see. "You always bring it."

"I know, but I didn't today."

"I'll run up to your room and get it," I said, disappointed that I hadn't noticed she was without the tiny tan knitted strap with a pouch at the end that held her prescription bottle. Like a small purse with a long strap, that was the last thing she always put on when she got dressed every morning. That way she'd be sure to bring her medicine and have it to take with lunch. And then when she'd go back to her room for a nap after lunch, she removed the pouch and set it next to her bed where she'd be certain to put it on again in the morning. She never forgot it—that we knew of. A pinch of concern made my scalp tingle. Was she starting to forget other things, too? We would need to pay close attention for any other signs of forgetfulness.

She shook her head. "Don't worry about it. I should be able to skip one day. Or I can just take it later."

I was on my feet. "There's no reason for you to skip your medicine, and you always take it at noon so you don't forget."

"I know. Thank you, Sunny."

Eve began a discussion with Mom while I was leaving the table, probably to discourage her idea of skipping her medication and also to distract thoughts of our sister who I was now also missing more than I had in quite some time.

The only stairs that I knew of were at the far ends of each hall. Since we were in the central portion of the manor, elevators were close. I was the only one riding up to the second floor. Things were quiet when I reached it. No one was visible in the long hallway.

Mom's room was just beyond the large room on the right that was used for working out or sometimes nondenominational church services. I glanced inside that room and saw no one.

A sound I recognized as a blow dryer picked up from the short hall to the left. That came from the little beauty shop used by those who didn't want to go out to a favorite hairdresser. Probably one of the usual ladies who sat at the table with Mom was getting her hair dried. I needed to hurry and get Mom's medicine down to her so I would have at least a little more time with her.

My mother's room, as always, was unlocked unless it was nighttime. Eve and I had urged her to lock the door when she left her room, but she had responded that was ridiculous. No one locked their rooms that she knew of here, and what would she do—walk around with her key every time she went right there to exercise or visit a friend a few doors down?

Her room smelled fresh. I made a quick run-through. Her coffeepot was off. So was her small stovetop. The four chairs were all straight against her little square table. The TV in front of her sofa was off. She had left her favorite soft afghan over the arm of the sofa where it waited for her. Her small bathroom was clean with everything put away, and as always she'd made her bed and placed two pink throw pillows on it right after she got up. The small tan pouch—knitted for Mom by a now-deceased friend—held the bottle of pills Mom needed for her heart to continue to work correctly. It lay forgotten today on the small bedside table.

I grabbed the pouch, squeezed it, and looked inside to make certain her prescription bottle was in it and hadn't dropped out and rolled under the bed. Satisfied, I hurried out, almost forgetting myself and locking the door behind me. I shook my head, wanting my mother to lock herself in her place just like she had done at home.

The whine of the blow dryer stopped. Voices picked up from the beauty salon and then a blow dryer started again. I needed to rush to have a little time with my mother.

"That was fast," she said when I sat again and gave her the knitted pouch. "I guess you didn't need to wait for an elevator, since everybody is down here."

"Not everybody," I said.

Mom smiled. "I know. Mac is at the doctor's office." She nodded toward the table four away from hers where he normally ate with other men.

"I meant the ladies whose chairs Eve and I are sitting in." My tone might have sounded more offended than I'd wanted to let on. "Where's Miss Clarice?" I nodded to her empty place.

"She went to the restroom," Eve said.

"But before that, she was talking again about my man." My mother was shaking her head with a crease forming between her eyes.

"Mom." I placed my hand on hers. "He's not yours."

Eve gripped her opposite hand. "That's what I've been trying to tell her," she said to me. "If she enjoys having a man to flirt with a little at her age, that's okay. I'm sure it's kind of flattering."

"You would think so," Mom told her, sliding her hand away. "But flirting is not what I want to do. Settling down and getting married is."

"But you've been married," I said, and she pulled her hand away from beneath mine.

"That was so many years ago, young lady. And if you ever decide to get married again, you can be certain I will support you. Now you two can just realize that I'm still of sound mind, and I do still get feelings I'm sure you don't want to hear about. So look." She pointed toward the bank of elevators. "The ladies whose seats you're in are coming back."

Yes, our mother wanted to get rid of us. Were my sister and I overstepping? I wondered in a brief thought. But then I recalled that we knew almost nothing about the man our one parent wanted a new life with.

Mom offered her cheeks for us to give her brief kisses on.

"Here's your medicine. Take some now." I handed her the knit pouch.

"I know what to do with it." Her annoyed response made an ache pinch my heart, but I understood. We were not trying to treat her as though she were incapable of anything because of her age. We only wanted to protect her as she had always protected us.

Outside the building, Eve shook her head. "You know what got her going so much about doing a rapid wedding again?" she asked but didn't wait for me to voice a guess. "That lady Clarice started telling me how she used to get boyfriends away from other girls when she was in school. She left it like that and just looked at Mom. From the anger in Mom's face, I was afraid she was going to get into a catfight."

I shrugged. "What do we do?"

Neither of us came up with an answer as we walked to Eve's car and got in. Once we were on the road, Eve glanced at me. "Maybe we can talk to the administrator and tell her what's going on now."

"And then what?" I asked, wanting some solution.

Her eyes looked unsure. "Possibly they could sit one of them at another table. Move Clarice."

"Hm, but if they sat her closer to Mac, she'd get to flirt with him more."

"And maybe he'd take the bait. That would show Mom what kind of man he is." We didn't know that ourselves. We both gave satisfied sighs. We may have found a solution to stopping our mother from getting badly hurt.

"Oh." My tone had deflated. "But suppose they'd want to move Mom instead, and she would get even closer to him?"

While Eve drove and peered ahead, her face lengthened. We would need to work much harder to find a solution.

Chapter 12

Eve pulled to the curb in front of my house. "I'm going to go home and call my grandbaby." Her smile was warm. "And then I'll paint. Maybe while I'm doing that, I'll come up with other ideas about how to improve Mom's situation." Only painting for her own benefit, she used to cover her canvases with flowers, ovals, and anything that came to mind when she considered the men she'd been dating. After she decided Dave was the soulmate she had awaited all along, her artwork became explosive, striking, bright colors filling every inch of the canvas. That was how she was expecting her relationship with him would become, she had told me.

But then she became a grandmother and things changed. She seemed to transfer some of her intense love to her grandchild. It wasn't the same kind of love. But now she coated her canvases with hearts representing her love of that adorable baby boy and his name *Noah* in tiny print between them. I'd watched to see if she'd print *Dave* between any but hadn't noticed that name yet.

"Good idea. Tell the little one hi for me."

Her smile widened. "I sure will." Of course he was still too young to understand.

"Oh, and Eve, let's start keeping a closer eye on Mom to make sure she isn't forgetting other things."

Her silent gaze told me she knew the severity of what I suggested. What if our mother had begun getting some dementia? That might also affect her intense feelings for a new man.

"She only forgot one thing one time that we know of," I said, trying to reassure her and myself. "I've done that lots of times."

"So have I."

Relaxing a little before she pulled away, I considered asking whether she had spoken to Dave lately. Second thoughts made me stop myself. I preferred not to get her talking about him or asking the same thing of me. Life would be much simpler in that regards if she knew *and accepted* that he and I had started dating each other. After three marriages and divorces, she still believed in falling in love, and she believed her true love was the man I was seeing.

He had come into this house with me and ate there with me, I considered, walking inside and through the kitchen. I glanced into the den at the spot where he'd been, and I leaned against him. He held me in his arms.

Going to the fridge for a water, I noticed movement beyond my window's shut curtains. A man's shadow crossed them.

Dave. I rushed to the door and with a bright smile, pulled it open.

"You look happy today. What's the occasion?" Detective Wilet stood at my doorstop, head leaning to the side while he looked as though trying to figure me out.

"Oh. Hi, Detective." I released a deep breath. "I was just... It's a beautiful day, don't you think?"

He turned around to look behind himself and then at the sky. It held dark clouds. "I guess. If you like rainy weather. Looks like we might get a downpour."

I considered my newly planted azaleas. "I'm sure our plants could use the rain."

His eyes pulled closer together. "We've been getting some rain fairly often."

"Yes." Many other things had been occupying my mind. "Did you want to come in?" I hoped he did not, but he stepped forward, so I stepped back to allow him inside. I moved into my kitchen, where he joined me at the table. Mouth closed, I let out a deep sigh. What was this about? Were Eve and I in even more trouble?

He laid his thick hands flat on my table and looked me in the eye. "I felt I owed it to you to come and tell you—I found out who relayed that rumor about Edward Cancienne knowing of a girl from here prostituting sometime back in New Orleans."

I sucked in a breath. "Oh, it was only a rumor?" Then we were still in trouble, still considered suspects, probably even more so since it would seem that I tried to put the blame on someone else.

His shoulders pressed forward, allowing his thick frame to come partway over the table and closer to me. "Since you told me the woman who passed on some of that information lives in Sugar Ledge Manor, I need to admit I thought she might have been kind of senile."

I rushed to respond. "Some of the residents do get forgetful, but most of them are just older people who just don't want the upkeep of a house any longer."

To my surprise, he was nodding. "I should have realized that. In fact I did know that, but I hadn't been around the place in quite a while, so I'd forgotten. But I did find Big Bub Richards's neighbor's aunt there, and I spoke with her. It was hard to do."

More discouragement. "Why? Is she one of the few there who have problems remembering?"

His barrel chest's sudden quiver over the table grabbed my attention first, making me concerned about a possible heart attack. I swung my gaze up to his face, expecting contortion and maybe graying. Instead his lips pulled back and up at the edges. Without a sound, the man was laughing.

"Detective?"

"Okay, here's what happened. I found out the name of Big Bub's neighbor's aunt and went over there yesterday evening to talk to her." He watched my eyes for long minutes as though he was building up to a big announcement. "She wasn't there."

"Oh. Well maybe she went out for supper. A lot of people who live there do that on a regular basis."

His shoulders quivered as he pulled back in the chair and gave an apparently silent chuckle. "She went out all right. When I got there, it was late, way past the time most people would eat." He again wore a smile while he shook his head. "It seems she and two other ladies there like to kind of sneak out every Saturday night and go dancing at Eric's Place."

"Wait." I set my hand on his, needing to straighten out his thinking. "Nobody needs to sneak out. The residents can leave whenever they please. And Eric's Place is where all the kids go."

"Yes, the older teens and those in their early twenties usually frequent that lounge. But the lady you told me about and two of her buddies get together in one of their cars and go dancing with young guys there." He snickered and gave his head a shake. "I'm sure the guys get a kick out of that. And probably some of them sometimes try to make out with those old gals just for fun."

I pulled back. "That would be terrible."

"Yes, but the ladies are too smart for that, and they're not interested. At least that's what Big Bub's neighbor's aunt told me when she got back to the manor." Not waiting for me to ask the question reaching my mind, he went on. "I'd left a message on the phone in her suite that I needed to speak with her right away. She had to call me as soon as she got in."

"And was that late?"

"Absolutely. But I waited up, wanting to see this lady instead of just asking her questions on the phone. When she called, I went over there." He smiled again. "She isn't bad looking for being her age. That's amazing. When my momma got to be in her eighties, she looked about ready for a nursing home. Not this lady."

"Okay, so tell me what happened."

His demeanor grew serious. "She told me in detail about Edward Cancienne knowing Tommy Jeansonne's daughter was hooking in the city, just like you told me. Today I checked up on some of those things. I believe them."

I was pleased, but sad about that girl and any others.

"Nothing is solved yet. We're continuing our investigation into Edward's death. It's just that since I seemed to make you afraid that we were after you or your twin, I wanted to maybe put you at peace a little bit." He offered a weak smile.

"Thank you for doing that. If you find out anything else you can tell me, would you?"

This smile of his was broader and showed his side teeth. He was being nice.

"Would you like some water or coffee?"

"I need to get back to work." He pushed back in his chair and rose. "But maybe next time?"

Once he was out the door, I leaned back on the wall. It was good that he had gained other suspects in the murder. But he had almost seemed interested in me, or was I only believing that, since this was the first time I saw him laugh and smile so much? I knew little about romance. He was not a man that I would be interested in in any way, and he was married, I believed. Then I recalled that a few months ago my friend, Amy, told me his wife left him.

I got Eve on the phone and told her everything the detective said to me. We laughed together about the three women who lived in the manor sneaking out to get their dancing done, and while they were out at the place younger folks frequent, maybe some of them also had a few drinks. But having the detective believe Edward knew about young teens becoming prostitutes in New Orleans and not telling their parents here made us both sad. But more assured about Edward's dark knowledge saddened both of us.

"Oh, I need to go. Nicole's calling me back." She clicked off. Nicole, her only child, hadn't been available to talk earlier when Eve phoned her. Now, obviously, she was, and little Noah would be available to hear my sister's sweet babble.

A little growl came from my stomach. I looked at the clock. It was well past lunchtime, and I never skipped meals. There was a little shrimp and eggplant casserole in my fridge. I had cooked the dish a couple of months ago and defrosted what remained of it three days ago. I added a couple of tablespoons of seasoned breadcrumbs over it with a pinch of butter and let the microwave work. While enjoying my tasty meal, I considered what I might do next.

Another glance at the wall clock assured me that my mother should be sound asleep by now. Her naptime always came soon after she ate, and her nap lasted awhile.

Without taking the time to wash my plate, I hurried out to my truck. While Mom slept, with any luck I would be able to get help for slowing down her plans from the person who ran the place where she currently lived.

Chapter 13

The area where Mom and her friends sat to visit was empty, as I'd hoped. All the ladies who were normally there went to their rooms after lunch, just like most of the other residents. Several of them would take a nap while others just rested, maybe caught up on favorite TV shows or knitted or worked crossword puzzles. A couple of diehard men always lifted weights right after they ate. Some of Mom's buddies occasionally drifted off for a few minutes while on a sofa or in a wheelchair and the others gossiped— gossiping being a major source of entertainment for many of them.

But now a hush dropped over the otherwise boisterous open area. Only scattered bits of sound carried. A group of men spoke quietly while they hunched over, playing cards at a table. One loud *clack* sounded like someone dropping a heavy pot. The odor of disinfectant reached my nostrils right before I spotted the yellow triangle at the entrance to the administrative area that warned of a wet floor. The shine on a small section in front of the counter suggested that area had recently been mopped.

Nobody was visible anywhere behind the counter. The three doors to offices back there were all shut.

I tapped on the counter to get the attention of the woman who normally sat behind it. I wanted to speak to the administrator, who was probably behind the closed door to her office. I didn't want to yell or knock harder. Instead, I went to the square cut section at the end of the counter, unlocked, and lifted it. The square of wood wobbled. I looked close and saw that two hinges were bent. I'd have to replace them. A staff member in navy blue came at a brisk pace down the hall. She looked at me with a frown, probably to say I wasn't supposed to be back here.

No matter what, I needed to ask my questions. Turning away from her, I knocked on the door marked Administrator.

The door didn't open, so I knocked harder. "Ms. Hebert, it's Sunny Taylor. I need to talk to you."

I watched the doorknob and listened while waiting for it to turn.

"Yes? What is it you need?" Instead of coming out of her own office, she came out of the one belonging to the nurse. The nurse and assistant-administrator came out with her. All of them waited, looking at me.

"There is a situation here with my mother that my sister and I need help with."

She tightened her lips and shook her head. "I'm sorry. Like I already told you, we can't stop your mother from being interested in any of our clients, whether male or female."

An image popped up, one I hadn't considered before. Even though the people who lived here were older, some of them probably had same sex partners. Well, good for them.

"No, it's something else. Something that's troubling her this time."

"Y'all come into my office," the nurse said. "We don't need everyone hearing about anyone's problem."

I pointed toward the section of the counter that I'd lifted to come back here. "A couple of hinges on that need to be changed. I'll get some and do that."

"Good. Thank you. Now I only have a few minutes before an appointment with someone," Ms. Hebert told me.

We gathered inside the nurse's office, all standing in a clump. Nobody suggested we sit, so I knew this probably needed to be quick with all of them. I faced the other two. "I've spoken to Ms. Hebert about my concern and don't know if the others are aware of the situation here with my mother and one of your fairly new male residents."

Rita Picou, the assistant-administrator, spoke first. "We all know about Mac's nephew dying. And we heard about a ruckus that had taken place here between him and you."

The nurse nodded. "We know Miriam and Mac are interested in each other."

"Yes, and my sister and I surely don't want them rushing into anything, unless we know more about him." I tilted my head toward the administrator. "She couldn't tell me anything about him. And I respect that."

Ms. Hebert glanced at her watch. "What is your concern now?"

"Things seemed to have slowed down between them after what took place with Mac's nephew, who died. We were really sorry his nephew died, but glad our mother wasn't rushing into a marriage any longer. But now another one of your female residents, a Ms. Clarice, seems to want Mac."

A small grin touched the nurse's lips.

I looked from one to the other of them. "Since she wants to get him, and she isn't bad looking, and she's not shy about telling Mom about that, Mom seems to want to rush things with him again."

A wider smile came from the nurse. "Just like childhood rivalry." She placed her finger on my chest. "You want him?" She removed her finger and set it against her own. "Then I want him more. And I'm going to show you I can take him away from you."

The head lady spread her hands and dropped them against her long skirt. "Just what is it you want us to do? You know there are things that we're capable of, but we can't tell adults what to do or not do unless it harms them." While protests worked through my throat, she added, "You wouldn't want us to do that to you if you lived here."

Her last statement, although true, made me sink back. It was the first time I ever considered that one of these days I might find myself in a place such as this. Maybe this place, if I was fortunate once I became older. Sugar Ledge Manor really was a fine establishment.

But was she suggesting that I was getting old?

The assistant pressed her face closer to mine, making me notice the wrinkles I hadn't paid attention to before. "And you have a suggestion for us?"

Yes, I could have suggested they keep my mom and her male friend apart. That wasn't going to happen.

"The woman who's pushing lately to try to take Mr. McCormick's attention away from Mom sits at the same table with her in the cafeteria. Even though Mom might not run into her much otherwise, while they share a table at every meal, it seems this Miss Clarice keeps saying how much she wants him. That's pushing Mom to want to get more serious with him than I believe she was before."

The women all looked at each other with frowns.

The nurse spread her hands as if she was ready to solve the problem. "Okay, so we'll get your mother assigned to a different table."

"Not one closer to Mr. McCormick's," I said.

The head lady spoke up. "First, we'd have to find someone who's willing to move to the place where she sits. You know people here get attached to a group. They don't like change much."

The nurse let out a sigh. "And the others at your mother's table might not be pleased to have her leave and get somebody they don't like very much take her seat. Most people here are really sweet, but some can be unkind, you know."

"Yes, I do."

The administrator stepped to the door and opened it, letting me know this discussion was over. "And even if we manage to achieve what was suggested in here, that still doesn't stop Miss Clarice from going after your mother's boyfriend any other place while they're here."

A lump sat in my throat. I managed to swallow past it. "No, but it would be a start."

"Yes, it would." The frown lines deepened outside her lips.

"And you can't let Mom know why." When deeper lines creased her forehead, I added, "At least don't let her know I'm the one who suggested those moves take place."

All of them looked at me with drawn faces, so I went on. "You could speak to her in private and tell her you know that Miss Clarice is being unkind to her. Tell her you want to be helpful and move her away from that lady."

The administrator's chest heaved. "This might take some time."

"I know."

She turned to her assistant. "Would you see what you can do to start taking care of it?"

The woman she'd spoken to didn't look happy with that chore. None of them appeared pleased with this new problem I had brought them.

I called my sister while I drove away from the manor. "Eve, we're old."

"Do you think since I have a grandchild, that makes me an antique?" Her tone hinted of insult but held a suggestion that she smiled when she spoke. She smiled every time she mentioned her grandson.

"No, I'm just kidding. Kind of. I was just at the manor and talked with the people in charge about Miss Clarice wanting to take Mom's beau, which seems to make Mom want to make a permanent commitment with him sooner. The nurse said that was how young kids acted." I told Eve more about our discussion and how they were going to try to get Mom moved. "And Terri Hebert asked if I lived there, would I want changes."

Her laugh was light. "You think the lady in charge of that place was saying you and I might be putting in our applications there soon?"

A car sped by in the opposite lane. That made me check my own speed. I was creeping along, driving like an aged person?

I shoved my foot against the accelerator. "I have to admit, she made me imagine us living there. I pictured you and I at a table surrounded by other old people."

"But you know Mom. She's intelligent. If they suggest that she might want to move to a different table, she's going to suspect we had something to do with it."

I sighed. It was a concern that had flared. "I know. But even if she learns I suggested it, I think she'd forgive me. She doesn't seem too attached to the other ladies she eats with."

"Right. The good friends she's made all sit at other places."

"Eve, how about if I call the manor and make reservations for us to have lunch there tomorrow? Then we could see what takes place with Mom and the others at mealtime."

"That's a great idea."

The wobbly section of wood on the counter in front of the three women's offices came to mind. "I'll pick up some hinges and screws to do a little job at the manor. Maybe we can do it after we eat and Mom goes for her nap. There won't be as many people moving around that we'd bother."

I understood the people who ran the manor had a lot more pressing problems to deal with than the one I had given them. Romantic rivalry between a couple of women who lived there probably sat low on the list of what they needed to do.

"While I was painting little hearts, I thought of calling customers we've already worked with. Josie wants us at her diner again. I'm going to run by there and see for myself exactly what she wants done."

"I'll come with you."

"No need to. If you don't have anything pressing for the rest of this afternoon, maybe you can come up with some ideas for ads. We could put something in the newspaper soon and maybe on the local radio station."

I agreed and disconnected. We had spent months working with plans for Edward Cancienne's house. We had done a lot of the work ourselves and hired subcontractors to fix up other things in that place he had wanted to move into. I was grateful that at least he had paid us some of the money upfront. But we still owed a lot to other people we had hired and companies where we charged flooring, lights, and kitchen fixtures.

Where was that money going to come from? Fear struck—everybody was going to sue us to collect for all those things and work done. My face muscles tensed. I thought of a song. Lesley's certainty came that I could handle fearful situations in much more positive ways. I tightened my throat, not allowing a tune or a hum to come through it.

I was proud of myself for squelching that long-held instinct. That pride was short lived. We still had the problem of owing everyone. Our Twin Sisters Remodeling and Repair business was growing, but our account didn't have anywhere near the money we would need to pay out if everyone sued us. Eve and I would probably need a lawyer to help us get out of this mess. Legal fees would add to our debts.

Was anything being done to the house Edward had us remodeling? Possibly it was up for sale. A sale of the place would cover much of its debt. Did Edward's uncle, our mother's beau, own it now? And if he did, wouldn't he also possess all the debts Edward incurred? If too much money was owed, he wouldn't have to accept anything. Yes, we would need to talk with a lawyer to sort through the situation.

I whipped my truck around at the next bridge. The small suspension bridge sank a little when I drove across it, and then I headed to the place my sister and I had spent the last few months fretting over. I would see whether anything was being done there, or whether a For Sale sign was out. Or better yet, a sign that said Sold.

And if no one was there, I could go around the house to look through the windows, since none of them would have curtains yet. I'd see if anything new had been done inside. If I was lucky, the key would still be where we left it, and I could let myself in. Possibly I could find some clue that the police missed, some small detail that might point to whoever murdered our client.

Chapter 14

Guilt crept through me like I was a thief when I drove onto Edward's property. I had driven down this long drive many times over the past months, normally with hope, expectations, and visions of how my sister and I could take this large traditional house and mold it into a spectacular home. We had slammed walls out and opened spaces into more inviting rooms, like wide-open arms that might draw a person in.

Today, I wasn't supposed to be here. The police or maybe Edward's uncle would probably be the only people allowed.

I found myself shutting my truck door quietly so as not to draw attention, even though no houses stood near. The late afternoon shadowing of the sky wiped away the sun's spotlight and lent an air of cover for me, although there actually was nowhere to hide.

Nothing appeared out of place out front. A few extra tire tracks created dents and small mud holes in the bright-green grass we had suggested that Edward plant to replace the weeds sprouting through what had been mainly Johnson grass. As this new grass grew, it would give the home an attractive frame.

I scurried onto the front stoop. To the right of the door stood various types of ferns with leaves now drooping like dead octopus arms over the sides of their pots. Edward had kept them watered. An urge struck to do that, but I didn't have time. Anticipation jamming my throat, I lifted the pot that held the asparagus fern.

Nothing was there except a little dirt. I went to all the pots and raised them, searching underneath. We had told Detective Wilet where to find the key to the front door. Surely the detective took it. Possibly after the police finished searching this place, he gave it to Edward's uncle Mac.

Edward probably also had keys in his pocket when we found him in the tub. And what about that man Carl who had argued with him? Could he have been one of Edward's lovers, a person Edward would have given a spare key to?

So far Detective Wilet had not discovered him that we knew of.

Not losing hope for getting inside, I tried the front door. It held tight. No one accidentally left it unlocked. I looked through the windows out front, expecting some item may be out of place. Possibly things could be strewn about as though someone had been searching for something that could prove important.

Little furniture had been placed inside. None of the pieces appeared overturned or removed. I didn't want anyone in passing cars to see me standing in front of the house peeking in its windows. I ran to the side, noticed nothing new, and tried to open the backdoor. It was locked. I dashed to the other side and again found not one thing looking suspicious inside. If I could get upstairs into the bathroom where he died, that might be different even though police surely inspected that room more than any others.

Muggy air pushing my wavy hair onto my face made me recall branches I had noticed moving back here. A few thick sweet olive bushes and a few trees rimmed the large rear lawn. I stepped across the grass to the right. Even though Eve hadn't seen any branches moving, my eye for detail made me certain I had spotted some soon after we discovered Edward dead.

I walked along the fragrant sweet olive bushes. My sinuses immediately protested and clogged, warning me to get away from them. Too late. I would need to pop an allergy pill.

The bushes were numerous, tall and thick, and I had no idea which ones a person might have walked through or if someone did. I stared up at the window to his bathroom that I must have looked out from. Doing that made me doubt myself. Had I really been able to see such a movement down here, especially when I was so unsettled from finding Edward?

Maybe I could. I walked close along the bushes, trying to determine where motion could have come from. The last two I looked between made my heartbeat quicken. A low branch of the one on the left had been snapped. Still connected, it bent back and leaned toward the ground.

Someone had run through here. My breaths stilled. That trespasser was the killer.

I stooped low and checked the grass, looking for any footprints, especially that might be in mud.

Disappointment flooded my chest when I found none.

Still, this discovery might prove fruitful. Detective Wilet answered on the fourth ring.

"I've found something that might help you find out who killed Edward," I said without greeting. He would know my voice by now. I hoped what I'd said would excite him.

Instead, his tone was dull. "Ms. Taylor, I'm in the middle of something. I can get back to you."

"No, this is important, and it'll just take a minute." Without waiting for a negative response, I continued. I told him about the snapped branch and that it was low, so maybe the killer was a short person, although while I was making this suggestion, other possibilities came to mind. A large dog might have gone through those branches. A child may have run after a tossed ball. The strong wind we experienced a few days ago could have done it.

My voice was less assured when I finished my statement. "Possibly you'd want to go out there and check it. I didn't see any dried blood on the snapped branch, but maybe there is some. And there could be footprints that I missed but you might see down there."

When he said nothing, I held my breath and felt the flush flooding my neck and cheeks like I had when I was in my third grade reading class and our teacher went down the rows, telling each student to read the next paragraph. She'd had no idea about my dyslexia and the difficulty that made me stumble over simple words and phrases. I could anticipate the laughter.

His exhale was loud. "Anything else?"

"No."

"Please leave this case alone. Getting involved could be dangerous for you."

"I'm already involved." A shiver ran through me. "I found his body."

"You did. Now leave the rest to me, okay?"

"I'll try." I was ready to hang up when he again spoke.

"Are you crying? I don't want to be mean to you, Ms. Taylor, but you need to realize we're dealing with a very dangerous person here. If that person believes you're getting close to pointing him out, he could come after you."

The compassion in his voice and his concern made the back of my eyes warm. "Thank you for everything."

Once we hung up, I pulled a tissue out of my purse and used it for my sniffles. I'd hated to tell him they came from my allergy to the sweet olives. I dug an allergy pill out of my purse and swallowed that, wishing I had some water to make it go down easier. Thinking of water caused me to look up again at the attractive curved top windows we'd had installed in Edward's bathroom. How he liked them and would have enjoyed looking out of them once he moved into the remodeled house. Or would a lover of his do that?

I got into my truck out front and started it, trying to recall what I was supposed to do this afternoon. Before I could remember, my phone rang. Seeing *Dave* as the caller, I smiled and answered, assured that my voice would portray my smile.

"What's wrong?" he said. "Are you crying?"

I laughed. "Not at all. I have sniffles because I was close to a bush I'm allergic to. I just took my sinus pill, and it hasn't had time to work yet."

"That's a relief." Relief also sounded in his voice. How refreshing. "You know what else might help clear your allergies?"

"What?"

"Fresh air. And catching a couple dozen fish with me."

Ah, anything with him sounded so much better than anything else I might do. I stared up at Edward's house as I backed down the long driveway. "I'm coming to take that medicine right now."

* * * *

The drive beside Bayou Boogie Woogie toward Dave's fishing camp made peace start settling inside me. I lowered my windows to get the scent that could not be matched anywhere else. The algae-tinged water gave off a pungent, though tempting odor. The air smelled fresh with undertones of dried shells of crabs and shrimp. The white shrimp boats moored along the bank with large weathered bald cypress trees leaning their branches toward the water sprouted the assurance of being here in Cajun country. Tall lavender irises and fan-shaped palmetto lined sections of the shore. The sound of a large splash alerted me that either a fish jumped or a large bird landed. I saw it was the latter—a white pelican sitting on the water.

"Dave," I said once I parked on his driveway and rushed out to him waiting for me with a wide smile. "I just saw a pelican. Not a brown one like our state bird. I've seen hundreds of those, but this was a white one. It was pure white."

His smile grew even wider. "I've seen a number of them out here." His lips met mine.

Still excited, I pulled my head back to talk. "Are you sure? Lots of white ones? Around here?"

"Yes. Come on, maybe you'll get to see more of them while you're waiting for a fish to grab your hook."

He had my line ready and handed the pole to me while we walked to the rear of his camp and onto the wharf Eve and I helped him build after he bought this place. He had two folding chairs set up side by side. "Look," he said and pointed.

I did just in time to view a bald eagle swoop low, riding a ridge of air right above the water. I dropped into a chair. "I felt stressed before. Now I'm all healed."

"I thought we were supposed to cure your allergy problem out here."

"You've cured both. Thank you." I glanced at the plastic bucket holding bayou water that sat beside his chair. "I don't see that you've put any fish in there."

"I haven't caught any yet. I just got off work, changed clothes, and drove out here." He did look good in those jeans. "I was waiting for you to get them to start biting." He held out a pint-sized foam container. "Have one?"

I took it from him, removed the top, and dug in the mud. I found the gray tip of a worm's tail and grabbed it. The slippery thing slid from my fingers and sank deep into the black muck.

"Need some help?" Dave asked.

I had shown him how to fish myself, since he wasn't from the South but wanted this camp. I'd helped him buy the right kind of tackle for fresh water fishing, which is what he had here. Together we had searched and located the right kind of boat he could use for going into other nearby bayous and canals. It also seemed perfect for some of the brackish and salt water at the edge of the Gulf. The boat shop in town was making sure it was ready to go. We would try it out soon.

I was also the person who'd taught him to use worms. Replying to him with a grin, I returned my attention to digging around in the mud. I uncovered a small worm and drew it out before it could wiggle back down to safety. This little fellow could provide us with the start of a good meal.

"The neighbor said the perch were biting yesterday evening with only a white jig head and no live bait." He nodded toward the camp that sat half a football field away. "Would you want to try like that first?"

I let go of the worm. Like a magician, it disappeared. After capping the container, I set it down and then wiped my fingers with the towel Dave held out for me. We cast our lines at the same time, me to the right and he a few yards to the left of mine. Our small round corks sat on top of the still water.

With a tight grip on my rod, I watched that cork, expecting it to get yanked down at any second. When it stayed in place, I glanced at Dave's. His wasn't moving either. Beyond our corks, a trio of turtles sunned themselves on a floating piece of branch. A great blue heron flew down and stood at the edge of the woodlands on the opposite shore. Near it, I spotted movement. A large rodent-like animal with what I knew would be two large orange front teeth was digging. It would be getting to the plants' roots. Oilfield workers had unknowingly brought those nutria here inside pipes from another state. The creatures had multiplied quickly and chewed up so many roots it caused the loss of a lot of our wetlands.

The slight breeze against my skin, the calming water, nature's creatures. Dave beside me. The last traces of sunlight falling into the swamp. All of it gave me such peace from the concerns I'd been experiencing. I was ready to tell him I could stay out here all the time when I noticed the muffled sound and realized it was my phone inside my closed purse behind my chair. I gripped my pole with my knees and got my phone out.

"Hey, you gotten everything done?" my sister asked.

I blinked. Glanced at Dave. Glanced at my cork. Couldn't think of what she was talking about. "Uh, have you?"

"Yes. I went over to the diner. Josie does need a few things done in there. I ate her delicious red beans and smoked sausage. Now I'm on my way home. I'll take a shower and then make a list of the things we'll need for her place."

While she spoke, I stood and set my pole across the seat of my chair. I gave Dave the tiniest quiet kiss on the cheek and pointing, showed him I needed to go. He nodded and took my rod. I jogged around the side of the camp to the driveway, still on my phone. "I'm glad you saw about that."

"And I called the manor and made reservations for us to have lunch there tomorrow. We'll get to visit Mom. Then we can change those hinges you bought." She stopped talking. "Sunny, are you short of breath?"

"No, I'm fine. I'll see you in the morning." I clicked off before she could hear me slamming myself into my truck and gunning the motor. I threw it in reverse and got on the road back to town before I noticed how dark the sky had become and called the lumberyard, hoping it was still open.

Their phone was answered.

"Hi, I need to get some things there," I said and then realized a man's voice on the other end had started speaking at the same time. His recording said they were closed but would reopen in the morning at six.

I would need to be there right afterward. Eve was such a great business partner and a wonderful sister. I felt blessed. She had always taken up for me. She took my place in a reading class once for an important test. After our older sister died, Eve snuggled up closer to me than she ever had before. We gave each other comfort.

If I could help it, I wouldn't let her down. I would set my clock to get up earlier than normal to make sure I'd purchase what we needed from the lumberyard. Anticipation swept through me like a power drill pushing its way through thin lumber. Tomorrow morning, we would also get to visit with our mother. Maybe we could get her aside and manage to convince her that she had been happy with her single life, and it was still working just fine.

But was it?

Either way, we would be able to check out the other woman who seemed to be after the man our mother wanted as a husband.

Chapter 15

Up early and dressed, I was ready to speed out to the lumberyard. When I walked outside my house, a mist lit on my face and arms, wrapping me in moisture. A gray fog had rolled in last night. It sat thick and heavy, enveloping the town. I found it almost impossible to see the houses beside the roads I drove on. I squeezed my fingers around my steering wheel and leaned forward, trying to make out the road better. Knots formed in my shoulders from the strain.

Taking the shortest route, I turned onto the street next to Bayou Bijou, instantly wishing I had not. A thick condensed soup of ghostly white swallowed the water. It took care of the air above and any land beside it. One pair of faint white orbs after another came toward me. In the eeriness, it took a second for me to realize they were headlights. A little farther along, a smaller ball of light came toward me before I heard the sound and determined it was a rider on a motorcycle who also could not see the road well and almost ran into me. I needed to get away from the water to a less-traveled street where I might be able to see where I was going. I watched for the next street sign so I would know where to turn.

I spotted one, but by the time I did, had driven past the street. Up ahead I spotted something that brought me relief. A trio of brighter lights from a service station came through the gumbo of misty air and called to me. I pulled in close to the station and parked. Then sighed, releasing a long-held breath. My arm muscles felt fluid.

At first, I wasn't certain of where I was. Not that it mattered. There were lights. I was off the road. Safe. And others were safe from me.

Two raps on my door's window made me jump.

"Hi, good morning. Can I help you?" The man beside my door was clean-shaven. He wore a bright, genuine smile and a blue-and-white striped cap that said Best Prices, the name of this gas station. Someone had recently spoken about this place. I couldn't recall why.

I opened my door. "Good morning. I'm going to get some gas, but I couldn't even see the pumps." Filling up hadn't been my plan, but I was certain my gas tank wasn't full. "I just needed to hurry and get off the road."

He pulled off his cap, revealing a shock of thick blond hair, and used the back of his wrist to wipe his brow. The air was cool, so he wasn't wiping sweat. "That fog really is thick this morning. Yesterday it burned off real quick."

I hadn't gotten up early enough then to notice.

"Come on inside. You can grab a cup of coffee and sit down a bit."

"Thanks. I think I will." I walked inside his small brightly lit building, glad to have shelter from the nearly invisible roads.

He came in behind me and pointed to a coffee pot with a carafe filled with a dark blend. "Look, I just made it. Get yourself some."

I poured myself a cup and added creamer and sugar, recalling Eve telling me how bad sugar might be for me or at least for my waistline, and my rebuttal—all the sugar cane farmers around here needed me to enjoy some of their crop.

"It's kind of scary out there. I could barely see where I was going." And I mentally patted my back. I had been frightened but experienced no thoughts of carols or hums.

"Yeah." His cap was back on, but he lifted it again, repeating the gestured he'd done outside, surely a long-held habit like my singing when in fear. "Almost had a wreck right out there yesterday morning. The guys got away with bumper taps."

"I don't think I've met you," I said to this kind man and put my hand out. "I'm Sunny Taylor. My sister and I own a remodeling and repair company called Twin Sisters."

His handshake was firm, his palm rough from his work. "Yeah, I've heard of y'all. I'm Tommy Jeansonne. Been living around here all my life."

His name and the name of this place on his cap that he was replacing on his blond hair brought back a story of concern. I scanned the rear wall behind his checkout counter. Advertisements of different products hung back there along with a license, and different from those things, an eight-by-ten framed picture of a young teen. The girl was pretty with hair the color of his that was set off by dark brown eyes.

My thoughts flashed back. Big Bub had told me that Edward Cancienne knew this man's daughter had become a hooker in New Orleans long before this man found out. How furious he must have been.

He stood so close to me I almost bumped into him when I turned. I smelled the oil on his skin mixed with a citrusy tone that might have been aftershave. "Pretty, isn't she?" He stared at the picture.

"Beautiful." I took a small step to the side, getting into a more comfortable space than so near to him. "She must be about what—fifteen? Sixteen?"

Dullness replaced the pleasure in his face. "No, she's a few years older now, just about ready to start graduate school." His lips smiled. Not his eyes. "She wants to be a psychologist."

Of course she would. The poor child had experienced such misery while prostituting in the city. Now she wanted to figure out why people like her were so taken in by the lure of such a profession.

Her daddy appeared wilted while he stared at her face.

"I know you're proud of her," I said and tossed my empty cup into a nearby trashcan. Barely glancing out through a large window, I walked to the exit door. "The fog is clearing. I'll move my car to a pump and fill up. Thanks again for the coffee and shelter."

He muttered words I didn't make out as I stepped outside. The defiled young woman's father remained inside, maybe still watching her, remembering her innocent youth and wishing he could bring it back.

I pumped a few gallons in my tank but didn't need much.

It seemed that an invisible hand with a large rag had rubbed the fog off the roads. I could finally see where I was going. I needed to center my thoughts to recall where I'd been headed.

Large bulky trucks were pulling away from the lumberyard, probably going to some construction sites. I knew where to find almost anything I needed inside, so I went straight to get the hinges and extra screws I might need with them. While I was at it, I looked around a bit to see if I noticed anything else we might require soon. Last night Eve told me Josie wanted us to do more work at her place. I could call and ask Eve what we might need.

Second thoughts made me hesitate. I wasn't ready to talk to her yet. Maybe because I felt so unsettled after being around the manager of Best Prices and seeing his daughter as she must have been before men defiled her. Maybe something else.

Chills skittered across the top of my back. I sauntered around the building, glancing at items, lifting a few tools, and adding a large crescent wrench to my purchases.

Much of the morning had passed by the time I headed to the manor. The sun blazed and sent glitters off people's windshields. Still, a cloak of sadness draped heavy on me. I was pulling along that young teenage girl's misery, wishing I could take away all that had stolen her youth.

And I believed I had told Detective Wilet what I had heard about her and her father and Edward. Now that I had met the kind, anguished man and seen his daughter's photograph, I wished I had not mentioned anything about them.

Chapter 16

The manor was filled with more motion and noise than normal. Residents and staff members and people I had never seen before were moving about, their voices loud. Probably the sunny day brought out more visitors and made people lively. A few of those who lived here had been sitting on benches outside, chatting and taking in the pretty morning that had started out with nasty, thick fog.

Even before I saw Mom, I spotted Eve standing near the counter that ran in front of the nurse and administrators' offices. She was lifting the uneven square section of the counter and telling the secretary who normally sat back there that we would take care of that problem right after lunch.

Seeing me, Eve said, "Good morning, sleepyhead." If she only knew how early I woke up this morning. "You bought the things we need to take care of this, didn't you?"

"Of course." *Just not yesterday when you had expected me to.* "I left them in my truck for now."

"That's fine." She lowered the section of wood. "I took care of putting our names on the list that says we ordered our lunches for today."

"Good. I'll pay for them." I unzipped my purse.

She held up a hand to tell me to stop. "I already took care of that. When I called in to make our arrangements, I paid for our meals with a credit card."

"That was sweet of you." I wouldn't offer to repay her since she always refused when this happened. She definitely had more money than I did, although with our business growing as it had been, finances were looking much better for me and also increasing for her. *If* money came through for the work we did at Edward's house. If not, we might both be in trouble.

I glanced at the rear doors. The first two to the left were shut. The nurse's door was open. She was checking in a filing cabinet in her office.

"And you came up with ideas for ads we could place in the paper, right?" Eve asked as we moved on.

Concern spiked through my scalp. My thoughts fell to yesterday fishing with Dave when I was supposed to be taking care of a couple of things. Getting hinges and screws for this place had been one of them. I knew I had forgotten something else. Writing ads.

Eve's clear blue eyes opened wider, expectation showing in them, the smile on her lips saying she knew I had taken care of business. She could count on me.

"I know of some things we could put out to advertise our business more," I said. Certainly words for them would come to mind when I was in a quieter place, like my home. "I'll let you know about them later."

"Okay, great." She squeezed my hand, letting me know I had done a good job and making me feel worse for having forgotten. "The work Josie wants us to do will take a few days, so we can schedule that in. We'll just need to grab another job or two to fill in the time we had put aside to take care of Edward's place."

I nodded toward the administrator's office. "She'll want us to remodel her office fairly soon and then I'm sure we'll get more calls as soon as we get new ads out."

My twin grabbed my hand. "Sunny, you sounded so short of breath when I talked to you on the phone." Concern pinched the skin between her eyes into folds. "You need to get checked out."

"No, I'm fine."

She squeezed my fingers. "I want to make sure you're okay, sis." The cry in her voice and concern in her eyes let me know she was thinking about our older sister.

I nodded, squeezed her hand back, and let go. "Look," I said, noticing a man walking alone beyond her that I had never seen here before and raising questions in my mind.

"He looks familiar. Who is he?"

"Emery Jackobson. He and that fellow Nelson were eating together at Josie's Diner. I believe they're a couple. Edward supposedly made him lose his wife and put him out of business and made him start drinking again."

"But if you're correct, Emery never should have married a woman in the first place."

"Right. I'll check the sign-in sheet to find out who he's here to visit." I stepped closer to the counter. The notepad that every visitor was supposed to sign sat front and center. As usual, we seldom signed in when we came here. Probably most regulars didn't either, although those sticklers for following rules would provide the date, time, and resident they came to see.

I skimmed through today's page but didn't see the name *Emery* or *Jackobson*. Feeling the secretary's stare, I signed in for both Eve and me with the time and that we were visiting Mom and eating here. When we moved on, I no longer saw the man in question.

"Hello, Daughters." Our mother wore a large smile as she strode toward us.

We smiled back, both putting our arms out to hug her.

Instead of reaching out for us, she turned back and grabbed the hand of someone else. "You remember Mac," she said, having him step forward. He had held back a moment to let a woman struggling with her walker move past him.

"Yes. Hello," I said to him, and Eve nodded. Struggling with my feelings about the man with our mother, I reached my hand out. He took it with his hand that wasn't gripping his walking cane. Eve did the same with him.

Mom's expression had withered a little while she watched our hands. I got the feeling she wished that instead of shaking his, we would have hugged him since we did that with her.

"It's lunchtime," she said, her words abrupt. Surely she was annoyed because we hadn't shown more interest in the gent standing beside her. "I don't have any time to sit and visit with y'all."

A snub, a shove from our mother. Oo, that hurt.

Maybe the way we'd hurt her?

Mac faced her. "Miriam, I'll leave you three to chat together the few minutes you have left before our meal." Although her mouth opened as though she was ready to protest, he stepped away.

She spun around toward us. "You two don't have to be so cold to him. He really is a sweet gentleman, and no matter what you think—" She stopped herself from saying more, but I and surely Eve knew what she was about to express. Whether we liked it or not, our mother was going to marry him.

She would. That fact sat on my brain. It slowed my heartbeat. Tugged at my heart.

I swallowed. "I'll try to behave better."

"Me, too." Eve nodded at her.

Mom gazed at us with steady eyes as though studying us, possibly seeing us for the first time. "Thank you. I would appreciate that." She pulled herself up straighter. The tan knitted strap that held the pouch with her medicine blended with her tan dress, making it almost invisible. "Was there any special reason for a visit from you two at this time? You know they really have started serving lunch."

"Yes, we know," Eve said and grinned. "And we know you'll head up to your room for a nap right afterward."

"I will," Mom said.

"We've been wanting to come and have lunch here, so we finally made reservations ahead of time."

Eve spread her hands. "We're eating with you."

"But there's no room for anyone extra at my table."

"We know," I assured her, "but the table next to yours will have two people out today. We'll be taking their places, and that way we'll still be close to you."

Mom took that thought in for a minute. "How sweet."

People had begun moving to the area set up as a cafeteria. The two chief administrators, other staffers, and residents headed there. As we fell into step with the crowd, I spied our mother's beau walking up ahead. A slender female resident spoke to him with a large smile. I recognized her as Miss Clarice, the person who wanted him for her own. He gave her a slight smile in return, and I felt a pinch of annoyance. Why?

Mainly I experienced a sense of relief mixed with dread. Since our mother hadn't started fussing at us for meddling in her business by trying to get her moved to another table, she obviously didn't know about those plans yet. She would probably be pleased to get away from Miss Clarice, but wouldn't be happy if she discovered we encouraged such a move. She wouldn't know our motive was to get her away from that lady whose interest in the same man might make Mom want a permanent situation with him much sooner than she might be planning.

He sat with three other men a few yards away, his back toward Mom's table. That was good. Maybe. To my surprise, I realized I continued to accept that they would be together. Still, something inside me tugged against that taking place. The cafeteria was filling. I looked around but didn't see Emery Jackobson. He probably only stopped by to visit someone. He may have already left.

A half dozen people gave Eve and me double takes. Most people in town knew us as identical twins. These who stared obviously didn't. Unless they'd heard we were linked to our most recent customer's murder or had heard us here arguing with him.

The clatter of dishes called my attention to staffers who had already begun serving trays of food to people at their tables. The enticing aroma of homemade bread made my mouth water.

Mom took her seat at the table where we had seen her sit before. Nobody else was with her.

Eve and I walked close. "Is anyone else coming" Eve asked, "or can we join you?"

Mom shook her head. "No, you can't. The others often get here late." She moved her fingers like she was shooing us away. "Go on and join those ladies. The staff will be serving meals at your table, so go get yours while it's hot."

Checking the table a few feet away, I spotted two staffers carrying trays holding plates and glasses and rolled napkins that would hold silverware. They set them in front of two who sat there.

"Here's my meal. Go ahead. I'll be fine." Mom waved her fingers as though wanting us to go on. A woman in navy served Mom a tray holding a meal that looked scrumptious. Shrimp stew on rice, lima beans, cole slaw, and a plump brown roll that smelled like it was right out of the oven sat on her plate. A tall glass of iced tea stood beside her rolled paper napkin, and next to the glass sat a bowl holding what had to be crunchy cherry cobbler.

"Yum, that all looks terrific," I said. "We came on the perfect day."

"I'm sure it will be. Now let me eat," Mom said, "and go eat yours."

Some of the servers moving to tables carried bowls of vegetable soup and tuna sandwiches instead of the main entrée, a choice guests were also given at each meal. Although some of the people here must have stomach problems or other ailments that made them watch their diet, I couldn't imagine eating what came out on those trays while others devoured shrimp stew and cobbler.

Not far from us, the woman we'd met who carried her urn set it in the center of her table. I wondered how her seatmates felt while they ate, knowing a dead man sat in front of them.

Eve and I stepped over to the table where we had been assigned. Both ladies seated there gave us warm greetings. They were friends of our mother's that we had known a long time. They chatted with us, asking which one was which.

"How is your love life going?" the woman who always wore long pearls asked Eve while she unrolled her napkin and set it on her lap. "Are you dating anyone now? Getting ready to get married again?"

That question made me squirm inside. We were used to a few of the residents asking sometimes rude questions that people in other settings normally avoided. It was like many believed that being of a certain age gave them permission to do so. That was ordinarily fine with us, but now Eve would tell them how much she loved Dave.

"You've had what, four, five marriages already?" The one with shoulders so thick they made me think of linemen on professional football teams lifted her fork and looked at my sister.

"Only three." Eve shrugged and added, "Who knows when I might get married again? But I'm not ruling it out."

"Way to go," the lineman lady said with a nod. "I'd get married if I ever had the chance." She stabbed two lima beans and chewed them. Using her empty fork, she waved it back and forth at both of us. "Either of you know of any available man I might get to join me?"

I do, I thought, my mind going to our mother's beau. I saw Mom's eyes turning to where he sat and feared she did not want him available much longer.

"I'll look around and let you know if I find any available man," Eve told the woman with us.

"I'd appreciate that."

Our other seatmate kept quiet once her food came. She attacked one item on her tray after another. Her cherry cobbler was one of the first things that almost disappeared, leaving only a trace of red and a few brown and tan crumbs behind in the white bowl.

"What do they do about people with diabetes?" Eve asked her. "That cobbler looks too tempting to serve to people eating with you if you can't have any."

"They make some with a sugar substitute. They do that with a lot of desserts." The food stabber lifted a forkful of rice with two medium shrimp.

Our mother's seatmates had joined her at the table, I noticed. Eve and I hadn't been served our food yet, but they had gotten theirs immediately after they sat. The people serving meals were doing an amazing job, getting plates out to everyone so quickly. Ours were probably slower in coming because we weren't regulars.

"This all looks so great," I said to Mom a couple of feet away from our table.

"If I ate like this every day, I'd weigh five-hundred pounds," Eve, the spoilsport, chimed in.

"Ladies," Mom said to the other ladies who had filled in her table, "you've met my daughters, haven't you?"

"Yes," one of them said. Another one nodded. Clarice, who wanted to take Mom's man, only stuck her nose in the air as though she had sniffed some offensive object. Nothing smelled foul in those plates, so I imagined she was reacting to Eve and me. I was disappointed in myself for having the urge to go over there and twist her skinny nose.

Our food arrived. We thanked our servers and didn't hesitate to get started. Words at our table and at others quieted while we all ate. The shrimp were wonderful, the stew seasoned well with bell pepper and garlic. I enjoyed a bit more of a garlic flavor in any stews, so I used the garlic powder from the center of the table and also sprinkled on a dab of the hot pepper provided. The well-shouldered woman had eaten all her food except for her stew. Before even tasting it, she added lots of salt and four shakes of hot pepper. She took a tiny taste, smiled like a woman who had just found love, and set one forkful of stew after another into her mouth.

I thought I could do the same thing. My stew was so tasty, I started to eat it rather quickly, but then took time from it to try my lima beans. Seasoned perfectly with pieces of salt meat, they were wonderful. The coleslaw swam in more mayonnaise than I was used to, but my bite of cobbler made me forget any complaint. Nice and sweet with the cherries, it had a crunchy crust on top and even a thick bottom layer of crunch. Before I knew it, I had finished my dessert. Then I looked up and saw Eve grinning at me.

"Yes, I love sweets," I told her.

"So do I." Those were the first words spoken by the pearl-wearing woman in a long time. Almost all her food had been devoured.

I was going to ask Mom what she liked best and already knew what she would say. She loved any kind of cobbler. When we were young, she would make peach or cherry cobbler as a special treat. She always ate as much of it as we did.

Coughing came from her table, making me look there even though our seatmate who'd made her meal disappear had begun telling us a story about her newest great-granddaughter. I wanted to make certain it wasn't Mom getting a cough or choking. It was not. The woman coughing was her competitor. She took a swallow of her drink, and her coughing stopped.

I returned to tuning in to the story being told at my table about a little girl who had gotten really sick last January with the flu.

"Clarice, what's wrong? You don't look well," a lady at Mom's table said in a loud voice, causing the four of us to look there.

The chair nearest us got shoved back as did most others near as projectile vomit spewed onto plates. Miss Clarice continued to vomit, making people nearby scramble. A few in the area rushed toward her, but most scattered away with utters of disgust.

I hurried close hoping to help, grabbing my unused napkin and Eve's to wipe the sick lady's face. Someone from the cafeteria area would probably bring towels.

"What can we do for you?" Eve stood on her opposite side.

"Clarice, do you want my daughters to help you to your room?" Mom laid a hand on her arm. Without warning, more vomit gushed. Some of it just missed Mom's fingers

Staff members wearing navy were helping residents who required assistance move to other places. The administrator and her assistant rushed near.

"How do you feel?" the administrator asked the ill person, who appeared barely able to give her head the slightest shake and seemed unable to voice words.

Rita Picou, the assistant, carried clean wet towels she'd brought from the cafeteria. She wiped Miss Clarice's cheeks and chin. Using another towel she'd carried in over her shoulder, she wiped what she could off the ill lady's hands and dress.

Miss Clarice began to cough as much as she had before.

"Let me through." The nurse rushed forward between those parting to give her a clear path. "Move aside," she told those of us still standing close.

Stooping near the woman who'd gotten sick, she asked, "Do you feel real bad, Miss Clarice?" Getting a slight nod in response, she said, "Then you don't feel like it's over. Do you hurt anywhere?" Before waiting for a response, she leaned close and used a stethoscope to check the her chest. The woman heaved on the nurse's cheek and long black hair.

She jerked back. Face pinched in annoyance, she told the administrator, "Get an ambulance. She needs to get checked by a doctor."

Most of the people who lived here had scattered. Staffers ordered everyone to leave the room. While Eve and I headed toward the nearest bank of elevators with Mom, I spotted the woman and man who did most custodial work around here and felt sorry for them when they came carrying buckets and mops.

"Miriam, are you okay?" Mom's beau had stepped up behind us. He took her hands when she turned to him.

"Yes, I'm fine. The poor thing must have come down with a bad virus."

"I certainly hope you don't catch it."

"Thank you." She let go of his hands and gave him a small hug. "I'm fine."

Eve cleared her throat. He pulled back from Mom and looked from my sister to me. "You two take good care of her." He smiled at her. "She told me you always do."

"She always took the greatest care of us," I said. "We'd never want anything or anyone to hurt her."

"I'm sure you don't." He returned full attention to our mother. "You're going down for your nap now, and I'll see you much later?"

"You know you will."

"It was nice seeing all of you today." He spoke to Eve and me, and we nodded in return.

One elevator had just taken off. "You two can go home now," Mom told us. "Everything will be fine here." Her eyes flitted toward the silver-haired man using a cane to walk away. Yes, she did care about him. She returned her attention to us.

"We'll go up to your room with you," Eve said, "just to make sure everything's okay."

Mom fisted her hands on her hips. "Young ladies, just because one person became sick at my table does not mean anything puts me at risk. And I do not need my daughters to take care of me." Her lips pinched into a thin line. "No matter what you may think, I am not an invalid, and I do *not* need you seeing about me or telling me what I can or cannot do."

Ooooh, this mother was different from the gentle one who was always sweet to us with her actions and words. This one seemed much more independent than the softer one. Maybe her ill rival caused it. Maybe her daughters were in the way here, and she instead wanted to be with her intended.

An elevator door dinged open. "Let us know if you need anything," I said and kissed her cheek and then watched her lips relax.

"Yes. Stay well." Eve kissed her opposite cheek.

"And when you find out, let us know what Miss Clarice has," I said, and Mom assured us she would. We walked off before the elevator doors shut to take her and anyone else who got on with her away. The halls we passed were clear. Probably almost everyone went to their rooms or suites.

"That was almost a good meal," Eve said once we stepped outside.

"Almost."

"He seems to care about her."

"Yes." I considered a minute. "I only wish we didn't feel so concerned about his reasons."

Eve frowned. "I know."

I sighed. "I hope Miss Clarice's all right and it's just a little stomach bug."

"Me, too. And Mac was sick. Let's hope Mom doesn't get it."

My own frown deepened with that thought. I headed for my truck, about to open the door when a siren called my attention toward the far end of the parking lot. It sounded like the ambulance would come in from there. As always when I heard one of them, I said a silent prayer for the person needing help.

My main concern was our mother. She had sat right next to the woman who'd seemed so violently ill. After we found out what that illness was, we could be more assured that Mom wouldn't come down with the same thing. Illnesses struck older people harder than those much younger.

Chapter 17

A phone call came soon after I got on the road. I dug in my purse, found my phone, and answered.

"Sunny, it's Dave. Your mother is all right, isn't she?" Concern strained his voice.

"Yes, she's fine. Why are you asking?" My stomach muscles jerked tight. Could something have just happened to her that he learned about but I didn't? Spotting a driveway ahead, I whipped in. I threw my gears in reverse and was backing to turn and speed back to the manor when he replied.

"I'm working near the manor and just saw an ambulance there."

"Oh." I pulled my foot farther back from the accelerator. "No, she wasn't in it."

"I didn't want to scare you. I was just concerned about her."

"That was sweet of you." What a great man who'd look after my mother. "Where are you working?" I glanced at houses to the right of this one but didn't see his truck at anyone's house.

"My crew and I are installing an alarm system in a new house near the Baptist church."

The church was to my left. I aimed my truck in that direction.

"Do you know if the person they brought away will be all right?" In the background, two men began speaking to each other, probably members of his crew.

Would she be all right? "I think so. Nobody died. One of the female residents got sick."

"Good. Then maybe I'll get to see you again soon?"

I reached the corner and turned right. His truck and his work van sat in the driveway of the house I'd noticed going up.

"Sunny? Are you still there?"

I slid my window open and pulled into the driveway Dave stood next to. When he saw it was me, his lips curved into a wide smile. He put up his phone and came to my door.

"No, I'm not there. I'm here." I gave him an even wider smile.

"How great to see you." He stepped up to my door and pushed his face toward me as though he was going to give me a kiss. A few feet behind him, a young man holding equipment that they used for jobs watched us. Dave and I had never really kissed in public. He obviously didn't care. Neither did I. I pressed my lips against his.

"It's good to see you, too." My peripheral vision let me see the worker grin. He turned and carried his things into the house.

"Did you have lunch yet? I could slip away for a few minutes and take you out to eat."

"Nice. Thanks, but I ate at the manor."

He placed his warm hand on my shoulder. Um, the effect he was having on me made me feel that being anywhere with him now was a nice place.

He squeezed my shoulder and grinned. "Guess what? You caught a fish."

"What? When?"

"Right after you left my camp, something started taking your pole. I grabbed it right before the whole thing went in."

I couldn't imagine how large the fish must have been. "What was it?"

"Catfish, a big one."

"I wish I could have caught it. I love the way they attack your bait and pull it down and put up such a fight. The big ones really bend your pole."

He laughed. "You've lived down here a lot longer than I have and had that experience much more often. If you keep coming to my camp with me, I'll let you catch another one."

"I'll need to do that soon. Fresh-water cats make great eating."

"We'll have it for supper sometime soon." His lips pressed into a small pout. "I didn't catch anything, but I stopped trying after you left."

Behind him, the young man walked out the front door. "Mr. Price, I'm sorry, but we need you in here."

"I'll be right there," he said to his helper who returned inside. Dave looked at me with a shrug. "Guess I've got to go." He gave me a parting kiss.

I watched him take long steps toward the door. The way he walked, his stride, his concern for my mother, the image of him grabbing my fishing line as it was being pulled away—all of it made me smile. I wanted to be with this man. Even though I had been married once briefly, I had never felt this way before. No man had the same effect on me. Soon after my marriage, my husband had started making me feel even worse about myself than I had from the early years with dyslexia and that horrible trait I'd picked up as a child when my oldest sister died. Dave made me feel totally opposite.

I looked at the doorway he'd gone into, hoping to see him again. I did not, so I backed onto the road and headed down the street when my phone rang. He was still thinking about me like I was doing about him. "Hello," I said, voice chirpy.

"Hey. You're in a better mood now," Eve said.

"Oh, yeah." My mind returned to the manor, to the woman who had been carted off by an ambulance. "I'm sure she'll be all right."

"Hope so. When you get home, would you look at those ideas you have for ads we could use? We need something better than we've used before, maybe something that'll pop when a person sees it."

Oh my gosh, advertisements never came to my mind. "I didn't get to my house yet, but it shouldn't take long."

"Good. Call and let me know what you came up with."

Does thinking more seriously about Dave count? That was surely an idea she did not want to hear. "I will," I said and hung up. Tugging my thoughts away from Dave, I knew I needed to put more effort into trying to get us more business. Too many distractions had attacked my ideas.

Arriving home, I went straight to my pen and legal pad. Many people were much more technically advanced than I was and could use their devices much faster and easier, but paper and pen worked best for me.

What words could we use? I stared at the blue lines on the long yellow sheet, tension building from knowing I needed to write something.

Dave I penned. I wrote the word small, but on the next line wrote it bigger. I found myself doing like Eve on her canvases and drawing small hearts. Doing that made me feel like a schoolgirl, a little adolescent with a large crush. Happily, I used a curvy print to make his name prettier and then framed it with hearts that contained a smile.

"Hey, are you here? I'm coming in." It was Eve's voice at my kitchen door. Her key jiggled in the lock.

My eyes speared my work. I sat at the kitchen table, my words and drawings concerning the man she was in love with right out there.

I ripped the page off the pad. Heart throbbing in my throat, I jumped up, wadded the page, and threw it in the trashcan. Its top was silently closing when my twin stepped inside.

Wearing a jogging suit, she sounded slightly breathless. "You got it?"

"You ran over here?" I asked, a question with an obvious answer. Of course she had.

Eve came up and looked over my shoulder at the pad on my table. "You didn't write anything?" The look on her face said she was disappointed in me. She had always been my big supporter.

Inside, I felt as though I had shrunk. "I had some ideas," I said quickly. "But I didn't write them." Those words came out slower.

She stared at the blank page in front of me. What if she could see the name and hearts I'd created on the page above this one?

I slid my forearm above the legal pad. "Did you have ideas for anything that we could use?"

She pulled up a chair and sat. "We'll put this ad out in papers in the surrounding parishes, too, this time so we can get broader exposure." Elbows on the table, she placed her hands together under her chin. "Let's see. We need to have Twin Sisters Remodeling and Repair in it. But do you think the words all need to be together? Or what about something like this: Need any remodeling or repair done to your home? Call Twin Sisters. And then write our phone number."

"That's a great idea." I wrote what she said. She and I stared at the words.

"Hm, I'm not sure I love it," she said, her eyes turned up to mine. She was asking for my true opinion.

I gave it. "That would be nice. But since we're two women running this kind of business, maybe we could mention our years of total experience because we worked so long with Dad, and say they could call and ask about referrals. I don't believe our customers would mind telling others how satisfied they are with our work."

"You're right. But how would we write that? It needs to be something clever."

We watched my unmoving hand gripping the pen.

"Sunny." Eve sounded sad. "I hope Mom doesn't find out we tried to have her assigned to a different table."

I set down the pen. "I know. Even though she might be happy to sit somewhere else to eat, I really don't believe she'd want us meddling."

Eve agreed with a slow nod.

My phone's ring surprised and satisfied me. I saw it came from my friend Amy, who must be at work in the gumbo kitchen. At least for a few minutes I could stop worrying about Mom and quit trying to concentrate on how to write creative ads for any newspapers.

"It's Amy," I told Eve and then answered. Getting up and away from the pad that screamed for my full attention, I wandered over to the window and peered outside. Dark clouds had moved in.

"Hey, girl," I said.

"Sunny." Her voice was frantic. "Something's happened at the manor." My heart jammed my throat. "There's no problem with my mom—unless you heard there is."

Eve rushed up beside me. Face pinched, she stared at the phone. I put it on speaker so she could listen.

"I heard some lady got real sick in there after she ate, and I thought of your mom. I hope she's okay. I hope it's not food poisoning."

My sister leaned closer to my phone. "Hey, Amy, it's Eve. I'm with Sunny at her house. We were there when it happened, and the woman didn't seem too sick. At least I don't think so." Her eyes turned to mine. "Do you, Sunny?"

"Probably not. She threw up after she ate. It was a lot and it really gushed." Recalling those moments made my stomach queasy again.

"It could be food poisoning. Wait, what were you doing over there when she was eating?"

"We ate lunch there, too," Sunny replied before I could.

"Then y'all need to get tested. Your momma, too." Worry made Amy's words louder and faster than normal. "I had a client who died from that. Her whole family got really sick."

"We're doing just fine, Amy. Don't worry." Eve had slipped the phone out of my fingers and into hers. She looked at me with narrowed eyes. "Right, Sunny? You're feeling okay, aren't you?"

"Yes, I am." I took my phone back from her. "Amy, the woman at the manor got sick not that long ago. How did you hear about it so fast?" After all, she worked at our community center that served the needy. Probably many of them were still eating lunch there or maybe playing cards right afterward.

"I heard a couple of men talking about it, so I asked where they were talking about. The fellow who knew what happened there was Nelson. Why? Was it supposed to be kept quiet?"

"Not at all. I just wondered how word of it spread so fast. We live in a fairly small town." I'd stepped away from Eve, but she could still hear with the speaker on.

"Okay, I need to get back to work. Y'all just keep an eye out for symptoms, and if you start feeling bad, get to a doctor or hospital right away."

"We will. I promise." I nodded at Eve, who nodded back at me.

"And you'd better keep an eye on your mother. The elderly get hit hardest, you know."

I said I did and I would; then I thanked her and hung up. Eve and I stared at each other.

"What?" she said. "Tell me your thoughts."

"The person who knew about what happened there so fast was Nelson. Remember he was one of the two men I introduced you to at Josie's? I'm certain Nelson wasn't at the manor, especially since as usual, he was eating at the gumbo kitchen. I believe the person who let him know what happened was Emery Jackobson. Those two men are close, it seems, and I saw Emery at the manor before lunch. I didn't notice him eating there."

"But that doesn't mean anything."

"I know." I pushed the legal pad aside. "I don't feel very creative right now."

Eve shifted her shoulders up a bit and lowered them. "Neither do I."

"I can't stop thinking about Miss Clarice, especially since Amy mentioned food poisoning, something that can be deadly. I want to check on things there."

Eve nodded, giving me the belief she felt the same way. As I paced with my phone with the speaker on, she walked near, listening. The secretary answered. "Hello, this is Sunny Taylor. I need to speak with the nurse."

"I'm sorry. She's really busy right now and can't come to the phone."

"I know what she's busy with. My mother is a resident there, and I was there for lunch today. I saw what happened. That's why I'm so concerned."

"I understand. But there's no way I can put you through to the nurse. I'm sure you understand that she's especially tied up right now."

My eyes flitted to Eve's.

"Ask for the administrator," she said, the same thing I was thinking.

"All right," I said into the phone, "but then let me talk to Terri Hebert. Tell her it's really urgent that I speak with her."

A sigh sounded. Long seconds passed. "Here she is."

"This is Terri Hebert, Ms. Taylor." Her tone that was normally pleasant and smooth now sounded snappy. I understood. She didn't want to talk with me.

But I would make her. "You know my sister and I were there for lunch and saw what happened. Since we were right there with our mother, we're especially worried. What's going on there now? Has anything else happened? Did anybody find out what made Miss Clarice so sick?"

She hesitated a moment in which I imagined her filling out reports about what occurred with one of her residents and possibly seeing a lot of movement out there. What was everyone doing?

"We haven't received any news from the hospital yet. Rita Picou, our assistant- administrator, followed the ambulance to the hospital and is staying with her while they're running tests. Miss Clarice's son has been notified, but he lives out of state."

Eve's right eyebrow lifted while she stared at me. Like me, she might be surprised to know the woman had once married. Or possibly she hadn't. But she had a son.

"What we've been doing over here," the administrator said, "is getting notes out to everyone telling them to let a staff member know if they feel sick, especially if they get nauseated."

Worry spiked through my scalp. "Why? Do y'all think it was food poisoning?"

"Just as a precaution." Her words returned to their usual calming nature. "We don't believe that was really the cause of her getting ill. The nurse thinks it's probably a touch of the stomach flu or something similar. Miss Clarice could be sent back here by this evening."

"Some conditions can be really contagious."

"We do know that." I could hear the deep inhale through her nostrils. She wanted to hurry and get off the phone with me. "What we've been doing is writing that notice about illness in the central areas on all the white boards that usually announce people's birthdays, and we've had pages about the same thing typed in extra-large print and slipped under all of the residents' doors. I believe your mother went to her room."

"Yes. She was going to take a nap, so she won't see the page."

"If she's asleep, then she won't need to be reading it. Listen, I understand your concern, but I'm sure your mother will be all right, and I believe our sick resident will be, too. Now I really need to go. There are things I need to tend to."

"Okay." I checked Eve's face to see whether she was trying to get some other concern in. Her expression remained calm, her eyebrows both down.

"Thank you for calling."

Words flowed from my mouth before I determined she remained silent and had hung up. I pressed the red off symbol on my phone. Eve and I stared at each other.

"I'm going to jog a bit and see if any ideas pop up," she said. "Even if they don't, I'll have a good workout." She pushed the chair she had sat in against the table. "Want to join me?"

I gave her a small grin. "No thanks. Maybe another time."

"You always say that," she said on her way out and then shut the door.

Maybe it was time for me to start working out again, I considered. Instead of running, I walked out my backdoor. The air was cool, invigorating with the rainclouds so close, but just passing by, it seemed. Maybe I should start running or at least taking daily brisk walks like I had done awhile back. I'd just gotten out of the habit of doing it at a certain time each day.

I needed to start before the temperatures and humidity rose so much that being outside would feel like walking into a sauna.

A few more of the fuchsia flowers had opened since the last time I'd walked out here, making that azalea bush more attractive. The number of tiny buds on it and the other bushes held lots of promise. Maybe they weren't as horrible as I had believed. The yellow snapdragons stood out most in my small garden to the left. I didn't find the orange or red flowers on the spiked plants as appealing, but they were all lovely. All of them could probably use water. I unwrapped the hose and gave a good sprinkling to all the plants while the sun came out and chased the dark clouds away. A slight breeze blew against my face. One couldn't ask for a nicer day. But then why did my back tense with worry? I asked myself, shutting off the hose and winding it where it belonged. Mom should be fine. Her seatmate should be fine. I had no reason to be concerned. I needed to let my uneasiness go.

There was nothing I could do at the manor right now. The staff seemed to be doing everything it could. I couldn't go and sit beside my mother while she slept in her bed. I wanted to. She wouldn't like it. I wanted to go and satisfy myself that she was fine and would continue to be physically healthy.

In the storage room behind my carport, I took out the worn tool belt that my father always used when he was a carpenter. Fingering its threadbare lower right corner, I told myself I needed to get that section changed. At the same time, I knew I would not. I tied the stained thing around my waist, grabbed a pair of sawhorses, and placed them on the carport in front of my parked truck. After returning inside the room, I retrieved the large nails and placed them and my favorite hammer Dad had used in each of their slots on the belt. I grabbed leftover chunks of two-by-fours, set them across the sawhorses, and slammed some nails in. My workmanship wasn't needed here since all I wanted to do was get some of my frustrations out. *Slam. Wham.* The bunching of muscles in my shoulder felt good. Familiar.

I whacked nails in, one after another, until I had filled in the space across the wood. Then I began another row. The nail heads were dark gray. The flowers out back were pink and red and yellow and orange. Orange. The truck that somebody fired a bullet out of that killed my older sister was orange.

Whack. Whack. Unease squiggled down my spine.

I yanked off my tool belt and replaced it and the other items I'd brought out back into the storage room. Then I ran back to my truck and jumped in, unable to shake off the concern for my mother.

Driving to the manor felt like it took longer than normal although I raced there. I reached its parking lot and saw what I'd feared. *Emergency vehicles.* Only these weren't ambulances to carry more people to the hospital. What now filled the space normally left open near the entrance were police cars.

Chapter 18

I threw my truck in park and raced inside. The place was brimming with men and women in blue. Some residents scattered and others converged and stood gawking to see what was going on. The only time people here saw so much excitement was whenever someone died or that time when Mrs. Jackson won the Louisiana Powerball. She cashed in a thousand dollars of it in tens. Then she returned to the manor and strolled around, tossing money as though she were a rider on a Mardi Gras float, and everyone in the place flailed their hands in the air to catch a few bills or scattered to grab those that fell on the floor.

"What's going on?" I asked a male resident, the first person I came across inside.

His response was a shrug.

A young deputy stood in the foyer. "What happened here?" I asked him.

"Ma'am, we're in the middle of an investigation and can't discuss it right now. Please don't block this area." He moved his straight arm backward as though to show me I should do as he said.

"Why? Is another ambulance on its way? Is someone else sick and being taken out on a stretcher?"

An angry expression replaced what previously seemed his little boy face. "Please just do as I told you." His grimace suggested he hadn't wanted to use such a nice request.

Terri Hebert came out of her office. The minute she lifted the counter's cut section of wood and came through, I grabbed her arm.

"Why are all these police here? Something serious happened."

She looked at other staff members gathered with some police officers and glanced back at me. "Miss Clarice has gotten worse. They need to investigate."

My heart went out to the lady. "That's so sad. I hope she gets better."
"So do we." She scanned the gathering. "Now I need to go."

"Why do police need to investigate?" I called, but she had dashed off
into the crowd of others that included Detective Wilet. I got Eve on the
phone while I ran to the closest elevator.

She answered with a smile in her voice. "Guess who I just spoke with?"

"Your grandson. Eve, get over here to the manor. There are police all
around. Miss Clarice hasn't gotten any better."

The elevator door slid open.

"How's Mom?" she asked, worry replacing her cheer.

"I'm about to go up there to find out." I hung up, counting off the
extended time it took to move upstairs. Pressure built inside my head
during this slowest ride the elevator ever made.

A couple of female residents using walkers moved slowly down the
hall. "Have either of you seen my mother?" I asked.

"She's probably in her room. They made an announcement that we should
all stay in our rooms or suites. And you know Miriam. She follows the rules."

"But we were downstairs when they said that," the other one said, "and
it takes us longer to get where we need to go."

"Thank you." I ran past them to my mother's room. I beat on her door,
fearful that she wouldn't be there. If not, where would she be? I envisioned
her in a small room on the first floor with dark brown curtains and sofa,
her beau seated at her side.

Much worse, she might be in her room, retching in her toilet or sprawled
out on the floor.

Too many strong thrusts of my heart later, the door opened. Mom's
eyebrows rose with her quizzical expression.

I flew into her room, pushed the door shut with my foot, and wrapped
her inside my arms. "You're safe," I said against the side of her head.

She gave a squeeze to me and then wiggled to back out of my embrace.
"What's happened, Sunny? Did they call you to come here?" I had
seldom before seen fear trace my mother's face and her eyes. "Why are
we in our rooms?"

"Have they ever ordered y'all to do that before?"

"I told you we had an announcement like that after the last hurricane to
make certain they knew who had returned if people had left here, but that
became a fiasco. Residents who have trouble with walking went rushing
and one man fell. He broke his hip and after he recovered, he needed to
move into the nursing home."

"No, you didn't tell me about that."

"Then it must have been Sunny."

Even if my sister and I were identical, our mother never ever got us mixed up, not even when we were adolescents looking for something to do during that long, boring summer, and we made everything different about ourselves. I wore Eve's favorite peacock blue short set, and she put on my black and gold Saints T-shirt and jean shorts. My feet weren't comfortable in her sandals covered with large clear stones and an irritating strap that slipped between my first two toes. Hers surely felt good when she showed up in my tennis shoes with socks. She'd placed a touch of blush on my cheeks and left her own face plain. Eve placed her hair in a ponytail held with a rubber band that day, and I left mine down. We took each other's places at the table when it was time to eat, having told each other to be careful of what we said.

Mom showed no sign of recognition of our changed states—until we finished eating and were carrying our used plates to the sink, giving each other winks on the side. And then our mother said, "Oh, Sunny, you know that when you tried some sandals with the strap between the toes like that before, they gave you blisters on the side of your big toe that hurt for a week. You might want to put them back on Eve's side of the closet." She wore a small grin and said nothing else about our attempted stunt.

Over the years we had fooled a few people, but this was our mother.

"I'm sure I told Eve to tell you about it. She must have forgotten. And I guess you didn't come around here too soon after that." That little dig she'd gotten in about me not visiting as often as she'd sometimes like let me know she wasn't too scared about today.

"Eve's on her way here," I said, and Mom's eyes opened wider, concern returning. "This is all I know. I got worried and decided to come and check on things here, especially to try to find out how Miss Clarice was. And when I got here, I found a lot of police."

"Why are the police here? Did something else happen?"

I searched my mind. What had I discovered downstairs? I needed to be honest. "They found she's sicker than she had been."

"Oh no." Tears rimmed the lower edge of her eyes. "What could have caused her illness? And why would the police be here?"

"I have no idea, but if she's not doing any better, I imagine they'll be admitting her to the hospital, at least for a day or two, instead of sending her back here too fast."

Mom's body slumped. "Poor thing. I'll say a rosary for her." She glanced at the wooden crucifix on the wall beside her sofa and made the sign of the cross. And then she sighed and headed to the coffeemaker. "You'll need something," she said, although I had the distinct impression that she was the one who did. By preparing this drink, especially so late in the day, she must feel a need for company. For me to stay longer. For me not to leave her alone up here now while everything was so uncertain. I wanted to stay with her, too.

"I can help." I went for her silverware drawer and took out two spoons. She waved me away from there. "You sit down. I need to wait on you again." As if she hadn't done that for so many years.

I nudged up right beside her and pressed my cheek against her soft one. "I'd like to wait on you now. I've had my turn the other way around."

Again she shooed me away from her space. "You and your sister tried to do that once my arthritis started acting up so badly." Her words made me glance at her hand with the large knuckles and twisted fingers that had made her slow down in the activities she could do for herself. Yes, we'd each insisted on having her move in with us, but she was such a strong-willed woman she wouldn't even consider it and had reserved a place here without even telling us about it until she was ready to move in.

I sat at her little square table. "Then spoil me."

"I shall." With the water hot in her single-cup brewer, she set a pod in the top section. "It's decaf so you don't have to worry about it keeping you awake tonight."

"I know."

Since she never wanted anything for a Christmas or birthday gift, Eve and I often brought her little baskets filled with her favorite pods of decaf and tea and hot chocolate. I sat back relaxed, recalling these same moves of my mother's around a kitchen, how her head tilted to the left whenever she checked stew or gumbo cooking on her stove. How her right arm seemed constantly in motion as she tossed in ingredients, chopped others, or stirred her pots. How the hem of her dresses swung one way, then another while she moved back and forth while she worked with those pots and pans. How the enticing smells began with the roux she was browning on the stove and then after she added onions, bell pepper, celery, and garlic, the whole room came alive with aromas.

Her upside pineapple cakes and apple pies with the crusts she had created by hand and laced over the top made me swoon. She had been a terrific cook with Cajun recipes that she created. Losing her big kitchen and stove were the main things she dreaded leaving in her home. That kitchen and stove had served too many fantastic meals for anyone to ever count.

"Here you go." She set a mug of coffee in front of me. "You know it's really hot. You might want to let it cool off. Or blow on it," she said as she had said so many times when I was a child and she gave me a hot drink or plate of food.

I grinned. "Thank you. I will." My gaze followed her quick motions to the overhead cabinet. From it, she retrieved white matching sugar and creamer servers. Mom set them in front of me. She placed another pod into her coffeemaker. A small, happy hum having no particular tune came from her while she watched it. I missed hearing those hums that came when I was a little girl and she'd wash my hair. Those weren't from fear. They let me know everything would be all right.

Stirring sugar and a dash of creamer into my cup, I felt more peaceful than it seemed I had in a long time. The coffee enticed me. What interested me more was having my mother sit and join me. Together we might share other sweet memories from all the years we spent together.

She set her mug at the place next to mine and smiled at me.

"I'm just waiting for you," I explained and nodded toward her chair.

She returned my smile with a sweet one of her own and was starting to sit.

Someone knocked on her door.

"Hey, Mom, it's me, Eve," my sister said from the hallway.

Mom went to her door and opened it. "How wonderful to see you," she said and gave Eve a kiss. "Look, your sister's here. You can join us. I'll make another cup of coffee."

Eve looked at me, folds in her forehead adding to the worry revealed in her eyes. Yes, she had seen all the police.

"Go on, sit right there." Mom touched the back of the chair she'd been ready to sit on. "Take that coffee. Don't worry, it's decaf. I'll fix myself another cup." She flitted around, getting another spoon, mug, and pod while heating more water. "What a wonderful surprise, having both my girls come to visit me in the afternoon in my room. This feels almost like old times."

Once she turned away, Eve and I exchanged concerned expressions. They were well founded. A moment later, a hard knock sounded on Mom's door.

She gave us big smiles. "Ah, how nice. More company." Without hesitation or looking through the peephole, she pulled her door open.

And then our mom's body shrank back.

Chapter 19

Eve and I scrambled to our feet when her caller came into view. We squeezed in close to her, pressing against her sides, letting her know we were there with her.

The man outside her doorway did not look directly at us, although the outer edges of his eyes certainly took us in. He looked directly at Mom. "Mrs. Gautreaux, I'm Detective Wilet with the sheriff's office. I'd like to ask you a few questions." During the long moments' pause he gave her to let that sink in, her upper body pressed harder against me and surely against my sister on her opposite side as though she needed support.

Then like the trooper we knew she was, she straightened herself and offered him her hand. "Hello, officer. Yes, you may ask."

"May I come in?"

"All right." She backed up to allow him entry. As soon as he walked in and shut the door, she said, "These are my daughters, Eve Vaughn and Sunny Taylor."

None of us tried to shake each other's hands. He gave us a brief nod. "I've met your daughters," he told her, and she started to open her mouth, surely to ask where, and then a dark expression flashed over her eyes as she probably remembered some terrifying experiences we'd been through, and she nodded. Yes, she was remembering our close calls with death and knew he had gotten involved. And we had found her beau's nephew dead beneath those lovely chandeliers in his new bathtub, so the detective could possibly still consider us suspects.

"Would you care to sit down, Detective? I'll fix you some coffee." Ever the polite hostess, she scurried to the coffeepot. "I'm sorry I don't have any donuts, but I do have a bag of small chocolates."

"I'll sit, but I don't care for coffee or chocolates, thanks. Please sit with me." His eyes aimed at the coffee mugs Eve and I had on the table. He left the chairs next to them vacant and took another one.

"I'm sure it's all right if we stay in here," I said to him, not asking.

"Yes." He pulled a pad and pen out of his pocket while the rest of us took places surrounding the table.

Mom sat beside him. She laid her hand over his, concern in her eyes. "This doesn't have anything to do with poor Clarice, does it? Has something else happened here that we don't know about?"

"Nothing else that we can tell you." He slid his fingers out from under hers.

Eve interrupted. "Detective, I don't know why police would question everyone about her getting sick." When he didn't respond, she continued. "I'm sure it will take forever for your crew to talk to everyone here about that."

He returned his attention to Mom, his gaze harder than before. "I'm sure you're aware that the woman you call Miss Clarice became ill soon after she ate her meal."

Mom nodded. "I was sitting next to her. My daughters were there, too, at the next table." She gave us warm smiles. "They came to join us for lunch."

"I understand that. Mrs. Gautreaux, I'm not sure if you're aware, but the woman we're speaking of has gotten much worse than she had been when she left here."

"Oh no, the poor dear." New deep wrinkles creased our mother's forehead. "But she'll be all right?"

"We don't know that. What we do know is that she ingested something she shouldn't have." He kept hard eyes aimed at Mom.

"What was it?" I asked.

Eve leaned toward him. "Do you all know what she took?"

Without looking at either one of us, he said, "We do. It was medicine that she shouldn't have taken." The detective retained eye contact with our mother. "Mrs. Gautreaux, we've put in a request for a subpoena to examine the medical records of people who reside here but it may take a few days to receive. Someone from here is extremely ill, and waiting to learn more might put her in a dangerous situation."

Mom released a sharp inhale. "Is there anything we can do to help?"

"Yes, ma'am. What we're asking people here to do is volunteer information."

"What do you want to know?"

I pressed against Mom's arm. "Wait," I said to her.

Eve was nodding like she agreed with my caution. "Maybe you should get legal advice first."

Mom pulled her head back. She gave us both a level stare. "For what? I didn't do anything wrong."

"I'm sure you didn't," I said, "but—"

She shook her head at both of us. "If everyone here has to get legal counsel before the hospital can learn what Clarice ingested, that might be too late for her." She lifted her chin toward the officer. "What is it you'd like to know?"

"Do you take medication for your heart?"

"Wait. Why are you asking her that?" I was ready to tell him to get out. While anger made me grit my teeth, my mother's composure remained calm. "Yes, I do."

Eve thrust her arm out, her hand raised like a stop sign aimed at him. "Probably at least fifty other people living here take prescriptions for their heart."

Detective Wilet's bulldog expression remained facing our mother with only the slightest shift of his eyes moving toward Eve and back to Mom. "How long have you been taking it?"

"Why do you want to know all that?" I asked, my voice not kind.

"Has anyone else gotten ill?" Mom asked him, the fear in her eye making me imagine she was thinking of the man she cared about more than any other person.

"No, ma'am, no one has notified the office here about that."

"But suppose," Eve said, "someone in their quarters here has gotten violently ill from the same thing, and nobody checked on them. They could possibly die."

"That's right," I said. "Would you like for me and Eve to go around and check on some people the office hasn't heard from?" I gave Eve a nod, like do-you-want-to-do-that-with-me, and she nodded to agree.

"We'd be glad to," she said, getting up.

Detective Wilet gave her a straight arm that suggested she stop. "We don't need your help, thank you."

She sat again. I took a big swallow of my coffee. It was cold, unpleasant, tasting more like instant than brewed, but that was probably because as Mom said, it was decaf. Why bother with coffee if you drink that? The situation here surely made it taste bad.

Mom tapped the tabletop three times and got the officer's attention. "What about all of the people in their rooms? How will anyone know if they've gotten sick?"

"My men and the staff here are contacting all of the residents to make certain they're okay." Seeing me ready to ask more, he said, "They're calling every person's room. And if anyone doesn't answer a phone, they're going to see about them."

A small breath sounding like relief left Mom's nostrils. The slightest quiver moved along her lips.

I reached out and clasped her hand. It felt chilled. "Mom, if you like, you can call Mac. Check on him."

"I'll do that after a while. After the officer leaves."

"He's surely okay," Eve said. When Mom didn't show relief from that statement, she added more. "Otherwise you would have heard."

The officer didn't ask who we were talking about or intrude in these assurances about a male resident. From the level look in his eye, I figured he already knew.

"Detective," I said, hands clasped together on the table, a pinch of fear making discomfort squiggle down my arms, "why did our mother luck out and have you come to visit her room instead of receiving a phone call like you said others in this place are getting right now?"

Mom leaned closer toward him. "Are you going around and seeing a lot of residents in their rooms?"

He held eye contact with her. Ignoring her question, he said, "Mrs. Gautreaux, you normally carry your medicine with you in a small pouch until you come to your room after lunch. Is that correct?"

Murmurs grabbed my throat and blocked real words from coming out. They would have formed lyrics from "Silent Night."

Eve's throat was obviously wide open. A pink streak ran up her cheeks from her neck. "Why do you want to know that?"

He focused his attention on our mother. "Ma'am, may I see that pouch?"

Eve and I shot to our feet.

"Oh, no," she insisted.

"You don't need to, Mom," I said.

She pushed her little self up. "There is absolutely no reason why I cannot show this police officer what he asked for."

"But—" I blurted.

She swiped her index finger across the air at both of us. "You two can sit right down. I am doing just like everyone else here is doing and letting an officer of the law see my prescription."

When Eve and I remained on our feet, she gave us that slit-eyed stare that dared us to defy her.

My twin and I swung our gazes toward each other. At the same time, we lowered our hips and sat.

Mom waited and watched us, seeming to make sure we weren't going to try to get up again before she made a move. When we did not, she turned and went into her bedroom, allowing little time for thumps from my heart to punch against my chest wall. I wanted this man away from our mother. *Hurry and go question someone else*, I silently told him.

Mom didn't need her blood pressure raised from having him stay in here.

At least he would soon leave, I knew when Mom stepped back in, her knotted fingers holding out her little tan knit bag.

Detective Wilet opened his wide hand and accepted it. He felt the pouch and touched its drawstring. "May I?" he asked her.

"Of course. Although I have no idea why you'd want to." She stood hands on hips.

He pulled the strings on the bow, and the bag opened. All four of us were leaning over, attempting to see inside.

The policeman stuck his fingers in there and pulled out the prescription bottle. He lifted the bottle closer to his eyes—probably needing glasses but not wearing them just like me. "I see your doctor's name," he said, "and the date and place where you had this filled."

"You probably know they deliver," I told him.

Mom nodded, a small smile playing around her lips. "My fiancée took me to get my prescription refilled."

My head jerked back. "He did?"

"He really owns a car?" Eve asked.

Mom turned her nose up, her only response to any of us.

Detective Wilet was writing on his pad. "He doesn't normally take her?" He glanced at me.

"Eve and I have been offering to get medicine for her or take her to the drugstore to get it herself so she could look around and see if there was anything else she'd want. It would be a little outing for her."

Eve explained more. "We've wanted to take her a lot of places. She used to come. She seldom comes anywhere with us anymore."

Three of us trained our eyes on Mom. The smile she offered in response was demure. She slid back down into her chair.

"This bottle also says how many pills were inside it and that you are supposed to take one pill a day."

"Yes, with a meal. My doctor suggested that since I sometimes felt queasy if I took it on an empty stomach."

"I didn't know that," I said.

Eve shook her head. "I didn't either."

"As I've told you girls, you don't know everything. About me—or everyone else." Her sharp response was surely concerning her male friend.

The detective made notes about what he read on Mom's prescription bottle like he had jotted a note here or there during our conversation. He pointed toward the kitchen cabinets. "Would you have two clean bowls that I could use to count these in?"

"Good grief," I said.

"All of my dishes are clean." Mom's tone hinted of insult. She yanked out two shiny white gumbo bowls and thrust them on the table in front of him.

"I didn't mean to insinuate otherwise." He easily unscrewed the bottle's cap that wasn't childproof. Lowering the bottle to set its opening close to the bowl on the right, he used slow motion to pour the pills in, a careful move for someone who looked so gruff. He mustn't have wanted to dump them in case any might spill to the floor and go undetected.

"Most of them are still there," Mom said. "We went to get them not long ago."

"Do I have your permission to touch them?" he asked Mom, reaching his hand toward the bowl of pills and ready to do that.

"If you wash your hands first."

With his mouth closed, what sounded like the smallest laugh came from his throat. "Yes, ma'am. I sure will." He shoved up and went to the sink near us. While he had his back turned, I stared at the pills and started counting them without putting my hands on any, only because I didn't want him to see me doing it.

"Use soap," Mom told him while the water ran, and he nodded. "And you can use that dishtowel to dry your hands." After a second's pause, she added, "It's clean."

Once he returned to his seat, all eyes aimed at the pair of bowls. "I'll count them twice," he said, "just to make sure." And then silently he lifted one round, white pill that would keep our mother's heart working well and help to prevent her from having a stroke. He set it in the empty bowl.

"That's one," Mom said. "Two," she counted when the next one made a slight clicking sound as it hit the bottom of the nearly empty bowl. She was the only person counting out loud. Eve was probably doing like the officer and keeping a silent count. I, on the other hand, distrusting my dyslexic tendencies, used my fingers. I straightened each one as a white pill dropped into the second bowl, my heartbeat thrusting harder, my jaw growing tenser. What count I was hoping for, I wasn't certain. I only wanted it to be the right one.

All the pills sat in a little pile in the second bowl before the detective wrote on his pad. Mom had stopped counting out loud when she got to sixteen, but then decided that pill might have been seventeen, and so she quit, leaving the numbers up to the man in the room.

He started again. While he took them from one bowl to the other, Mom did like me and stretched her fingers out to count. When he was done, he wrote on his pad. Air in the room seemed to still.

He looked at Mom. "Some of your pills are missing."

"What do you mean?" Eve asked.

"Are you sure?" I blurted.

Mom placed her closed fingers across her lips. The skin between her eyes folded. "I thought I always took them correctly," she said, sliding her hand away from her mouth.

"How many?" I asked him.

"A few." His bad cop expression took hold of his face.

Eve got up. "Maybe some of them fell out." She grabbed the knit pouch from the table, pulled it wider open, and looked inside. Obviously not satisfied, she reached in and ran her finger around the bottom. Then she turned the bag upside down and shook it. Nothing fell out.

"Let's go look in her bedroom," I said. Eve hurried with me, and we went straight to Mom's bedside table where she always kept that pouch. Hearing a slight noise, I saw Mom and Detective Wilet had followed us into her room.

From the small tabletop, I lifted Mom's Bible and rosary to see whether any pills got caught in them. Finding none, I raised her little clock, aware that it couldn't hide much.

Eve got on her knees and looked under the bed that our mother always made the minute she got up. She felt around on the carpet with a low pile under the edge while I checked the floor around the little table, hoping for once that our mother had spilled some of her meds.

Finding nothing, we exchanged stares with the detective. We stepped into her bathroom, and he and Mom came behind us and watched from the doorway of the small room while we searched everywhere—including the small medicine cabinet that held only her toothbrush, toothpaste, hairbrush, and pale pink lipstick. No pills lay on the floor around the toilet or tub or in the empty garbage can. I rubbed my hands one way and the other across the white rug beside her tub and raised it to look underneath. Slowly, I stood.

As though hearing each other's thoughts, Eve and I moved toward each other and stood in front of our mother, facing the man and blocking her from him.

"She must have accidentally taken more than she was supposed to," Eve said. I gave a hard nod to confirm her words.

"I understand that." Even while we spoke, his eyes zeroed in on the slim area between us at our mother. We automatically shifted nearer each other, closing in that space. He turned and walked out of the bathroom. The space felt like it expanded.

Both Eve and I gripped our mother's hands when we stepped with her into the kitchen area where he stopped.

"Thank you all," he said and looked at Mom. "I may be getting back with you."

A tremble ran through our mother's fingers.

Chapter 20

The three of us remaining in the room behind the door the detective shut once he went out released simultaneous exhales that might have been heard in the next room.

"Mom, do you sometimes take more than one of your pills in a day?" I asked her.

"Not without meaning to."

Eve moved closer. "Are you sure?"

Mom began shrinking back from us. "I don't believe I do."

"Then how come you don't have all of the pills you're supposed to in your bottle?" I asked.

She was shaking her head, lips pulled forward and face tight, fear in her eyes. "I don't know. I'm sure I take one of them every day right before I start eating my lunch. That's why I bring the medicine with me every morning."

Her eyes looked so fearful of us, of what we were saying, that I stepped away from her. Eve seemed to realize the same thing. She also moved and gave her space. Eve pointed toward the bowl holding pills on the table. "Do you have any idea why you have fewer pills left than you're supposed to?"

Slouching, Mom shook her head. Her eyes squeezed tighter until they became slits. She looked ready to cry. My mother, our mother. And we were doing this to her.

I wrapped my arms around her. "It's okay, Mom. Don't worry about anything."

"Yes, it's no problem." Eve used a sympathetic tone.

For the first time ever, our mother felt frail inside my arms. She was soft, except for the ribs in her back against my fingers. Her scent was light, the same enticing baby powder she had dusted her torso with after a bath ever since I could recall. Instead of lifting her arms and hugging me back as she had always done, she left her arms limp against her sides. A slight tremble ran through her body. I gripped her tighter. A soft whimper came from my mother. As though that sound gave the command, her whole body shook. Tears coated my eyes when I knew my mother was silently crying.

I couldn't remember seeing her cry, although she must have when Crystal died.

Mom stayed snuggled inside my grip, and I kept my head lowered against hers, creating a cocoon for her to feel safe.

Eve remained quiet and still. Sadness touched her eyes while she watched Mom.

"I'm all right." Our mother said this and nudged me to let go of her. My instinct was to keep sheltering her there, to keep holding her close, to take care of her as, for so many years, she had taken care of us.

She used a slight swipe of her fingers across her eyelashes to wipe away the moisture still visible there and moved her hands away from her face. She lifted her chin and straightened her spine. "Thank you both for your support. You can go now."

"Oh no." Eve stepped closer to her. "We're not going to leave you alone now."

"We can stay here a bit," I said.

"And do what?" Mom swept her arm toward the table. "Help count my pills again? Be really careful putting each one back in its container to make certain I don't spill any? Watch me to make sure I won't take another one even though I had one right before lunch today—as I always do?"

We backed away. "No, you can certainly take care of that," Eve said, and with a big nod, I tried to assure her I felt the same way. But our mother knew us so well; she could still sense our uncertainty. We'd want to believe she would be fine without us staying close. I feared that wasn't the case.

She took steps to her door. "I thank you both for coming. I really am glad you were here, but now it's time for you to go."

The slam inside my chest felt like panic. "But just let us stay here until they let all of you get out of your rooms. Then we could see what's happened with everyone else."

"I can do that myself. If anything important takes place, I'll let you know." She set her hand on the doorknob.

Irritating static dropped into the room. We all looked at the small speaker that was seldom used in the corner near the ceiling behind the door.

"Everyone, may I have your attention." The administrator's voice sounded uncertain. "Can I have your attention?" she said louder. The three of us in Mom's room looked at each other with pinched faces. "Due to unforeseen circumstances, we are asking all residents to stay in your rooms. Dinner will be served to you so you don't have to come to the dining area to eat."

I swallowed.

"I repeat. We want all residents to remain in your rooms or your suites, and dinner will be served to you by our staff members. A little later, your used dishes will be picked up so you don't need to bother to wash anything."

By the time the three of us gave each other quizzical stares, Terri Hebert spoke again. "Please don't get concerned about this situation. We've just discovered a small glitch in our system."

Mom, Eve, and I gave each other stares that questioned what the administrator was saying. Each of us had probably believed she would always tell people the truth.

"There's no major problem," she said right after a brief wall of silence, "but as always, if any of you have a need for any assistance, please let someone on our staff know. You could call the office, or in the case of an emergency, pull the emergency cord in your bathroom, and someone will get back to you quickly."

Mom stared at the floor while Eve and I eyed each other, surely none of us reassured.

"While we are dealing with this situation, we ask that you not invite others to come here. And we request that all guests should leave."

Muffled voices sounded, possibly grumbling residents in rooms on either side of this one.

The static came again and then the voice. "We do apologize. We hope to have this situation cleared by tomorrow. We'll let you know of any changes as soon as possible."

Who wrote those words for her to say?

Eve gripped Mom's hands. "Let us stay awhile. They won't know we didn't leave right away, and if they catch us going late, oh well."

"Yes, please." I touched my mother's arm.

She nodded toward the counter near her coffeemaker. "Do you see my phone? I want to use it to call friends I have in this place." Before we could suggest we remain while she'd do that, she turned the doorknob and opened her door. "I'll let you know what happens. I love you both more than anything," she said. "Thank you." She puckered her lips.

We both kissed and hugged her extra tight. She shut the door behind us. Her lock clicked.

The long hall on this floor was empty of people that I could see. Eve and I took our time walking past residents' rooms. Behind some of the shut doors, loud voices complained. One woman's high-pitched voice sounded extra high. She must have been on her phone, excitedly telling someone about what happened here and that she was shut up in her room. Calls like this—residents contacting family, calling friends, someone else who lived here—were probably being made by people living behind the doors. Our mother was surely on her phone, and just as surely, I imagined, getting her beau on the line. He would be downstairs, stuck in his room just like she was up here stuck in hers.

Instead of being paid guests in this lovely establishment, they were all being treated like prisoners.

Eve and I kept quiet while we walked, she, like me, certainly keeping her ears open for words we might hear. When we neared one door after another, we slowed, listening intently. Women's loud voices griped to people they called.

"And he asked to see my medicine bottle," one voice said.

We both stopped. The woman quit talking as though she could have heard us outside her door, but then went on, so she probably had listened to a question or comment on the other end of her line.

"Yes, I showed him all of them—the ones I take to regulate my heartbeat and the ones I take for blood pressure and cholesterol and even the things I take for constipation and diarrhea when I get that. Yes, he asked to see my medicines, so I showed him all of them."

Feeling a squiggle of guilt through my stomach like a thief must, I checked around to make certain no one was watching us, that nobody could see us standing here listening to someone else's private conversation.

The hall remained empty, almost tomblike. My heartbeat increased.

Maybe she had stopped talking, I decided, giving Eve a nod and tilt of my head to indicate we should continue. But then the woman again spoke loud.

"Yes, that's right. I showed him all of them. Ha, let them ask an old lady what kind of medicine she takes." She laughed, which I imagined the person she spoke with also did. "No, the only pills they were really interested in were the ones I take for my heart. He copied stuff off the front of the bottle and then counted them out on the table. It's almost time to refill them, so that didn't take long. I only had five pills left." She paused, and my eyes and Eve's shot toward each other. I held my breath. "No, he was satisfied. He said that's what the count was supposed to be."

We hurried past her room and reached the elevators right as a young male staff member wearing navy stepped out of another room down the hall. He stayed there and stared at us as though making sure we were leaving.

My sister and I said nothing to each other while we waited for the elevator's door to open and let us inside. While we rode down, we remained quiet, possible consequences of what we'd just experienced and heard running through my mind.

When the door slid open on the bottom floor, things were quite different. There was a lot of motion and noise and the strong odor of cooked turnips making me believe the cafeteria prepared vegetable soup. Three of the cooks pushed carts with two levels that held trays with drinks and covered dishes that I imagined held soup and sandwiches, defrosted soup and sandwiches that were quick to prepare. Maybe they also held a slice of angel food cake that wouldn't be too bad for diabetics.

Uniformed police officers strode across the area where tables and chairs were set up. Each table was in place, all the chairs pushed against them, all signs of the earlier panicked departure of patrons gone. No one was visible behind the counter that shielded the nurse and administrators' offices. Half a dozen guests walked toward the foyer to leave as instructed, one of them Emery Jackobson, who stood half a head taller than the rest. He must have still been visiting someone here.

I checked the hall to the right that housed mainly men and nudged Eve to show her Detective Wilet coming out of someone's room and then shutting the door. Her squinted eyes indicated she wanted to ask me about this. I gave my head the slightest shake to let her know I didn't want to talk about it until we were outside away from the others.

One officer with strands of gray in his brown hair stood right inside the main entrance. This was not one of the young recruits with pimpled foreheads. His dark eyes speared each of the people who walked out past him. Their piercing made a quiver run through my stomach, even if I had done nothing wrong.

Outside the building, I sucked in a deep breath but kept walking. Although the sun had set, the evening seemed especially dark. I looked above and to the sides of the covered entrance and saw Eve doing the same. The bright lights that were usually lit there at night were not. Spotted filtered lighting came from inside bushes and around the doorway so that people might see to walk, but none of the vibrant lighting invited anyone inside. Would the officer stationed there turn any visitors away? I had the distinct feeling he would.

Eve and I had arrived separately. Her car was parked farther away than my truck, so I gave her arm a quick tug to tell her to follow me. We waited until we sat inside my truck's cab before we spoke. There were so many things to talk about concerning what was going on in there that I found it difficult to pick one.

Eve blurted first. "Do you think they can keep people from visiting?"

I did a quick roll of that question through my mind. "I don't know why not. It's a privately-owned business."

"They're treating it almost like a crime scene."

Both of us quieted. She was right. That thought wasn't pretty.

I chose another one. "I believe the room Detective Wilet was coming out of just now belongs to Mom's friend Mac."

She shrugged. "He was probably questioning lots of residents."

"But I'll bet Mom got Mac on the phone the minute we left her room. I'll bet she was talking to him when the detective got there. Or maybe Detective Wilet was already in his room when she called." I gritted my teeth. The officer would have asked him who called. Mom didn't need her name mentioned again so soon.

Headlights of two cars leaving lit the darkened parking lot. Eve and I talked about what we had seen and heard and experienced while we were in the manor and how it all bothered us, mainly because Miss Clarice had gotten so ill, and some of our mother's pills were missing.

My phone rang, making my heart jump. Mom? I shoved my hand into my purse and pulled it out. *Dave* showed on the front. I recalled our last kiss, and my cheeks warmed. The phone rang again. I pressed the off button and dropped it back where it had been.

"Who was it?" Eve asked.

I gave my head a shake. "Someone I can call back later."

She eyed me and then my purse. Tension built inside me like hardening cement. I could imagine my sister reaching inside my purse and pulling my phone out to see where the last call came from. We had sometimes checked out each other's possible fibs or things we tried to hide when we were younger. But we were so concerned now about our mother that she did not need to hear about a romantic entanglement between Dave and me.

"Well then." Her gaze drifted over my purse again while she let me know she was questioning who or what I might be hiding. She grabbed the door's handle and opened it. "I'll talk to you tomorrow."

"Good."

Her phone rang. She pulled it out of her small bag. "Oh, it's Dave." Face brightened with a smile, she got out of my truck and slammed the door. I watched her walk away toward her car, a new spring in her step.

Dave had just phoned me, and now, before I had time to return his call and speak in private, he called my sister. What was that about?

Instead of watching her to see if she'd laugh while she spoke to him, I pulled away from the parking lot.

Streetlights appeared brighter than usual. Did it seem that way because of the dim lighting in front of the manor? I reached my house quickly and rushed inside, wanting to do something—but what? Jitters jumped around my stomach like a jackhammer slamming holes in the foundation beneath an old fishing camp. The image of a camp brought Dave to mind, but I did not want to think of him. Not while he was talking to my sister.

I took my phone out of my purse and checked it to see if he had called back and I'd somehow missed the call. He had not.

Setting the phone on the kitchen table, I grabbed a legal pad and pen. I stood at my kitchen counter and jotted quick notes about what happened—things I heard at the manor, what I had seen. I came up with fast questions concerning the whole experience. Shoulders and back tight, I left the list. Mom would be fine.

A small growl from my stomach let me know I'd missed supper. I threw together a peanut butter and jelly sandwich and downed it with milk.

Still antsy, I forced myself not to check the phone again. Not for Dave's call, not for one from Mom. I needed to move, to do something. I was grabbing the vacuum cleaner from the small closet where I kept it when I thought better of that idea. If the phone rang, I might not be able to hear it if I was vacuuming. I could set my phone in my pocket and have it vibrate, but with the motion and noise of the vacuum, I decided not to take a chance.

Instead, I grabbed my feather duster and pulled out the broom and dustpan. I had used all of them and the wet mop and other cleaners within the last four days. Nothing said I couldn't use them all again now.

I was wiggling my duster down along the leg of one of my dining room chairs when my phone rang. Mom? I dashed to the kitchen.

Dave showed on the top of my phone.

"Hello," I said, breathless.

"Can I come over?"

"Yes!"

The phone went dead. I threw all my cleaning supplies back in their closet, much more eager than usual to have a visit from him.

Chapter 21

The second I opened my front door, I knew he had heard. Dave's eyes were tight, his face concerned. He stepped inside and opened his arms. I leaned into them, my head against his wide chest. Words raised themselves and tried to pop out of my mouth—to tell him, to ask him—but I made them stay inside. I needed comfort now.

We stood inside my front entry, and he held me. At some point, I realized he had used his foot to quietly shut the door. I didn't care. I wanted only to experience peace, to feel like we would be safe. Mainly, my mother needed safety, I considered. That's when I finally pulled back from him.

"Something happened at the manor," I said.

He was nodding. "I know."

Awareness hit. "Eve told you. I saw that you had called me, but I didn't answer because she was with me inside my truck." I was sucking in a breath to say a whole lot more.

"Yes, she told me that."

"Why did you call her right after you called me?"

"Let's talk." He took my hand and led me to my den. Leaving the overhead lights off, he lit only one small lamp. Dave put his hand out toward the sofa, so I sat. He settled himself down next to me. "I had heard about what happened at the manor. I was worried and tried to call you. When I couldn't get you, I contacted Eve to learn how things were with your mother."

"Our mother?" Tightness returned to my stomach. "She's all right. I'm sure Eve told you that."

"She did. She told me a lot of things I was going to ask you about concerning your mother and the other incidents there."

"I guess I don't have anything else to tell you about it."

"Except how you feel." He stretched his arm out along the back of the sofa and rubbed my shoulder nearest him, a soft soothing motion.

"I feel great with you being here. And knowing you care."

"Of course I care about you and your mother. And your sister. Would you like for me to hold you?"

"Absolutely." I scooted my hips farther on the seat until I was against him. Dave wrapped both arms around me. I nestled my head into the space where his arm met his chest. The experience was what a content baby must feel like in a cradle. I stayed there, thoughts coming up or questions about what he thought, but still I kept quiet in my comforting space. Answers would come, probably not from him. For now, his arms were strong, his chest my refuge.

I had no idea I had fallen asleep until a light snore awoke me. I lifted my head and realized I had released it. "I'm sorry." I pulled myself out of the cocoon of him where I'd snugged. A small lamp provided only a spot of light in the otherwise dark room.

Dave gave me a small laugh. "It's no problem. You were worn out. You needed to get some rest."

"And you provided me with a good pillow." I smiled with him.

He tilted the top of my head toward him and placed a light kiss there. "Let me know anytime you need one."

More awareness of the late hour came. "Let me get you something to eat or drink."

"No, you need to get to bed." He reached his arms straight out to the sides and stretched. "Maybe I do, too."

He let me go ahead out of my den and then clicked off the lamp behind me. By the time we stepped into the foyer, my mind was working clearer. "Wait, why did you call me and Eve tonight? How did you know about what happened at the manor?"

"People have heard about it. Word gets around here pretty fast."

"Where did you heard about it?"

"We were installing security cameras at a house in a neighborhood where there have been a few car break-ins." He didn't mention the neighborhood, but I knew where he was speaking about. The newspaper had reported those incidents. "My customer told us about it. His mother lives at the manor. He got a call from her."

And my mother didn't call me. I glanced at the wall clock. It was too late to phone her to learn whether anything else had taken place.

Dave moved in close. He placed his hands on both sides of my waist, his touch sending a shot of warmth through me. "But I don't believe you have to worry. Things will take care of themselves over there." He cocked his head. "I really think the lady they sent to the hospital will get better."

"But we heard she's gotten worse."

"I'm not a medical expert, but I know some illnesses tend to get worse before they improve. That happened to my aunt. We were all afraid she might die, but after two weeks in ICU, she made a turn-around and improved." He smiled. "She's back to baking the best cherry pies you ever want to eat."

"Yum. I'd like to try one."

"Then you'll have to come to Connecticut with me when I go back there." I laughed. "That's a deal."

"And I froze the catfish your line caught after you left it. You'll need to come back to the camp so we can eat that."

"We'll do it soon."

All humor left his face. Dave peered into my eyes. "Sunny, you're really important to me. I want to spend more time with you, a lot more time."

I inhaled. Exhaled. "I want to be closer to you, too. Just right now let us get these things straightened out with my mother."

He gave a slow nod. "With her wanting to get married."

"Yes, to a stranger." I sucked in a deep breath. "And now this, the situation at the manor." A sudden idea struck. "You know if things don't get any better with what's going on with her over there, I might need to get her to move in with me."

He watched me without saying a thing. I couldn't tell how he felt about what I'd said. Both of his parents had died years before. Was he concerned about our situation—his and mine—that if my mother came to live with me things between him and me might become strained? If she lived here, possibly all romantic involvement between us may need to be behind closed doors? And how would he feel about that?

His hands came off my waist. "Hadn't you and Eve each invited her to move in with you when she started to need more assistance because of her arthritis?"

"We did. But now things are different."

He quirked a brow. "In what way?"

I didn't want a grilling from him. "Things are strange at the manor right now with police questioning residents. I hope the sick lady gets much better soon. But then there's that other thing."

He watched as though waiting for me to go on. I chose to stop. Dave offered a slow nod. "You don't want your mother to marry the man."

Ready to argue with him, I said, "Her mind isn't as sharp as it used to be."

"Oh." A crease folded in skin between his eyes. "I'm sorry. I didn't know."

"She's taking her medicine more often than she's supposed to."

"A nurse doesn't make sure she's taking the right thing?"

"No, the manor isn't a nursing home where they do that. Residents are responsible for any medication they take." I rolled my shoulders. "But it's okay." I gave him a quick kiss on the lips. "Thanks for coming over. I'll let you know what goes on."

"Please do."

After he walked out, I locked the door behind him and then pressed my back against the wall. Why had I told him that? I was never one to lie and didn't want to start now, especially to Dave, but why had I told him my mother was losing some of her mental capacities? Was it true?

She hadn't known some of her pills were missing. Had she begun taking more of them than she should have? Worry skittered around my back in a squiggly move like a worm made when I tried to pull it from the mud in a bait box. What if she sometimes took a pill before she ate her lunch but then forgot by the time she finished her meal and took another one right afterward?

Was our mother really developing dementia?

My whole body went stiff. The backs of my eyes warmed. What kind of care might Mom require? I had plenty enough room to bring her to live here. So did my sister. And while we worked on a job, one of us could stay back with her. Or would we hire a sitter?

My stomach jerked tight at the thought of losing the kind and intelligent mother we had always known. If more food had been in my stomach, I could have thrown up. The thought about that brought back the image of Miss Clarice seated at Mom's table, bending over the table, getting extremely sick.

I needed to check on her condition in the morning. Heading for bed, I knew I would barely sleep, but instead would toss around while I worried about my mother who I had to painfully admit was moving further into those senior years. I would be at the manor to see about her in the morning.

Chapter 22

When I opened my eyes and found slanted rays of sunshine forcing themselves through my bedroom curtains, my first thought was unspent words: *Dave, yesterday did you tell Eve you had called me before calling her?*

"Ridiculous," I said and threw off the covers. Was I reverting to childish jealousy? I had much more important things to see about this morning. *Our mother.* I grabbed coffee in my kitchen, and because I'd often get weak if I didn't eat soon, I took a minute to fix buttered grits in the microwave. With both hot, I remained standing with my food and drink on the counter. I took a swallow of coffee and a spoonful of grits, checking the local headlines on my phone.

The grits caught in a ball in my throat. Before I could stop coughing, I reread the opening of the lead story to make certain I had read right.

Large print above a long shot of Sugar Ledge Manor said what I already knew—"Local retirement facility closes during investigation." But right below that, the article stated *Police officers secured a retirement home located on the 500 block of Sugar Cane Street while they checked into the death of one of its residents.*

My breaths stopped. *Death?* The poor woman had died.

Tears rimmed my eyes while I tried to read more of the words that blurred. My phone rang, and I answered, fearing for Mom.

"Did you see the paper?" Eve said.

I swallowed the tears that were blocking my throat. "Yes, I'm just reading it now."

"Let's go see about Mom."

"I'm ready." A second thought made me glance down. I was wearing a lavender nightshirt. "I'll be ready by the time you get here."

"Okay. I'm coming over."

With another swallow of grits, I carried my coffee mug to my bedroom and threw on slacks and a shirt. It was good that I took time to brush my teeth, since that made me glance in the mirror. I wouldn't take time to use the little natural-toned makeup I normally used when I went out. My hair, though, would have frightened someone with it sticking straight out on the right as it did while most strands of my wavy hair lay flat on the left. I pulled a brush through it on the right side so it fairly matched.

Eve hit her horn right before I unlocked my door and ran out. She didn't look much better than I did. "What do you think happened?" she asked.

"I have no idea, but I am so sorry for her and whatever family she has."

"Me, too. Do you think they'll let us in there this morning?"

I stared at her and she at me. "If they don't, we'll have to find a way to sneak inside. I am going to see Mom."

She slapped palms with me to agree and her eyes speared the road.

"Eve, I hate to even think this, but do you believe Mom could be losing some of her mental capabilities?"

She kept her eyes forward, her body appearing almost totally still. After a long moment, she took a deep inhale that made her shoulders and chest rise. "God, I hope not. That would be so hard on her."

"I know." While we rode in silence, another thought came. "What if we get her one of those pill cases that some of those older people use? The ones that have a small opening for the medicine they take every day of the week."

"Yes. Then she could tell if she took one a day like she's supposed to."

When we were a few blocks away from the manor, she whipped her car into a parking lot. "Look, there's only one car here at the drugstore. Do you want to run in and grab one of those containers for pills?"

"Good idea." I fast-walked after she parked, knew where I had seen them, and went straight for the long narrow plastic containers. I paid for one and hurried outside.

"That should help her," Eve said and pulled onto the empty street.

The memory of police cars parked close to the manor came to mind. My back tensed while I imagined even more of them over there now. Last night they were investigating what Detective Wilet suggested made me believe was a resident's severe illness caused by her possibly taking someone else's medicine. Today they would surely be checking even deeper into her death.

What I saw made my chest expand with my deep breath. The main entrance to the manor looked exactly as it normally did. No police cars surrounded the entry. Not one squad car that I could see parked in the lot.

Eve and I gave each other small smiles before she parked. We rushed inside. The first thing that slammed against us was all the voices. Residents everywhere were talking. They talked to each other and to staff members and guests, and spoke loud. Everyone seemed to be scurrying about.

"What's going on here?" I asked once we'd walked past the foyer and approached Mom's group of Chat and Nappers. Mom wasn't sitting with them. Two others who normally sat in this gathering weren't around either.

"Oh my God," said the woman I almost didn't recognize, since she hadn't worn any pearls today. She pressed her hands to her chest. "It was horrible here last night, like a prison."

"They locked us in our rooms and wouldn't let us come out." A woman wearing a startling bright red dress sat on a sofa and lifted her walking cane. She held it straight out and swung it back and forth. I got the impression she was using it to let herself out.

"They locked you in your rooms?" Eve asked while concern came to me.

The little woman cuddled near in her wheelchair shook her head first, followed by some others. "They didn't really lock the doors," she said and then looked around. "Did they?"

"I didn't try the door to my suite, but it was wrong of them to make us stay in our rooms," the one holding her dead husband on her lap said.

"But they didn't actually make us," the woman missing her pearls said.

"Oh, yes they did." The one still holding her cane out slammed its tip on the floor. "If we'd have tried to come out, they probably would have stopped us."

Tears misted the eyes of a couple of them, while the faces of most revealed anger. I had the feeling the teary eyes were for themselves and the situation they endured instead of grief for the woman who had lived here but passed on. These ladies were friends of our mother. They had surely known that the person who died hadn't been very nice to her. She had insisted she wanted Mom's beau. But did she really, or had that been only talk, like an adolescent trying to get another girl's boyfriend? And did it really matter?

The group we stood between kept up their chatter, telling each other and me and Eve how ticked off they were about being told to stay in their rooms. "And the bread on my sandwich was stale," one said.

"My soup was cold," griped another.

More complaints flew from each of them while other people moved around. Staffers moved faster than usual. The nurse scurried past with rolling trays of medicines. The assistant-administrator, Rita Picou, always walked like she was in a hurry. This morning she seemed to move even quicker. Maybe she was trying to get away from thoughts of being at the hospital with their resident who died. Probably she needed to fill out many forms and contact people, just like I imagined the head lady had been doing. She was not scrambling around that I could see.

The men's deeper voices carried much more than usual. From where we were, I could see many of them sitting at tables where they often played cards or read the newspaper or a book. Now, though, they kept talking. Many of their voices sounded angry. Nobody here liked being told to stay in their rooms last night or any other time. And was that even necessary?

"I'm sorry you had to go through that," I said to the ladies seated around us and considered mentioning my sorrow for the person who died. But did they even know about that death? Had the administrators let people here know about it?

A man's raised voice made me look at the males in view again, recalling that Emery Jackobson had been here last night just like we were.

I didn't see him now.

"Do y'all know where our mother is?" Eve asked in the middle of these ladies' non-stop chatter.

Some of them looked at each other. Two of them glanced toward the hall with the men's rooms. My stomach clenched.

"Good morning, daughters." The cheerful voice came from behind us, from the direction of the elevator she always used to reach the floor to her room.

"Good morning," Eve and I told her, one after the other enjoying her hugs.

"What's wrong?" Mom asked her group of friends. "None of you wanted to let my girls sit down today? They're very nice, you know."

"We know that," one uttered, scooting to make room on a sofa.

"I'm sorry," another one said. "We were just so busy talking we didn't think to be polite."

All of them on the sofas tried scooting one way or the other and patting the seats they opened for us. The widest section to open up was where Mom normally sat in the middle of the central sofa. We squeezed in on each side of her.

"How are you doing today?" Eve asked her.

"I'm just fine. I slept well." So she mustn't know that a woman she'd known here died. She pointed to the small plastic bag I held. "You brought me breakfast?"

"No, just..." How was I going to put this so she wouldn't take it wrong? So I would not give away our concern? "It's just a little present." I held it out to her.

All the other ladies had gotten quiet. They all watched, expectation of something good in the package on some of their faces.

Mom pulled the long pill container out of the bag. She held it straight up from one end. "Why would you bring me this?"

I kept my eyes away from her, aiming them at the vinyl floor. My neck and cheeks warmed. I was certain they had become pink. My outer vision let me see that she turned to face Eve, again holding the pale blue pill holder almost as though she were gripping a weapon. She slipped the single prescription bottle out of her knitted pouch.

A little fake cough came from Eve. "We thought you might want to keep your medicine in there instead of that pouch." Her throat sounded constricted.

Mom caught me looking straight at her. "And why did you two believe that?"

I didn't speak. How do you tell your mother of your horrible fear that she could be losing the person she once was? The woman who had always held and nurtured you? Whose mind could be slipping?

The pearl-less woman broke my silence. "I keep all of my pills in one of those reminders."

"Me, too," a couple of others said.

"I have one like that for my morning pills and a clear case like that for all of my evening pills," said another.

They went on telling each other about how many pills they take each day and what all their pills were for, most of them taking something for high blood pressure and high cholesterol. Some had acid reflux, constipation, and diabetes.

Mom kept staring at me. We sat so close I could smell her light bath powder and feel her familiar soft hip against mine.

"But I only take one pill a day." Mom held up her prescription bottle. "And this isn't for birth control."

A few of her buddies laughed. "I wish I needed to take that kind of pill again," one said and others chattered about wanting to have sex again or dreading the whole mess.

"Well, Eve." My mother looked straight at me, seated right against her. "I'm waiting."

I'm Sunny! I wanted to blurt. A soft Christmas carol swirled around my throat. I had already lost my beloved mother? She didn't know me anymore.

"Sunny," she said, turning to my sister. "Why would you two choose to have me use something like this for the single pill I take each day instead of just letting me continue to take a pill out of its prescription bottle?"

My twin's eyes widened with panic. "Mom, it's me, Eve." She pointed at me. "That's Sunny."

I held my breath as I knew Eve surely did hers. The mother we had always known was gone. Who was this new person in her place?

Chapter 23

Mom looked from one to the other of us as though she were confused. The back of my eyes started to burn. And then Mom burst out laughing and handed the new pill container back to me. "Here, Sunny, you can bring this back to the store. I don't need it."

So she did know me. She was tricking us.

"I'll take that. Mine is old," the woman on my opposite side said. I handed the container for pills to her.

Eve and I both leaned in to Mom and squeezed her in a long hug, which she returned.

"Okay, I'm confused," a woman behind me said.

"About what?" asked someone else.

"About why Miriam is laughing like that. She smiles a lot, but she doesn't laugh very often."

When the three of us let each other go, all of us were smiling, Eve told the confused woman, "Mom was pretending she didn't know which one of us was which." Confusion remained written on the woman's face, so Eve pointed at me and herself. "Mom called Sunny *Eve*, but I'm Eve, and she called me *Sunny*."

"Well, I wouldn't know y'all apart," the woman without her pearls said.

"Me either," said another.

But our mother always would. We let the group take up their chatter about twins, about taking the wrong medicine and forgetting to take it while Eve, Mom, and I snuggled our faces close to each other in our semi-private conversation.

"We got you that pillbox so you'd be sure to take your medicine right," Eve said.

I touched Mom's cold hand with the twisted fingers. "Do you need a sweater or something?" I asked and she shook her head. Her hands often felt cooler than the rest of her body. "Mom, some days you must have taken more of your medicine than you were supposed to. That could really harm you."

"But I didn't take more than one every day."

Eve clasped her other hand. "Then what happened to those missing pills?"

"I must have spilled them, and they got vacuumed up before I noticed they'd dropped." Sadness touched her eyes. "You two heard about Clarice?"

"We did," Eve said.

"That is so sad," I said.

Mom nodded. "I know. It's horrible. I can't believe she's gone."

Everyone in our group quit talking at one time. The next voice, which came from the wheelchair-bound woman, carried. "I guess they'll be advertising another room available here. Or did she have a suite?"

"A suite," the woman beside her replied, and many of them began discussing where the newly available suite was located and maybe one of them would want to move up from her single bedroom to what the dead woman made available.

Thoughts of that were gruesome. They made me consider that even if our mother hadn't really developed dementia, she was aging. Those deepening lines in her face sucked her soft skin even farther down outside her eyes and into folds across her neck. Signs of her youthful beauty remained evident —in the twinkle in her eyes when she was happy, in her high cheekbones and cupid lips. But lines now folded all around those lips.

"Good morning, everyone," a man's cheerful voice called out. It was Mac, using his cane for a fast walk toward us.

"Good morning," most sitting in our group said to him. So did Mom and Eve and me.

Our mother's face had brightened with her wide smile. "Oh, it's getting time for breakfast already?" She glanced at one of the many large wall clocks.

"Almost." The intensity of his eyes, aimed at her, said she was important to him. And then he turned them toward me and Eve. "But I see that you have company this morning, Miriam, so I'll just talk to you later."

How many laters would our mother have for a man who seemed to love her?

"No, we were just leaving," I told him. Eve gave me a questioning look, to which I nodded. I hugged and kissed Mom. "Enjoy your day," I told her before she smiled her appreciation and gave a quick hug and kiss to my twin.

The most wonderful smell of sizzling bacon filled our space, making me not want to leave. But we exchanged good-byes with Mac and our mother's lady friends before I recalled something. I nudged my head to the side to tell Eve to follow me. We went straight to the counter separating the main staff from others. The secretary sat behind the desk.

She grinned at us. "Your mother and her guy friend are sure hitting it off, aren't they?" she asked and pointed.

We looked back toward where she'd aimed. Mom was walking side-by-side with him. They smiled at each other and held hands.

"They always do that," the woman at the desk said. "They take a little walk around before every meal and then when mealtime comes, they need to part, since they sit at different tables." Her smile spread. "But that will change once they get married."

Eve and I exchanged questioning glances. I wasn't totally sure how I felt about Mom and her man friend anymore. I'd thought I had begun to accept their escalating relationship, although when this woman spoke of her marrying, I felt as though someone slapped my chest, pushing the air out. I didn't want to feel that way.

Doors to two of the offices behind her were open. The nurse's door wasn't. The top official and her assistant both appeared busy on their phones at their desks. Their faces were tense.

"Can I help you?" The secretary looked at Eve and me.

"We wanted to see if Ms. Hebert is ready for us to fix this." I stepped near the end of the counter and tapped its uneven cutout section.

"I sure wish she would. That opening is so aggravating to go through since it's gotten uneven like that." She looked back at her boss, who now waved her free hand around while she spoke on her phone. "Now probably isn't a good time. I'm sure you heard something happened here last night, so there's lots of commotion."

"Yes, we know," Eve said. "Please tell her we'll be ready to repair this when she's ready."

The young woman looked back and then at us. "I will."

We thanked her and headed for the exit. I checked behind us before we walked out the door. Mom and her beau were nowhere in sight. Again outside, we looked around. "It's great not to see any police cars here again," I said once I slid into Eve's car.

"It is. That was a frightening image." She gave my arm a small pat. "I'm proud of you." In response to my quizzical expression, she asked, "Have you been seeing Lesley?" She referred to our friend the psychiatrist.

"I have."

"Good for you. It shows." She steered us out of the parking lot. "And as a little reward, I'm going to treat you to breakfast at Josie's. I'll even eat bacon with you."

After experiencing all the tension at the manor, it was nice to watch her smile and to consider the treat we would soon enjoy. The enticing aroma of bacon at the manor had made me want some, so now I wouldn't have to bother to cook it. I thought of Josie's flaky, buttery biscuits that we'd get with the meat, and my mouth watered. Eve was proud because even though events from last night had been fearful, I was almost entirely able to control my instinct of singing. She never ate such fattening foods as bacon, so she must also be feeling different. Events at the manor had been sad. Mom tricked us into believing she was no longer herself. Now she was with that man.

"Eve, what do you think about Mac?"

A small crease folded across her smooth forehead. "What do we really know about him? He was Edward's uncle." She glanced at me with a shrug. "He seems to make Mom happy."

"But is he good for her? Now with a woman she knew well dying at the manor, she might consider how short life can be. You never know when it will be gone."

"So this death might make her rush into going after what she wants."

Our mother could do that, just like when Edward was around and pushing them into that commitment.

Life was short. Dave wanted more of a commitment from me.

Eve nodded. "Since we haven't learned anything about him from the manor, and she might be wanting to hurry to be with him again, I'm going to do searches for him. I'll start online and take things from there."

"Great idea." Since my dyslexia often screwed up my ability to distinguish words in their proper order, she could perform tasks like that much faster than I could.

We pulled up to Josie's in town and found one car leaving a parking spot out front. Eve easily maneuvered her car into the space.

The sounds and aromas of breakfast foods—sizzling meats on the grill, powdered sugar covering fried beignets, and syrup on pancakes—made me lift my nose and let it lead the way to the nearest clean table. Bright lights filled the large cavity of a room, bringing out the reds and whites of similar old-style diners. The place wasn't too crowded.

"I see y'all," Josie called to us from across the room. She made her way to Eve and me. "I don't see any toolboxes in your hands, so I don't guess you're coming to do repair work for me."

"Oh, I'm sorry," Eve said. "We were out in my car and didn't have tools."

Josie smiled. "That's fine. Since I want some shelves built in the kitchen, I'd rather schedule when would be a good time for both of us." She eyed me. "Breakfast?"

"Absolutely. I was just smelling bacon and—" Second thoughts made me stop before I mentioned the manor. "And I would love to have bacon—crisp please—and a biscuit and milk."

Josie kept nodding, no order pad in her hand. "I know. You like it extra crisp. And you, Eve?"

"Give me the same."

Josie's left eyebrow lifted. "Fine." She turned to go off but turned and came back. "Your mother's at the manor," she said, eyeing one and then the other of us. "She must have known that lady who was killed."

My back jolted straight. "Killed?"

Eve leaned toward her. "A lady from there died either late last night or early this morning, but nobody said anything about murder."

"Yes, they did." She strode away from us and gave rapid orders to the cooks out front.

Eve waved to call Josie back. Josie gave her a brief nod and spoke to customers who sat along the counter. While we watched, Josie appeared to keep her eyes diverted from us. She went up to one person seated up there after another, talking to each one. Once she had finished that, she turned her back on us and fooled around with the cooks, even flipping some breakfast sausage herself.

"I don't think she wants to let us know who gave her that information," I said. "And I can't believe it's true."

"I can't either." Eve pulled her phone out of her purse. "I'll check the latest news and see if they say anything about that." She did rapid searches, shaking her head no.

A young waitress appeared at my shoulder. "Extra-crisp bacon and biscuit with milk, right?"

"Yes. Thank you."

She set my plate and glass down. "I'll go grab yours," she told Eve, who told her thanks.

"Josie's not coming back around us," I said. "Did you find anything on your phone?"

"Nothing." She put her phone away and made room for her meal that the waitress was carrying toward her. "She probably just heard gossip that somebody started. Anything to get people excited."

"I guess so." Ready to attack my food after Eve was served hers, I took a moment to glance around. Maybe someone was here that we knew of who made up stories, our nice way of considering people who lied.

A familiar older couple sat at a table. The wife was feeding small bites of a waffle to the cutest toddler seated beside her. A little red bow held up a small cluster of her hair. Four men with hair varying shades of gray sat together, drinking coffee and talking. I had seen those men together in restaurants. Surely some of them shared gossip. Checking to my rear, I discovered two college-aged girls at different tables with laptops. And at the farthest corner where we had seen them before sat Emery Jackobson and Nelson.

"I want to go talk to him—Emery," I told Eve and pointed at him.

"Yum," she said after swallowing her first crunchy bite of bacon. She lifted an eyebrow. "Why?"

"Emery was at the manor. He might have been the person who told Josie that Miss Clarice was murdered. I want to find out what he knows and why he was there."

"He might tell you it's none of your business." She broke off a piece of biscuit. "And he might be right." She licked her lips to get the smudges of Josie's special sweet butter off them, smiled, and used her napkin. Then picked up a slice of bacon.

Glancing back, I found Emery throwing his head back and laughing. That must have been a reaction from something Nelson said. Possibly something they planned to do. I was going to go talk to them and ask Emery what I wanted to know. Checking my extra-crisp bacon, I figured I should enjoy my meal first and give them a few minutes to talk.

I buttered my biscuit and bit into flavorful goodness. I enjoyed another bite before nibbling on the crunchy bacon that tasted like it had been smoked. The milk was ice cold. After a long swallow of it, I started the round again—biscuit first, then bacon, and then milk. Eve had finished her biscuit and had almost devoured her second slice of bacon when her phone rang.

Both of us frowned. She shook her head and didn't make a move to get it from her purse. "I can call back once we're finished," she told me.

"But it might be Mom."

She pulled out her phone and answered. Her eyes clouding over made me stop in mid-bite of my biscuit. The part of it that was in my mouth felt mushy when she said, "Yes. Yes, sir. We're coming there right now."

I wiped my mouth and shoved my napkin from my lap to the table. "What?" I asked the second she hung up.

"It's Detective Wilet. He went to both our houses and couldn't find us. We need to get over there to see him."

Chapter 24

Eve pulled out some bills and threw them on the table. I saw Emery looking at us when we hurried to the exit, but the minute I made eye contact, he looked down. I didn't have time to get with him.

"What did he want?" I asked Eve once we stepped outside.

"He didn't say, but maybe we could guess." She barely took time to strap herself in and then pulled away, driving above the speed limit. A couple of blocks later she must have realized that getting stopped now would not do well for us. She glanced at her speedometer and slowed.

Still, it didn't take long before we were sitting in the detective's office.

"You know why I wanted to talk with you two?"

"Why don't you tell us?" Eve said.

"You were both at Sugar Ledge Manor yesterday evening." He knew that. He didn't say it as a question. Still, we nodded. "You know that a woman there who sat beside your mother for meals became violently ill and had to be rushed to the hospital." Again he paused, so we gave brief nods. "We asked a lot of questions at the manor last night. I didn't want to try to track you down and speak to you there in front of anyone else again."

I leaned forward. "Why not?"

"What happened?" Eve asked, the angle of her seated body now exactly like mine.

"The ill resident has died."

"Yes, we heard," I said.

"We are so sorry," Eve added, and I nodded.

He slapped his palms against his desk, his upper body leaning toward us. "But is your mother?"

"What?" Eve blurted

"Of course she is," I said, anger ringed by fear roiling around in my stomach. "Detective Wilet, why in the world wouldn't our mother be unhappy to learn that any person, especially someone she knew fairly well, had died?"

The sound that came was air leaving his nostrils. He pressed back in his chair. Voices carried of two women talking while they walked beyond his shut office door.

"A number of people at the manor seem to know that your mother hopes to marry a resident there, a Mr. McCormick."

"That's right," Eve said with a nod.

"Some of them also have heard the woman who died telling others, including your mother, that she hoped to get him for herself."

A soft carol swirled around my throat.

Eve thrust her upper body so far toward him I thought she'd slip out of her chair. "But that was just like girl's jealousy. I did that when I was twelve or thirteen. If a girl got a boyfriend, I wanted him. It was childish."

He gave me a harsh look. "You two might also have heard that the lady they call Miss Clarice got so ill from taking some medicine that she shouldn't have. It was the medicine that probably killed her."

We looked at him, at each other, at him again, shaking our heads no.

He picked up a pen from his desk and put the back end of it in his mouth. He chewed on that a long minute. Setting it back down, he went on. "You were there when I questioned your mother about any medication she took. And some of her pills were missing."

I quit breathing. My gaze shot to Eve.

A hard knock came from the door. "Detective," a man's voice called.

"Not now." His voice came out gruff.

I shoved up off my chair and reached his desk. "But lately Mom is different."

The harsh look in his eyes made me sit back in my chair. "Sit down please," he said.

I sat again at the edge of my seat. "She might be forgetting some things, but she certainly knows better than to give any of her medicine to someone they weren't prescribed."

"What did she forget?" He gripped the pen he had chewed on to begin making notes.

I shot a sideways glance at Eve. I'd spoken without thinking, and now I needed to come up with something, something that might keep our mother out of trouble. "Well, she seemed to forget which one of us was which." I pointed toward Eve and myself.

"How is that forgetful? I can't tell you apart. I doubt that many people can."

"Right," Eve said, shaking her head, "but our mother, the woman who gave birth to us and raised us? She has never ever in her entire life gotten us mixed up. Until this week."

I wasn't certain Mom really confused us. On second thought, it seemed she pretended. But we needed something. And he was making me angry. I spoke up. "Detective Wilet, why are you so interested in our mother? You can't possibly think she murdered that woman, can you?"

He didn't say a word. He sat staring at us while we stared at him, a swirl of fuming emotions twirling between him and us like waves from hurricane-force winds pounding the gulf's shore.

Eve and I looked at each other, her steely face revealing the same fury I felt.

"Here's the information I gathered," he said. "Yesterday's lunch at the manor included cherry cobbler." We nodded, and he went on. "The other two ladies who were assigned to the table with your mother and Miss Clarice said anytime cobbler was served there, Miss Clarice told those eating with her that it was her favorite dessert, especially the crunchy kind the cafeteria made there with cherries."

I looked at Eve, then at him. "So?"

He leaned forward, clasping wide hands across the papers on his desk. "They said your mother really liked it, too." He eyed my twin and me while we gave him nods. "But yesterday your mother removed the bowl of cherry cobbler from her tray. She said even though she loved it, she should be watching her waistline, since she hoped to get married soon."

A boulder of dread dropped into my stomach. We hadn't known this.

"She set that large bowl of cobbler on the table right next to Miss Clarice's tray and said if anyone wanted it, they could have it." The pause in his story let me picture that bowl of dessert—the tasty, sweet treat filled with lots of cherries and thick red juice and a top and bottom layer of crunchy loose bits of crust—Eve and I had eaten with our meal there yesterday.

"Miss Clarice ate that extra cobbler," he said in a quiet tone. "Medicine like your mother takes was discovered in Miss Clarice's system. It's what made the medical examiner suspicious, since that type of medication would prove deadly to someone so slim and with a kidney condition like she had."

I shoved up to my feet, needing to push away the ball of fury and fear wrapped inside my throat. "What are you suggesting?"

"Some pills could have been crushed and shoved under the top layers of that dessert. Not having a taste, they wouldn't have been noticed."

Feeling Eve's hand gripping mine, I realized she had also risen. "And what? What are you saying to us, Detective?"

"Some of your mother's pills were missing from her prescription bottle, and she couldn't account for them. We all searched for them in her room." He gave his head a slow shake. "We couldn't find any of them."

"But—" Eve and I said together. Neither of us found words to come after that.

Hard knocks came from his door. "It's really important," said the same man as before.

"Just a minute."

"Detective, does our mother need a lawyer?" I asked, my voice firm.

"Are you charging her with something?" Eve's words were as steady as mine.

He shoved himself up and strode around his desk. "No. We don't have enough evidence to charge her with anything right now, and we're still early in our investigation. I wanted you aware." His eyes went hard. "Make sure she keeps all of her medicine where she can keep track of it."

He opened the door, and we shot out of the room toward the exit. If the police considered our mother could be a murderer, we desperately needed to do something to disprove that theory.

Chapter 25

We were back at the manor. While Eve and I were walking inside, my phone rang. I didn't want to answer it, especially if it was a customer calling about work. That wasn't anything we'd want to speak about or even think about right now. After it had rung four times, I slid it up and glanced at the caller.

"Hello, Dave," I answered once we had reached the foyer. I normally avoided saying his name if he called while I was with Eve. Right now, that didn't seem to matter.

I stopped walking. So did Eve. She watched me and listened.

"The woman from there really did die, and the police suspect that she could have been murdered," he said.

"Yes."

"You know about it? What can I do?"

"Just hang tight for now. Keep good thoughts coming out for everyone at the manor."

"I will. Do you want me to come over to be with you?"

I looked at Eve. She could hear his words. "No, thank you. I'm not home. I need to go. I'll keep in touch and let you know what I learn."

"Good. And Sunny, I really care about you. I want everything good for you and your family."

"I appreciate that." Hanging up, I made brief eye contact with my sister. She slid her gaze to my phone, but made no comment. I slipped my phone into my purse while we strode farther inside to locate Mom.

People moved around during midmorning with their stomachs filled from breakfast. Most residents and people who worked here looked lively and fresh.

Rita Picou walked around from behind us and reached the counter to the main offices. She got to the end of it beside a wall and lifted the cut section. "Ow," she said, dropping the wood and pulling her hand back.

"What happened?" Eve reached her seconds before I did.

She sucked on the side of her index finger. With her other hand, she shook a finger at the uneven hinge that must have squeezed her. "Y'all need to fix that thing."

"We will," Eve said, "but we're not in Sunny's truck. I don't have any tools with me."

I stepped nearer. "And we didn't think y'all were ready to have any work done with everything that's happened." I hoped my comment might get her to tell us anything more than the detective did. Doors to the administrator's and nurse's offices were open. Both women moved around inside those rooms.

Rita lifted the cut piece of wood. "Well, I hope you can get this fixed before I retire."

"You're retiring?" Eve asked.

"I hope so. I'm getting older." She stepped through the opening. Before she could let it down, I held it open. She barely glanced at me as I, and then Eve, followed her into the area. The secretary wasn't around. Rita walked into her office ahead of us and shut her door.

The administrator glanced at us as we walked through the sheltered area. When she saw us heading for the nurse's doorway, she continued whatever she had been doing.

Before I could tap on the nurse's doorframe, the nurse looked out at Eve and me. "Can I help you?"

"I hope so." I didn't wait for an invitation to step into her office. She shut a file drawer she'd had open.

"Can we close your door?" Eve asked, hand against it and ready. The nurse nodded, and Eve pushed it shut.

"What can I do for you? I'm really busy."

"We know," I said. "And we know the police suspect that your resident was murdered."

Her face showed no change of expression. Probably everyone in town had heard about what Detective Wilet told us by now. But probably not about our mother being a possible suspect. The people in these offices knew more than most. She didn't seem to want to give away anything.

"Do many people who live here take the same kind of medicine that our mother takes?" Eve asked, mentioning its name.

"I'm sure you know I can't tell you anything specific about any of our clients' medical history." She eyed the door, making me feel she wanted us to leave. "But you know that a lot of people also work here. I won't look up your mother's medical records right now, but some of the staff may have a similar condition and take the same prescription."

We stared at her. Her comment opened up a world of possible new leads to offer the detective. Or did he already know this?

"Just one other thing," I said, a thought occurring. "After leftover food is thrown out here, could anyone dig through it and find out if any kind of medicine was in any individual item?"

She frowned. "Not likely. No, I don't think so, and I can't imagine anyone going and digging through all the garbage bags that are thrown out. Also, that could be really dangerous." She glanced toward the filing cabinet and stepped to the door. "Now if you'll excuse me." She held the door open.

"Thank you," we both said, although she might not have heard. We were barely out of the room when the door shut behind us.

A man's voice came from the head lady's office, so even if her door was still open, there was no reason to try to speak with her now. We walked a few feet away from Mom's Chat and Nap buddies, but didn't see her with them. They appeared so intent on their lively conversation that none of them seemed to see us. None looked our way while the woman in a wheelchair spoke.

"So if she decided to get rid of her competition, good for her," she said, making some heads nod and Eve and I jerk our faces toward each other, our eyebrows lifted.

"That's right," another one of the ladies said. "I mean it wasn't nice to kill anyone, but I don't think she knew it would do that. Maybe make her sick, but not dead."

We hurried our clip away from them, Eve shaking her head while she spoke. "If the other two ladies Mom is assigned to eat with told the detective about her offering her cherry cobbler to the rest of them and Miss Clarice getting it, Mom might be hesitant about eating with them until this mess is cleared up."

"Yes. Why don't we take her out to lunch?" I said.

"Good idea."

"In fact, I'll suggest that she come and spend a couple of nights at my house. I can cook for her and keep her away from this place."

Eve nodded. She pointed to show me our mother was standing at the opposite side of the large room that held a few loveseats, tables, and chairs where residents sat to read the paper, play a game together, or just chat.

Mom stood beside a group of men who were betting red and blue plastic chips while playing cards. The only problem was the man she stood behind was Mac. And he was wearing a pale orange shirt.

I thought of red cherries and an orange. My eyesight returned to his shirt. Mom tilted her head and gave us a look of surprise. "You're here again?"

Legs shaky and feeling my frown, I pointed at Mac. "Your shirt is reminding me of our sister who died years ago. Recently I remembered that the man who shot her was driving an orange truck."

He glanced down at his shirt and then up at Mom. "I'm sorry, Miriam. I'll get rid of it."

"No, you don't have to," she said, although she just stared at the shirt.

The bald fellow seated across the small table looked at us. "I know who drove an orange truck a lot of years back. I think he was the only guy in the parish to ever own one that color."

I didn't imagine this man knew about someone driving past our yard when I was eight and playing basketball with my beloved sixteen-year-old sister that the driver shot and killed.

"How long ago was that?" Mom's beau asked him.

"It was some time back. The fellow drove that truck for a really long time. Let's see, my daughter Angela had started high school, I think. And my son...."

While he went on, a card player beside him kept nodding.

"Wait. What was the man's name?" I asked.

"Fred. Fred Zydeco. Isn't that something? Never heard of anyone with a name like that before. He lived down the bayou, but he sure wasn't Cajun. Nobody I know got a name like that. It's just the music some guys play with a washboard."

It took Mom only an instant to step to the speaker and grab his shoulder. "Where is he? Where is this person now?"

He pulled his head back and looked at her hand. Looked up at her face. "Humph, he's serving time in the pen. Shot up a couple of people. That guy's never getting out."

Mac folded the cards in his hand together and set them down. "I'm out." He was up and at our mother's side. A whimper sounded from deep inside her when he wrapped an arm around her. We all stepped away from the table and moved farther away from all others.

He stopped near a wall and looked at my mother's sad face. "Miriam, I can call the sheriff's office and get them to match the bullet that killed your daughter with those used by that Zydeco person in the other murders."

Tears swam over her eyes. Mine burned.

"I'm sorry," he said and held Mom in a hug, while Eve and I stood by and watched. I wasn't sure what to make of his offer about matching bullets but liked seeing him take charge and giving her comfort. "I'm sure this is painful to think about, but knowing who did it would give you closure for your daughter's death." He tilted his head toward Eve and me. "And for your other daughters, too."

She watched him, face sad, and nodded.

"I'll get on it."

I stepped near him and touched his arm. "How would you think to even do that?"

"I was involved with the court system."

Eve moved closer so that we formed a tight circle. "The court system?"

"Back home I was a district judge."

My sister's expression told me she was as surprised as I was. Instead of being a man who wanted an older woman he could mooch off of, here was a man who could take control. He was a man of strength in his own right. And he was comforting our mother.

"We wanted to take Mom out to lunch," I told him. "You could come, too."

"I'd like that. Only let me make that call first. Tell me where you're going, and I can take Miriam in my car and join you two. We had thought we'd go shopping today anyway."

I looked at my mother, viewing her in a new way. She was still the person who gave birth to me and my sisters, and no doubt loved us and our father who had died. She was getting older, that was certain, but I saw her beside this man who appeared to also love her and she him. Their love for each other would not take anything away from her feelings about us. It might even strengthen our ties.

While Eve kept watching Mom, I got the feeling she was experiencing similar thoughts and emotions. Our twin minds ran so close together.

"You decide where you'd like to eat," Eve told Mom.

"Miriam, would you sign us out?" Mac asked, and she nodded. Using his walking cane, he took firm steps toward the wing of the building that mainly housed men.

"Dad-dy!" a woman's voice called, making him stop. From the entrance, a woman who seemed a few years younger than we were with fluffy brown hair and the rounded face of a person with Down syndrome came with a wobbly run to him. They threw their arms wide and grabbed on to each other in a bear hug.

Tears moistened my eyes while I watched.

A MANOR OF MURDER 173

A younger woman came in right behind Mac's daughter and stepped up to him. "I'm taking her to the dentist, but she insisted on stopping here to see you."

His daughter gave him a big smile with her nods.

"I'm so glad you did. I'm always happy to see you, sweetie." He gave her a kiss on the forehead. "Now I want you to meet some people."

She gave us the widest, most genuine smile I had ever seen.

"You know my friend, Ms. Miriam," he said, and she nodded. "And these are her daughters, Ms. Sunny and Ms. Eve." He didn't try to indicate which one of us was which and probably couldn't tell that with the few times we'd met. "This is my daughter, Belinda."

Eve and I greeted her. To my surprise, she grabbed each of us and our mother in a tight hug.

"Belinda, we need to go," the young woman behind her said.

"And this is Amanda," Mac told us, and we exchanged greetings.

"Daddy, we need to go," Belinda said to him as though he hadn't just heard those words. Father and daughter held each other in tight hugs again. She gave us little waves and ambled out with her friend.

"She's adorable," I said to her father who kept smiling at her while she left.

"Yes. How old is she?" Eve asked him.

"She's your age," Mom answered.

What a surprise. Belinda looked so young. She also looked happy, and I imagined she stayed that way a lot.

Mac faced Mom, his smile no longer evident. "I'm going to go make that call to the sheriff's office. Would you sign us out?" She nodded, and he thanked her and stepped away.

I took note of the thin, knitted strap on her shoulder with its attached small pouch. "Mom, you need to start using a pill container like I'd brought you."

"I thought I made it clear that I don't need to do that."

At her raised angry voice, Mac turned back to her. "You have a problem?" he asked.

She swiped her hand backward to include Eve and me. "Even though I only take that one pill a day, my daughters think I need to use one of those long daily reminders so I'll remember to take the pills when I should."

"But Mom," I said, telling more than I had planned to. "Detective Wilet wanted to talk to us. He said medicine like what you take was in Miss Clarice's system, a lot of it. He believes that's what killed her."

In silence, all of us stared at each other.

Eve took up the story. "And you had a number of pills missing from your prescription bottle that you couldn't account for."

"You put your cherry cobbler aside," I continued, "and she ate it."

Mac eyed us. Was he afraid that the woman he cared so much about was a murderer?

He clasped our mother's hand. "They believe those missed pills could have been broken into pieces and blended into that crunchy cobbler. Miriam, your daughters have an excellent idea. For a while at least, it would be a good idea for you to put your medicine in one of those containers to make certain you—and the detective, if he's interested again—can see that you've taken one every day."

"We'll get you another container. Just leave the top open each day that you take a pill," Eve said.

"Wait." Mom's hands reached out to Eve and me. "Are you all saying I'm a murder suspect?"

"Join the crowd." I said the words before better thoughts arrived. When Mom and Mac eyed me, I went on. "After Eve and I argued with your nephew here that day and then we found him dead in his tub, Mr. McCormick, police believed we could have murdered him."

He grew quiet, staring down, possibly judging us as killers. Slowly, he shook his head. "No," he said, looking at us, "you wouldn't have done that."

How kind of him to say, especially since no one had located Edward's murderer yet.

He took Mom's hand and gave her a small comforting smile. And then he lifted his face toward Eve and me. "By the way, if you'll get me the bill for all the work you've done on my nephew's house, I'll pay you for it."

I released a breath. "Thank you. We will."

His eyes filled with alarm. He turned them on Mom. "Miriam, someone must have gotten hold of your pills and taken some and crushed them and mixed the pieces in that cobbler." He stopped, looking even more concerned. "All of your extra pills in that cobbler were meant for you."

My body grew still as a board. "Someone tried to kill Mom?"

We all stared at each other.

Mom shook her head, facing her beau. "But how can I prove I didn't do anything to Clarice?"

Again, he sandwiched her hands in his. "The burden of proof isn't on you. We'll figure out who's a better suspect to give them." Letting go of her hands, our mother's betrothed wrapped an arm around her back. "And I'm going to be watching you closer. I'm more concerned about someone trying to hurt you than trying to prove you're innocent."

Was he suggesting that he might want to move in with her? If so, did that idea bother me? Not if he protected our mother.

Cooks preparing their early lunch made pots and dishes clatter. Some residents were making their way to where they would eat. Their shoes, walkers, and canes struck the floor and their voices lifted while they spoke of food or other things. The scent of spaghetti sauce wrapped around the air.

A man walking across the opposite side of the room made my scalp tighten. Emery Jackobson was around again. Did Mac know that his deceased nephew had put Emery out of business? And also that his nephew knew Tommy Jeansonne's young daughter was prostituting in New Orleans and hadn't told him?

What would we discuss when we all sat across from each other at a restaurant? Could I tell Mac? Should I?

I needed more time to sort through my thoughts, to talk them out with my sister. I imagined forcing myself to withhold those things from him and was sorry we had suggested taking them out to eat.

But someone wanted to kill our mother? We needed to keep her away from here.

A thump sounded to our side. The nurse had come out of her office and lifted the wooden piece of the counter. It obviously slammed down, again the uneven piece of that long flat surface.

Behind the nurse, the two head ladies stepped out of their offices and headed toward the offensive piece of the countertop. I anticipated another loud thump and their unhappy faces, and stepped farther away from the office area, hoping the administrator didn't see us and loudly complain. None of us were in the mood for something like that.

She frowned at the offensive loud part once she came through it, but then headed toward the men's corridor, her long skirt sweeping the floor. Her assistant came out behind her and did her quick walk toward the dining area.

"She isn't very nice," Mom said, an unusual comment for her. She seldom used negative words about anyone.

"Not to me," Mac said. "Rita is always extra sweet."

Mom's mouth opened, her look at him holding disbelief. "Then she must really like you and not me."

He shrugged, tilting his head, and lifted his silver eyebrows in that way people do to suggest *Oh well, I can't help it.*

"She wants to retire," Eve said. "She looks way too young."

"Rita is just lazy and doesn't want to work." Mom's comments drew our full attention. "The ladies I spend the most time with all say they don't know why she gets paid, since she doesn't do anything."

Rita strode between tables that now held a few people and appeared to be heading to the kitchen.

"She just oversees the meals," Mom said. "That seems to be the only job she really takes care of around here."

"Wait," I said. "She's around all the food in the kitchen. She also has access to all of your rooms."

Eve frowned. "And she wants to retire early."

"She's really sweet to you." I pointed at Mac. "And she must have access to all the residents' records, so she knows you were a judge. I hate to ask this, but you aren't hurting for money, are you?"

Lips tight, he gave his head a brief shake. "No, I am not."

All four of us turned toward the assistant-administrator when she was about to go around the wall and step into the kitchen.

"Rita Picou!" Mac called, and she stopped. Her eyes narrowed when she watched the four of us storming across the room toward her.

"Stay there!" I yelled

"I need to go," she said.

"No, wait, stop!" Eve yelled at her.

As though she perceived evil closing in, Rita darted toward the front exit. As fast as she was, after she got outside, she could take off and might be hard to stop. I hoped I wasn't wrong, but she could be a killer.

"Stop her!" I screamed, and residents looked at me thrusting my finger toward her. "She's dangerous. Don't let her get away!"

Mom's Chat and Nap buddies and others all shoved walkers and canes in front of the frantic woman.

Arms flailing, she went down.

Chapter 26

Dave rushed into the manor shortly after policemen took the administrative-assistant away. He found us sitting with our mother's buddies and came straight to me. "You're all right? And your mother's okay?" His gaze located Mom, who smiled at him, bypassed Eve, and shot back to me. "I heard there had been a lot of sirens here."

"Pull up a chair, young man," Mom's fiancée told him from the chair he had pulled up for himself beside Mom, "and we'll tell you a story."

Dave grabbed a nearby chair and sat on it beside me to complete our large circle.

Mac started first. "We'll learn a lot more once Detective Wilet completes his investigation."

"The main thing is," I said, "Rita Picou wanted Momma's man."

Dave scanned Mac, a slight grin appearing with his nod at the elder man, many of the women in our group now smiling.

"It's not because of my looks," the elder gent admitted, one man to the other.

She wanted him for his money, we would learn. He and Mom never discussed their finances with each other, but as assistant-administrator, Rita Picou did know of their worth from the forms they submitted when they applied to move in. As Mom had said, Rita was lazy and wanted to stop working early. She had been trying to figure out how to get Mac to marry her. Then she could live an affluent lifestyle as she'd always wanted.

Mac and Mom became interested in each other, which Rita didn't see as a major problem as long as things between them didn't get too serious. She would figure out a way to break them up.

But then Edward came around and started pushing the two to hurry and get married. After they seemed interested in doing that, she went to the house Eve and I had been remodeling. She asked him to show her around. When they were in his lovely upstairs bathroom, she insisted he stop pushing Mac and Mom and, instead, discourage their marriage. When he vehemently refused, she shoved him. He fell backward into that freestanding tub beneath the chandelier. His head bled, and he lay still. Panicked, she turned the water on full blast and ran.

She might have even killed Mac after she married him, after she realized how easy murdering a person had been. In the meantime, she decided to get rid of our mother.

Chills crawled over every inch of my skin when I tried to comprehend that fact.

Rita had gotten into Mom's room when Mom wasn't in it on the afternoon before the cafeteria would make the cobbler. She took a handful of pills out of Mom's prescription bottle, enough of them that she figured would stop our mother's heart. Crumbling them, she easily mixed the tiny pieces into the crunchy coating and base when she went into the kitchen to inspect each tray of food that was labeled for residents or guests. She shoved the deadly dose of medicine into Mom's dessert. Only Mom didn't eat hers, since she wanted to watch her weight before her wedding day.

When Miss Clarice ate it and later died, Rita decided that would also serve her purpose. Because Miss Clarice wanted Mac, her interest probably made Mom want to marry him sooner than she had originally planned. Our mother would be blamed for the other woman's death and sent off to prison. Then Rita could actively pursue him. Surely he would like a younger woman wanting him.

All this information sent cold water rushing through my veins. This wasn't a cop show on TV they were talking about. It was real life. It involved my mother's life.

I had suspected Emery Jackobson of wrongdoing in what was going on, but he had only been visiting a friend in the manor. Detective Wilet had located the man named Carl who we'd seen arguing with Edward that day we went to Edward's house, and then Carl showed up at Edward's wake. It seemed he was only another lawyer, one from a nearby town. He had no involvement in anyone's death.

When we left the manor for a late lunch, Dave agreed to join Eve and me, along with Mom and her intended. Mom's preference was Swamp Rat's Diner, so that's where we went. After we all placed our orders for different seafood dishes, our table went quiet.

I wanted any discussion except about what almost occurred, and turned to Dave. "I hadn't thought to ask. Have you gotten your boat out of the shop yet?"

"You have a boat?" Mac asked.

"Yes. I needed help to figure out what kind I needed." Dave kept his eyes trained on me. "They'll have it ready soon."

Should I admit our growing relationship to my twin? She was the person who'd made me hang around him in the first place when I was hell-bent about never wanting a man again since my divorce. And she had been attracted to many men who also cared for her, but then she'd met Dave and decided he was her soulmate—the perfect man she had been looking for all along.

Only he hadn't gone along with her pushiness. He had let me know he cared for me. And patiently waited for me before we took our relationship to another level.

I dreaded telling her. I had to tell her. "Dave was waiting for me to help him decide on a boat," I said to everyone. I aimed the next statement at Eve. "He and I care for each other. A lot."

As though I had said someone dropped a *remain-silent* sign on our table, everyone grew quiet. Still. And then came smiles and laughter.

"Sunny, I'm so happy for you," Mom said from her seat beside mine, gathering me in her sweet hug. "I was afraid you would never find true love."

Her intended was grinning and patting Dave on the back.

Dave kept his pleased smile aimed at me.

I did a slow-motion move of my head to face Eve. Her expression was noncommittal. We locked eyes. "I brought you two together," she said and her face broke into a weak smile. Her lips trembled. "Sunny, I helped you find a man you could love." The edges of her lips pushed back and up. "How wonderful!"

I could barely see Dave through the tears of pleasure coating my eyes when my sister laughed and held on to me.

Chapter 27

Mom let us choose whatever we wanted to wear for her big day. She had discovered a pale pink dress that brought out her eyes and still-lovely pale complexion. Mom even let Eve put makeup on her face, a trace of blush on her cheeks and a deep pink on her lips.

We wore ankle-length eggplant gowns Eve selected. The slenderizing dresses fit her and me and Mac's daughter Belinda, our sweet new sister, very well.

In the manor's largest area, chairs had been lined up on both sides of a center aisle. A white trellis at the opposite end of the aisle had been decorated with flowers. A judge friend of Mac's stood facing those of us about to walk toward him.

Most residents of the manor and other friends of our family and the groom's took seats in those folding chairs. Lots of chatter came from happy voices.

Strains of music began, and everyone looked back. Bursts of laughter came as our mother's Chat and Nap buddies, who had insisted on becoming flower girls, walked or rolled forward, cheerfully tossing rose petals.

The person behind them carried a small satin pillow with a ring tied to it. Everyone laughed when the little fellow stopped and turned back. Right behind him, Eve chuckled and took his hand. They walked together to the front, she and her grandson, Noah, the little man who now fulfilled her.

Dave looked extra fine in his navy suit. I hooked my arm in his. Enjoying his strength and our growing relationship, I walked proudly beside him behind my sister and the others.

Mac stepped up under the trellis. The gentleman appeared dapper with his light gray suit that matched his silver hair. His black walking cane with a gold grip was fancier than his usual wooden one. This day was extra special. So was the wide smile he gave our mother who now faced him from the opposite end of the aisle, giving him a similar smile.

Eve and I left our partners in front and returned to the rear. We took our places on both sides of our mother and wrapped our arms through hers. Music intensified while we walked forward to the man whose eyes never left our mom. There was no doubt that with him, she would remain content.

Meet the Author

From the bayou country of South Louisiana, June Shaw represents her state on the board of Mystery Writers of America's Southwest Chapter and has served as the published author liaison for Southern Louisiana's chapter of Romance Writers of America. She previously sold a series of cozy mysteries to Five Star. Publishers Weekly praised her debut, Relative Danger, which became a finalist for the David Award for Best Mystery of the Year. June gains inspiration for her work from her faith, family, and friends, including the many readers who urge her on.

For more info please visit juneshaw.com.

Fatal Romance

See where the Twin Sisters mysteries by June Shaw began . . .

Fixing up homes can be tricky.
Finding true love can be even trickier.
But finding a killer can be plain old deadly . . .

Twin sister divorcees Sunny Taylor and Eve Vaughn have had their fill of both heartaches and headaches. So when they settle down in the small Louisiana town of Sugar Ledge and open a remodeling and repair company, they think they've finally found some peace—even though Eve is still open for romance while Sunny considers her own heart out-of-business.

Then their newest customer ends up face-down in a pond, and his widow is found dead soon after. Unfortunately, Sunny was witnessed having an unpleasant moment with the distraught woman, and suspicion falls on the twins. And when an attempt is made on Eve's life, they find themselves pulled into a murder mystery neither knows how to navigate.

With a town of prying eyes on them, and an unknown culprit out to stop them, Sunny and Eve will have to depend on each other like never before if they're going to clip a killer in the bud.

Chapter 1

I stood in a rear pew as a petite woman in red stepped into the church carrying an urn and stumbled. She fell forward. Her urn bounced. Its top popped open, and ashes flew. A man's remains were escaping.

"Oh, no!" people cried.

"Jingle bells," I hummed and tried to control my disorder but could not. Words from the song spewed out of my mouth.

"Not now," my twin Eve said at my ear while ashes sprinkled around us like falling gray snow. She pointed to my jacket's sleeve and open pocket. "Uh-oh. Parts of him fell in there."

I saw a few drops like dust on the sleeve and jerked my pocket wider open. Powdery bits lay across the tissue I'd blotted my beige lipstick with right before coming inside St. Gertrude's. "I think that's tissue residue," I said, wanting to convince myself. I grabbed the pocket to turn it inside out.

"Don't dump that." Eve shoved on my pocket. "It might be his leg. Or bits of his private parts."

"Here comes Santa Claus," I sang.

She slapped a hand over my mouth. "Hush, Sunny."

The dead man's wife shoved up from her stomach to her knees, head spinning toward me so fast I feared she'd get whiplash.

"Sorry," Eve told her. "My sister can't help it."

Beyond the wife a sixtyish priest, younger one, and other people appeared squeamish scooping coarse ashes off seats of the rough-hewn pews. An older version of the wife used a broom and dustpan to sweep ash from the floor. People dumped their findings back into the urn. Other mourners scooted from the church through side doors. A boiled crayfish scent teased my nostrils. Someone must have peeled a few crustaceans for a breakfast omelet and didn't soap her hands well enough.

Ashes scattered along the worn green carpet like a seed trail to entice birds. "Look, there's more of him. I'll go find a vacuum," I said.

The widow faced me. "No! Get out."

"But she's my sister," Eve said.

"As if I can't tell. You leave with her. Go away." The petite woman wobbled on shiny stilettos, aiming a finger toward the front door.

I sympathized with her before this minute. Now she was ticking me off. I'd been kicked out of places before, but never a funeral. "I didn't really know your husband, but Eve did. I stopped to see if she wanted to go out for lunch, and she asked me to come here first. She said y'all were nice people."

"We are!" The roots of the wife's pecan-brown hair were black, I saw, standing toe-to-toe with her, although my toes were much bigger inside my size ten pumps. I was five eight and a half. She was barely five feet. Five feisty feet. "But you're not going to suck up parts of my husband's body in a vacuum bag." She whipped her pointed finger toward me like a weapon. "And you need to stop singing."

I wanted to stop but imagined parts of the man that might be sucked into a vacuum cleaner and ripped out a loud chorus, my face burning. Nearby mourners appeared shocked. Mouths dropped open.

"You don't know my sister," Eve told the little woman who'd just lost a spouse. Actually, lost him twice. "Sunny can't help singing when she's afraid. And that includes anything dealing with sex, courtesy of her ex-husband."

"What does sex have to do with Zane?" The wife's cheeks flamed.

Should I tell her about his privates possibly being in my pocket? Second thoughts said not to. "Who knows? But you don't need to worry. I certainly wasn't having an affair with your husband," I said, quieting my song to a hum.

"Just the thought of sex makes her sing," my sister explained. "Maybe it's a good thing she doesn't think of it often."

The widow shook her finger. "Zane was always faithful to me."

"I'm sure he was," I said, working to get my singing instincts under control. Nodding toward the carpet, I spoke without a hint of a tune. "I'd really like to help you get those pieces of him out of the rug. If we can just find an empty vacuum bag, I'll—"

"Go! Get away!"

I stomped out of the church into muggy spring air. Eve clopped behind me toward her Lexus in the parking lot.

"You told me they were fine people," I said.

"They are. At least he is. Or was." Eve shook her head, making sunshine spread golden highlights over her flame-red waves. Her clear blue eyes sparkled. I was glad few people could tell us apart. "I only met his wife that day I laid their pavers, and Zane stayed and helped a little. When she got home, he introduced us. She seemed pleasant."

"I guess you never know."

"Good grief, Sunny. You kept singing after she spilled her husband."

I lowered my face toward the chipped sidewalk.

Eve touched my arm. "I know, but maybe you can try harder."

I nodded. She knew how long I'd fought to stop the songs that began when a major tragedy threw my life into an unending tailspin. Junior high had been especially painful.

At the next corner, we waited for a truck to pass. I checked my sleeve in the sunshine, relieved that if any ashes had been there, the breeze had blown them off to a better place. "There weren't many people in church."

Eve frowned. She started across the street. "They've lived here less than three years and don't have much family. Zane's job kept him out of town a lot. When he joined our line-dance class, he said his wife was shy and didn't like to dance anyway."

"I don't think she's shy. I think she was involved in his death."

"What?" Eve stopped. "The man drowned. It was an accident."

I spread my hands. "In his own yard? Why didn't he fall in that pond before now?"

"Because this week he tripped on a cypress knee near the job we did in their yard and knocked his head on the tree and fell in. He couldn't swim. And you don't even know his wife."

No, neither she nor her husband had been home when we created that seating area in their yard. I tugged on Eve's arm to get her across the street so oncoming cars waiting for us could turn.

She kept talking. "Darn it, Daria Snelling might not be the sweetest person right after her husband's ashes flew to the heavens, but that doesn't make her a killer."

"Eve, you know I have good instincts about people. And covers on burial urns are sealed. They aren't supposed to come off." I created a mental picture of what happened. "Besides, she was walking along carpet. There weren't any bumps for her to trip over."

My twin's face pinched up. Not a pretty picture. "How do you know that?"

"Her shoes. When the organ music started and everyone turned to look back, I noticed her shoes."

"I can't believe this, Sunny. You aren't usually that shallow." She stomped off ahead of me.

I strolled faster behind. "You know I can't even pronounce the brands of expensive shoes. I saw she was tiny but looked extra tall, so I glanced at her shoes. Her heels must be four inches. That's really showy for a grieving widow."

"Wearing stilettos make her a murderer?"

"And a bright red dress. Red?" I caught up with Eve. "I think she wanted to dump her husband so his remains couldn't all be buried together."

She threw up her palms. "You are so sick. The man was my friend."

"Geez, you worked for him briefly and saw him a couple of times in dance class."

"That doesn't give you the right to cut down his family."

"And if you hadn't made that dig about my unhappiness with sex, his wife wouldn't have gotten so upset."

Eve knew my limited experience with sex had come with Kev soon after our marriage. If I'd known how unpleasant one man could make the quick chore, I would have started chuckling in bed much sooner. Eve and I were both divorced—she, three times, her choice—and her admiring exes still showered her with gifts. Kevin left me with little and did so after my spontaneous laughter about frightening things escalated to include sex. But he made the intimacy so unpleasant I had begun to dread it.

Watching my sister, I saw myself a little slimmer, wearing dressier clothes and an unpleasant grimace. At thirty-eight, she was fairly attractive in a black knit top and skirt, emerald green jacket, and spike heels. I wore low heels and tan slacks with a white shirt and my favorite jacket, a rust-colored silk. With a pocket that now held parts of Zane Snelling.

"Sis," I said, "do you see any ashes in my hair? Or on my sleeve or other places on my clothes?"

She did a quick inspection of my hair and looked longer at my clothes, while I did the same to her. "I don't see anything anymore." She checked inside my pocket. "Except in there."

"You're clean," I said, voice dull from knowing I still wore parts of a man. I slid my jacket off and carefully folded it, not letting anything escape.

Eve wrenched her car door open and flung herself inside. I slid onto the passenger seat. "Buckle up." She waited until I did before pulling onto the street.

"Do you want to go out for lunch?" I asked.

"My stomach's too upset. I'm going to change clothes and hit the gym."

Positive news came to mind. "Anna Tabor wants us to give her a price to replace the picture window in her den with a glass block one." It wasn't much of a job, but we were still pleased with every one that came in.

"Why does she want that?"

"She said it would be unusual and attractive. I'll do the estimate this evening."

"Okay. I'll check your work tomorrow, and we'll schedule her in."

I nodded. Our deceased father had been an excellent carpenter who made us enjoy working with our hands. We'd done quite a bit of work with him and liked changing the design of some of his jobs. Ever since I convinced Eve to join me to start Twin Sisters Remodeling & Repairs months ago, we were gradually building up our name and earning people's trust. We were both strong and knew how to use subcontractors and power tools. So far my estimates all turned out correct. Still, being dyslexic made me want all written work and numbers double-checked. Early struggles and some teachers' hurtful comments made me still doubt myself.

Most of the sugar cane stalks in fields Eve drove past stood three feet tall. On the opposite side of the highway, the brown bayou lazed along, shielding gators, turtles, catfish, and other water creatures. We sped by shotgun houses dotted between brick homes in our small town of Sugar Ledge and entered our subdivision. Houses were brick and stucco and most of the lawns well-tended, especially on Eve's street. She reached her house, remoted the garage door, and pulled in.

"I shouldn't have snapped at you. I'm sorry," she said.

I leaned over and kissed her forehead like Mom used to do to let us know anytime we were forgiven. "To make amends, can I see what you're working on?"

She considered a minute, then led the way through her picture-book house. The lingering fragrance from vanilla triple-scented candles made me want yellow cake. The spacious den held large windows and pale neutral shades, its main color from Mexican floor tile and Eve's muted-tone abstracts, which I determined she painted when she was between dating or marriage.

She kept most of her home with a colorless feel like a blank canvas, letting her imagination soar. Pulling a key from the second drawer of an end table beside the white marshmallow-leather sofa, she unlocked a door off the den.

Shell-shocked. Her studio made me feel that way even more so than usual. While the rest of her house gave off a bland feel, this room was infused with color, especially on a huge canvas on an easel in the center of the room. Splashes of color and bright dots of varying sizes filled almost every inch of the canvas.

"Intriguing," I said. "Who does it represent?"

"Dave Price. That man is terrific."

"I can tell. Y'all must have an explosive relationship."

"I only know him casually. Of course I'm planning to change that." Her grin widened. "This is how I'm expecting our relationship to become."

"Impressive."

The other dozen or so paintings on easels and standing on the floor represented men she'd dated or married. Some wore drab shades. A couple of canvases showed small vases. Others held crudely-drawn flowers or apples. She wasn't a proficient artist, but while our business grew, this gave her something to do with extra time besides line dancing once a week and working out at the gym. She didn't get to see her daughter in Houston often enough. A sex therapist would enjoy analyzing what she did in here.

"Thanks for letting me see your latest work. Sorry about the funeral ruckus."

"You didn't cause it." The fair skin between her eyes creased. "I'd like to know what happened after we left the church."

I'd prefer to know what really happened to the dead man before we went there. "Maybe you'll find out. See you later." I locked the stained-glass front door on my way out.

Ambling alongside her taupe stucco house, I paused in back to admire the fountain burbling on her patio. Inside it, a stone angel poured bleach-scented water. Again, I wished the fountain held live fish instead of the almost real-looking plastic gold ones. Angling through the little grass path between the yards behind her house, I passed a dog-eared cedar fence on the right and white solid vinyl fence panels on the left. Then I stepped across the next street, which was mine. Yards and cars here were less fancy than on hers. A couple of clunkers sat in circular drives. Even the air smelled less pure.

"Your petunias still look good," I told Miss Hawthorne, kneeling beside the purple blossoms lining the concrete path to her front stoop.

"Thank you. Oh, Sunny, look. The girdle you sold me still works great. Two years old and still holding me in." She struggled up to her feet. Miss Hawthorne was probably older than my mother and didn't like help. She'd insisted on a girdle, not that newer stuff she said was smaller than her gloves, and bought it from me while I still worked at Fancy Ladies, our town's only upscale dress shop. I'd needed to quit that job since I had developed excruciating heel spurs that wouldn't get better until I stopped standing all day every day, and surgery wouldn't correct them.

The top of Miss Hawthorne's plump face hid beneath the wide floppy brim of her straw hat, which didn't hide her pleasant smile. Dirt tumbled off the knees of her slacks. The girdle pushed her stomach up and made the thick roll above her waist more pronounced through her knit shirt. I'd learned to notice details while I fitted ladies with undergarments and determined she had gained fifteen pounds since I sold her that girdle.

"You look good, Miss Hawthorne. But next time you're at Fancy Ladies, you might check out the newer styles. You could find a control panty or shaper that's more comfortable."

"Oh no, hon, this works just fine."

"Good. I'll see you later." I strolled off, pleased to know her smile finally returned after her misery because a relative's pet she had been keeping escaped from her fenced backyard.

A couple of houses to the left, I reached mine, a gray brick with a darker gray stucco entrance. I entered, experiencing the same stir of unpleasant emotions as every other time I returned from Eve's. My place was pleasant, yet now felt like it held too much clutter, even if there wasn't much extra. The house even smelled dull. I plugged in a vanilla-scented air freshener.

Standing beneath the foyer light, I yanked my jacket pocket wide open. Course grayish bits of a man lay inside. I strode to my kitchen trashcan and stepped on the pedal to pop it open, ready to turn my pocket inside out.

No, that wouldn't be right. I let the can's top close. Where else might I put these powdery flakes? I couldn't dump them in my yard or even think of flushing them.

This was part of a person that needed to be treated with respect. I hung the jacket in the foyer, grabbed a phonebook, and looked up a number, relieved to find the person listed. I punched in numerals and listened to the phone ring. A click sounded.

"Snelling residence," a woman said. "We can't get to the phone now, but we will return your call as soon as we're home if you leave your number." Daria Snelling sounded much more pleasant on the machine than she had in church.

I hitched up my chin and tried to sound cheerful. "Hello, Mrs. Snelling. This is the tall redhead who blurted a song this morning at St. Gertrude's. I'm sorry I sang and really sorry about your husband." I cleared my throat. "I called to tell you I have something of his. I'm sure it's something you'll want." I gave my number in case she didn't have caller I.D. and hung up.

My stomach rumbled, reminding me of why I'd stopped at Eve's in the first place. I considered eating leftover red beans and sausage, but instead yanked rice from the fridge, heated a pile of it in a bowl, and squirted my initials over it with ketchup. I munched on this entrée with a chunk of lettuce topped with a few raisins, fat-free ranch dressing, and crunchy chow mein noodles.

In my bedroom, I peeled off church clothes and struggled to snap my jeans, then yanked on a purple T-shirt with gold letters in front that said TWIN SISTERS. Small letters on its back said Remodeling & Repairs.

I slipped into my backyard, where flats of flowers waited. Sunshine and temperatures in the mid-sixties made the spring afternoon appealing. A cool breeze pushed off earlier mugginess that reminded us soon south Louisiana would treat us all to steam baths.

Digging up scraggly plants, I tossed them aside, noting sirens in the distance. A harsh memory trying to erupt froze me in place. I fought the remembrance from my youth and forced it away.

I stabbed soil with my shovel, knowing something was definitely not right with Daria Snelling. Years of working in close contact with women at Fancy Ladies let me learn much more than I wanted to about their private lives so that now my initial instincts were normally correct. Dragging topsoil to the flowerbeds, I mentally weighed the probability of what police decided happened to Zane Snelling and shook my head. Why had he tripped and slid into the deep water in their backyard near the seating area Eve and I recently completed?

Uneasy about his drowning, I added weed preventer to my beds and topped the mounds with cypress mulch. Next came tall coneflowers as a nice backdrop. I set daylilies in front and filled in the closest section with coreopsis.

When the sun was dipping behind rooftops, my riot of color pleased me. I watered everything and kicked off my dirty shoes near the backdoor. Walking into the kitchen, I was ready to develop a bid for Anna Tabor's window that would add to our other pending jobs. A flashing red light on the answering machine caught my attention. I pressed the button, expecting Mrs. Snelling.

"Sunny! Where are you?" Eve yelled.

My heart slammed against my ribs. Something happened to Mom?

I played the next message. "Sunny, it's Eve. I need you!"

My quivering finger pressed her number in Memory on my phone.

"Where have you been?" she asked with a sob. "I've been calling."

"Planting flowers. Is it Mom?"

"Somebody broke into my house!"

"What? Are you okay?"

"No. Come over."

"I'm there!" I raced toward my sister.

Printed in the United States
by Baker & Taylor Publisher Services